MISSING

Margaret Grimshaw shook her umbrella looking up at the rain clouds wondering if it ever really stopped raining in the north of England. She glanced up the steps of Ramsbottom police station undecided whether to enter or not when Doris her neighbour appeared.

'Margaret?' She glanced toward the police station. 'Trouble?'

Margaret shifted a little away from the steps. 'Trouble?'

Doris nodded toward the police station.

Margaret quickened her step. 'Goodness no.'

Doris walked with her. 'How's Bernard?'

'Don't ask.'

'Oh dear.' She wore a sympathetic - but perhaps inwardly satisfied her suspicions were correct - smile. 'I don't know, why do we allow ourselves-'

Margaret snorted. 'I swear he gets worse, if that's possible.'

Doris moved closer. 'What's he done now luv?'

Margaret pulled her coat tight and gave a little shiver. 'I don't want to talk about it Doris.'

'Oh dear.'

'Let's just say if he were like this when we got wed, he'd still be standing at bloody alter.'

'I feel for you luv. I thought mine was bad enough but…' she checked her watch, 'Anyway, better go or I'll miss the ten fifteen. Got knit and natter at 12.00.' She hurried off.

As soon as she was far enough away Margaret pulled her coat even tighter and bustled up the steps. The smell of the foyer (years of paint, polish, cleaner, dust from the well-worn carpet and battered bench seats) brought back uncomfortable associations with the police station from five years ago concerning the Penelope incident – something she regretted but had at the time felt justified. Unfortunately, the Magistrate did not. (She was not surprised when learning later that he was one of Bernard's friends from the winemakers' club). Bernard had of course tried to play it down, but she suspected it was more than he let on.

With distaste she tried to ignore the tattooed youth biting his nails on a bench inside the door and approached the desk. She waited patiently for a few seconds, studying the bald pate of the desk sergeant bent over writing, grew impatient and coughed to get his attention.

Sergeant Turner continued to write carefully and meticulously, seemingly unaware of her presence. Sergeant Turner had been around a long time. Sergeant Turner had seen it all. She coughed again, this time a little louder.

Sergeant Turner carefully placed his pen on the desk and looked up. 'Can I help you?'

'I want to report a missing person.'

'I see.' He smiled. 'Then you've come to the right place.' He picked up his pen and began a new entry. 'Your name please.'

'Margaret Grimshaw.'

'And the missing person?'

'Bernard Grimshaw.'

'And he is…?'

'My husband.'

Sergeant Turner had a habit of vocalising what he was writing; something his colleagues found both amusing and annoying. '…my husband.' He stood and stretched his back. 'Age?'

'Fifty-nine.'

'And when did he go missing?'

Margaret rearranged her coat a little tighter. 'Five days ago.'

'…Five days ago.' He straightened again and with tired, but kind eyes asked, 'Has he been missing before?'

Margaret sighed. 'Not really.'

'Can you be more specific?'

She glanced uneasily in the direction of the youth. Sergeant Turner smiled. 'He's one of our many "customers" insisting they do not require a licence or insurance to drive a motor vehicle. Also totally self-centred and oblivious of the world around him.' He sighed. 'Gone are the days when a beat bobby could administer a clump round their earhole. Nowadays they must be called customers and their rights respected, albeit increasing by the day, to be above all else. But that's just -'

She leant closer. 'He vanished for a day last year,' she huffed, 'he said he wer with friends at wine club.' She shuddered, 'But I'm sure he wer with that Penelope Smyth.'

He smiled kindly. 'Hmm.' He put his pen down. 'Do you think perhaps he-'

She snorted, 'I wouldn't put it past him, Midlife crisis my arse.' She glanced at the youth again and leaned closer. 'He's always texting but stops when I appear. Disappears for a few hours at the weekend, know what I mean?'

'Sadly, I do. A difficult time I must admit, not that I suffered from it, but my cousin George did. In his sixties he was and went off with a twenty-year-old.' He sighed. 'Didn't last like. Changed his whole wardrobe, he looked like', his face took on a look of distaste, 'an American. Do you have any contact with this Penelope? to perhaps verify if he is there?'

She gave a little shudder. 'I certainly do not. Anyway I couldn't. A restraining order or summat.'

'I see.' He picked up his pen, poised to write but hesitated. 'Was he under any stress?'

'No. Well he doesn't get on wi our son.' She thought for a moment. 'Come to think of it he doesn't really get on with anyone.'

A blip pinged on Sergeant Turner's radar. 'Has he got any enemies?'

She smiled tiredly. 'How long have you got?'

'I see.'

She looked into the distance. 'Even the cat doesn't like him.'

He gave her a kind look and began writing. '…a lot of enemies, possible kidnapping,' he paused, 'even the cat…'

Margaret was beginning to feel irritated by his habit. 'Do you have to?'

He paused and looked up. 'Sorry?'

'Never mind. So, what happens now?'

'I will alert my colleagues and see if we can find him. Do you have a photograph?'

She rummaged in her bag and produced a dog-eared picture of Bernard holding a wine glass with a group of men.

He studied it. 'Is he a drinker?'

'Oh yes. He thinks he's God's gift to the Ramsbottom wine makers club.'

FOUND

Bernard opened his eyes shielding them from the early morning daylight. He shivered and tried to pull his coat around him – only to discover it was not there. In fact, the only clothing he wore was a pair of underpants. He groaned and looked around recognising the Tesco carpark he was regularly forced to visit, usually under protest and carrying too many bags of *her* shopping. His mind refused to cooperate, and he sat staring into space in a sort of dream state.

PC May and his partner PC Jones were on a routine, and as usual, a quiet shift. He would prefer to police his way but had reluctantly requested PC Jones to be his partner because the thought of her being let loose given her predilection to automatically assume all men were sex offenders and therefore - in her world – guilty, was too much to contemplate. She had joined him straight from training bristling with all the latest terminology - which he hated. He considered himself an "old fashioned copper" willing to see the bigger picture, bend the rules if needed to avoid cluttering up the courts and ruining someone's life for an act of out of character stupidity. PC Jones was therefore a thorn in his side, but at least he could metaphorically speaking keep her on a leash…

They had been called to a situation in Tesco carpark and he tried to head off any likely confrontation. 'So, all we know is-'

She growled, 'Naked in a carpark at nine pm?'

'We don't know the situation yet PC Jones.'

She snorted. 'I do.'

He sighed as he pulled into Tesco carpark and spied a figure huddled against a row of trolleys. 'At least he has underpants on.'

As soon as the car stopped PC Jones was out one hand on her riot stick, the other on her pepper spray. PC May hurried after her. 'PC Jones!'

The figure stirred as she reached him prodding him with her stick. 'Pervert!'

PC May moved her to one side and gently helped the figure to his feet.

Margaret arrived at the police station to be greeted by the familiar sight of the top of Sergeant Turners bald head.

He looked up as she approached. 'Mrs Grimshaw. Come to collect your husband?'

She sighed but bubbling beneath was anything but concern. 'Hmm. What's this about him in't carpark in underpants?'

'Staff at the store out for a quick smoke spotted him.' He looked deep in thought, 'Health and safety rules …mind you I don't condone the habit, just the eroding of -'

Margaret sighed impatiently, 'And?'

'They saw him sitting against the trolleys. All he was wearing was his underpants.'

She shook her head. 'Bloody underpants, int winter, in bloody carpark. Tesco an all.'

'Quite. Just wait a moment and I will get someone to see you. We can't release him unless we know he will be safe you see.' He smiled thinly. 'In this time of political correctness and "duty of care" we must ensure we are complying with the regulations regarding our "customers". Even when in their underpants…'

She asked sharply, 'Was he drunk?'

'Not that I am aware of Mrs Grimshaw.'

A female pc entered with the sorry figure of Bernard clothed in a bright multi-coloured blanket. Even beneath the blanket his portly figure was evident giving a striking resemblance to a Christmas pudding.

Sergeant Turner said, 'All the paperwork is complete so you can take him home.'

She nodded curtly as she grabbed Bernard by the arm and hustled him out of the police station.

Sergeant Turner called out after her, 'Mrs Grimshaw?' She turned giving him an impatient look. 'I'm afraid the blanket is on loan. Once upon a time we would have gladly let you keep it but budgets, costing etc ...'

She nodded as she hurried Bernard down the steps, stopped realising he had no shoes and paused then muttered, 'Serves you right,' before continuing toward the carpark.

They arrived at the family focus and she bundled him into the passenger seat. 'Showing me up in public like that. Should be ashamed of yerself.' She started the car. 'Put the damn seat belt on.' Bernard sat staring into space seemingly oblivious. She said sharply, 'Bernard!' He jumped giving her a startled look. 'Seatbelt!'

He slowly comprehended the instruction.

She hurriedly pulled out of the carpark and braked sharply to avoid hitting an oncoming car causing the driver to toot. Being at the end of a very shredded tether she boiled over shouting, 'Get knotted,' and stuck two fingers up at the hapless driver.

With a screech of tyres Margaret drove on and turned to Bernard. 'You owe me an explanation, and it had better be good.'

Back at home in a leafy suburb of Ramsbottom, Margaret closed the front door and stomped into the kitchen. She looked around the door at the Christmas pudding inert in the middle of the room. She came back in and stood – hands on hips - in front of him. 'Well?'
He seemed in a daze staring straight ahead with a thousand-yard stare.

Tiger, a rescue cat - now living in luxury as a house cat - almost feral from the day it was released to Margaret and much to Bernard's disgust - weaved lazily around Margaret's legs arching its back as it eyed Bernard with a venomous glare, hissing and spitting at him angrily. Usually, Bernard would react with an angry outburst but today he didn't appear to notice.

She could see he was in no fit state to explain himself and she bustled him upstairs, into the bathroom where she snatched the blanket off him. 'Have a shower to wake you up.' She sniffed his breath. 'No booze anyway.' She looked disparagingly at the grubby underpants. 'What would happen if you'd had to go to hospital - in them? I'd be ashamed.' She left him to it.

Bernard sat in the bath, still in a daze.

Margaret fussed around in the kitchen making a cup of tea and paused, something was wrong. She marched to the foot of the stairs. 'Bernard! What are you doing?'
Silence.

She entered the bathroom to find him sitting in the bath staring at his feet. 'What the hell – where's bloody water? And you've still got them bloody underpants on. She turned the taps on and stood with arms folded. 'I don't know what game you're playing but it won't work. Get washed and come downstairs.'

Margaret sat at the kitchen table reading Women's Weekly and dunking a digestive when   Julien their fifteen-year-old son crashed through the front door and ran upstairs. Julien was - if there is really such a thing - a typical teenager but with the added problem of being gay and unsure how to handle it. A few minutes later he entered the kitchen. 'Why is he sitting in the bath and the taps running? It's all over the _'

Margaret ran upstairs and frantically turned off the taps tutting to find the floor was flooded. She looked at Bernard who continued to sit staring into space. Something was not right. She pulled the plug out and prodded him. 'Bernard.' He did not move. 'Bernard.' Nothing. 'Bernard!'

He seemed to jolt back to reality. 'Where am I?' He looked around bewildered.

Margaret got him a towel and said, 'Get dry and go to bed. Perhaps some sleep will sort you out.'

She returned downstairs to find Julien drinking from a bottle of milk out of the fridge. 'We all have to use that you know.'

He put it back. 'What's going on Mum?'

'Not sure luv. Something's happened to your Dad. He's not himself.'

Julien sat at the table. 'Got to be an improvement then.'

That night Margaret finished reading her latest romantic novel - perhaps in the vain hope that she might find Mr Right one day but certainly not in Bernard – and turned off the light. Bernard's snoring reverberated around the bedroom, and she sighed deeply, gave him a hefty nudge in the ribs and got under the covers.

The next day Bernard sat at the kitchen table while Margaret made a pot of tea. She said, 'So, are you going to explain yerself?'

He moved a crumb around on the table. 'Can't. Just a blank.'

She turned to him arms crossed. 'Blank? That's not good enough Bernard.' He shrugged despondently. 'What's the last thing you remember?'

He thought. 'I was walking to the club, about seven in the evening. It wer to demonstrate me blackberry and garlic wine.'

'And?'

'And then I was in't carpark.'

'Where's the wine then? It wasn't with you at the police station.'

He looked puzzled. 'Good point.'

'Even by your standards Bernard, you must admit it's a bit thin on detail?'

He sighed. 'I know.' He stood up. 'Thirsty.' He poured a glass of water and gulped it down, and then another. 'Can't go to work, too tired. Going to bed.' He wandered upstairs.

Margaret sat at the table deep in thought. For all his bluster, pomposity, arrogance, and downright awkwardness, he was different: something odd had happened to him. Perhaps tomorrow he would remember.

Margaret had considered the Penelope angle but there was no evidence with which to confront him - this time.

UNWANTED VISITOR

Three days later, Margaret arrived home from the vineyard to find a message on their answerphone from a woman asking Bernard to ring. Feeling a storm of anger appearing on her horizon she rang her friend Doris.
'Hi Doris. Have you got a minute?'
'What's he done now luv?'
'There's some woman on the answering machine for him.'
'Recognise the voice?'
'No.'
'It's not-'
'She wouldn't dare, not after-'
'I know you were on probation dear but she deserved that blackeye.' Her voice became unsure, 'Perhaps it's innocent?'
'Nothing involving Bernard is innocent Doris.'
'You're right there Margaret. Who would have thought he would be such a bastard?'
'My mother did. I should have listened to her and gone with Gerald.'
Doris tutted. 'Didn't he go to prison for fraud or summat? Can't remember where he worked.'
'Yes. He worked at the Congregational church. He was their accountant.'
'That's right. Mind you he always claimed he was framed by the vicar.' Doris took on a pious tone. 'Never liked that vicar, Margaret. Shifty eyes.'
'You're right Doris. Never realised what it was about him. Hmm. Shifty eyes. And too close together, always a sign in my book.'
'You could ring the number.'

Margaret remembered a newspaper article. 'What happened to the vicar?'

'He wer arrested in Brazil with charity money.'

'That's right.' She drifted for a moment. 'Gerald was never the same after you know…'

'Eh, there are some right nasty bastards in't prison.'

'You're right Doris.'

'I remember Fred from number 28, the things they did to im were something awful.'

'I'll ring it and see. Thank you, Doris.'

She disconnected and dialled the number left on the answer machine.

'Ramsbottom Gazette. Deidre speaking.'

Margaret was puzzled. 'You left a message on my phone for Mr Grimshaw?'

'Yes I did. I wondered if he would be willing to be interviewed?'

'Interviewed?'

'About the abduction.'

Margaret snorted. 'Abduction? You'll have to speak to im about that.' She slammed the phone down and went into the kitchen to put the kettle on.

Bernard entered and threw his coat onto the settee as he slumped down, 'First day back at work and I had to spend day in't car to avoid people asking stupid questions.'

'What do you expect, sitting in't carpark in grubby underpants. How many times have I said what would happen if you had to go to hospital?'

'I didn't go to damn hospital did I.'

'Police station's just as bad.' She poured tea for herself and sat at the kitchen table. 'There's a message on answer machine for you. Ramsbottom Gazette.' He groaned. 'They won't go away Bernard, these people never do. I remember Mrs Parker at number sixty-three when their lawnmower wer stolen. Hounded her for weeks.'

He jumped up angrily, 'Fine.' He dialled the number. 'Bernard Grimshaw. You left a message.'

'Thanks for ringing back. We would like to speak to you about what happened Mr Grimshaw.'

'Why?'

'It's important for people to know the truth.'

He grunted, 'I've got nothing to say.'

'It might have happened to someone else Mr Grimshaw, your account might be of comfort to them.'

Margaret sighed and stood behind him giving him a prod in the back of his neck. 'Just get it over with, they'll keep on otherwise and I haven't got time to keep answering their bloody messages.'

Bernard flinched as she prodded him. 'Ok. Come in an hour, but don't expect much.' He disconnected and cried out as Tiger embedded its claws in his leg hissing and biting furiously. 'Margaret! Get bloody thing off me!'

She knelt down and stroked the cat's head. It dropped to the floor and purred as she stroked it.

'Why does it bloody do that?'

'Because it senses your hostility. Let's face it, you're not the world's greatest animal lover.'

An hour later, Margaret opened the front door to a smartly dressed young woman and less well-dressed older man with a camera. She ushered them in.

Bernard was in the shed doodling forlornly on a writing pad. Margaret's dulcet tones brought him back to earth. He noticed the doodles were of dinner plates, stick figures and big black eyes. He scrunched the paper up and threw it on the floor. He noticed his hands were shaking. He entered the lounge and the young women greeted him warmly.

'Mr Grimshaw, I'm Deidre from the Gazette and this is Dave.' Bernard grunted and slumped onto the settee. Diedre sat opposite him with Dave beside her. 'So, what can you remember Mr Grimshaw?'

'Nothing. So you might as well go.'

'People often say that but gradually it comes back to them.' She opened a note pad. 'What was the last thing you remember?'

He sighed. 'Walking to the wine club down Hawthorn Avenue at seven in't evening.'

'Did you notice anything odd?'

'Like what?'

'Well, anyone suspicious nearby, vehicles,' she paused, 'odd lights in the sky?'

He eyed her suspiciously. 'Lights in the sky?'

'Hmm. People have been seeing odd lights, adamant that they were not stars.'

'How could they know that?'

'The lights seemed to move around in an odd way.'

Bernard stiffened feeling very uncomfortable. 'I've had enough of this. I was kidnapped by some idiot and let go, end of story.'

'And yet you can't remember anything?'

'Perhaps I was drugged.'

Margaret interjected. 'He was odd,' she almost said *even more odd*, 'for a couple of days. Like he'd been drugged.'

Diedrie was furiously scribbling as Dave checked his camera. Bernard sucked in his belly and straightened his back as Dave took some pictures. She stopped and studied Bernard closely. 'Do you have any marks on your body Mr Grimshaw?'

Bernard forgot he was posing and leapt up. 'Marks? I've had enough of this.' Dave snapped three quick shots of Bernard in full flow, belly in its natural state flopping over his belt. Bernard snarled, 'See yerselves out I've got nowt for yer.' He stomped out to the shed.

'I must apologise for my husband; he's been under a lot of stress since the… incident.'

'I understand Mrs Grimshaw, it must have been a terrible ordeal for him.' She glanced at the photographer. 'Perhaps it will start to come back to him. Perhaps we could have a picture of you? You know, supportive wife etc?'

Margaret touched her hair into place wishing she had been to the hairdressers as she had planned. 'Suppose so.'

The next day Margaret brandished the Ramsbottom gazette at him. 'Well done. You're a local celebrity.'

He snatched the paper and read the headline. "LOCAL MAN ABDUCTED BY ALIENS AND DUMPED IN TESCO CARPARK". He read further. "Local man Bernard Grimshaw, a council employee was found almost naked after being missing for five days. Residents have been observing strange lights in the sky recently. Could Mr Grimshaw have been abducted by aliens, and possibly subjected to horrifying probes? Should we all live in fear of the skies?"

Below the headline was Bernard standing with his mouth wide open mid rant and his belly in full repose over his belt.

He threw the paper on the floor. 'What the hell?'

Margaret fussed with the cooker. 'I think flying saucers are more believable than you being kidnapped. I mean,' she looked him up and down, 'who would bother?' She furiously scrubbed the hob - her marigolds squeaking. 'You have to embarrass me don't you Bernard.'

He threw his hands up in despair. 'Here we go.'

She rounded on him snatching off the gloves – he took a step back as she threw them at him. 'Not since the wine tasting fiasco have I been so shown up.'

'You just can't let it go can you Margaret.'

She smiled sweetly. 'Hmm I wonder why? Oh I know,' she angrily thrust her face up to his,' rolling around in't marquee fighting over a bucket with Tony, that's right.'

Bernard began to bluster. 'He-'

She glared at him. 'Don't. Your pathetic.'

'Thank you for that vote of confidence. I shall retire to the shed and do some secretarial business for wine club.'

'Sulk you mean?'

The shed was a place Bernard ran to for cover when he sensed trouble brewing on the home front. He spent a lot of time in it. The shed was a compact arrangement comprising a work bench, shelves and cupboards reclaimed from decorating projects in the house. The shed's main function however (apart from a bunker to dodge the regular bombardment of verbal, and at times, physical, attacks, not to mention regular assaults by the cat) was for wine making; his one passion and at which he was talented, enough in fact for him to be elected chairman of the Blackburn wine makers' club for the eighth consecutive year.

Safe within the confines of the shed, Bernard tried to ignore the horror that was becoming his life. How could he face his colleagues at work, the golf club and worst of all the wine making club? His wine making prowess - together with an innate belief that he was right on all occasions, bolstered by an aggressive defence of such a position - made it inevitable he would continue to be Chairman and re-elected until someone brave, or stupid enough, challenged him. Despite furtive discussions in dark corners of the Goat and Badger pub - the name defied any local to explain its origin - the more disgruntled members regularly plotted schemes to dethrone him. However, these plots inevitably withered away when an actual opportunity presented itself. After all, they had lives outside of the club, didn't they? Was it worth the lengthy, painful and embarrassing character assassinations they would have to endure in front of their peers as Bernard proved by lengthy explanations why he was the only one with the right skills to hold the office of Chairman? Such meetings would end in a heavy silence followed by the scraping of chairs over disgruntled mumblings. 'Next year definitely....'

Naturally, Bernard considered his role of chairman to be one of guidance of the lesser members and believed he set a sound role model by his modesty in reluctantly accepting re-election, something he secretly considered a well-earned accolade. He was aware of the annual plotting against him but this year his re-election was even more uncertain following the recent incident and press coverage which gave the plotters the ammunition they needed to oust him. He needed an ally to secure his position which would come in the form of Frank, Margaret's future brother-in-law. The tiny fly in the ointment was that Bernard despised him.

BAD NEWS

A week later, Bernard was back to normal – whatever that implied - driving, deep in thought, carefully adhering to the speed limit. He was not in a good mood; something was up with Margaret which he hoped was not to be a repeat of five years ago. That was too much to put up with again. Talk about an overreaction to finding messages from Penelope on his phone - and what right did she have to go through it anyway? Granted the messages were a little fruity - and his replies even more so – but it was only a harmless flirtation. Not that Margaret saw it that way.

He considered women's moods something they should keep to themselves; men had enough to put up with making all the important decisions. With early retirement around the corner he envisaged spending it perfecting his home-grown wine and of course the odd round of golf. He wasn't going to make the mistake of not expanding his interests like Margaret, also planning early retirement. The thought of being together every day filled him with dread. But something else filled him with dread although he was unaware of it: underlying memories that were deeper, darker, and much too frightening, hiding from examination concerning missing time, big eyes, weird smells…

He spotted the road he was looking for and turned into a housing estate checking for number 22. In the distance he could see a house with an extension nearing completion. 'Got to be it' he sighed. He pulled up outside and confirmed it was the right house. He checked himself in the rear-view mirror twirling his walrus moustache and noting with pride his full head of hair. He eased his portly frame out of the car and reached back in for some paperwork. He strode purposefully to the front door and gave the knocker a hefty bang. He adjusted his expression to that of a "representative of Local Government", something he took very seriously.

The door was opened by a young, very pregnant woman who, on noting Bernard's undeniable 'official presence' seemed to shrink a little as he announced in his official deep Yorkshire accent, 'Bernard Grimshaw, Blackburn building control'.

He tried to look past her, eager to undertake his responsibilities as she said, 'My husband is in the kitchen if you'd...' Bernard carefully edged between her and the door, ensuring he did not physically touch her, "that could lead to an accusation of assault" he had been told on his recent health and safety course. He strode purposefully down the hall uttering an official, 'Thank you'.

He entered an extension to the kitchen where, up a ladder, a young man was filling some cracks. The young man looked round in surprise. 'Mr Grimshaw, we were expecting you yesterday'.

Bernard sighed as he opened a plan of the building. 'My schedule is a busy one, we do our best. I'm sure the public would prefer representatives of their local government to be in two places at once, but I'll not be attempting it.'

Quickly apologetic the young man hurried down the ladder. 'I wasn't saying...'

Bernard continued as if he hadn't heard him and examined an exposed lintol over a door. 'That lintel is the right size?' he consulted the plan, 'It's specified here as a 200 by 150'. The young man looked relieved. Bernard peered at the lintel, '150 end bearings? Concrete pads, or engineering bricks?' The young man smiled again, 'Of course Mr Grimshaw. I want this to last us a long while, so I used engineering bricks'.

Bernard consulted the plan again, 'That's as maybe. Forgive me for doing my job but the regulations are in place to ensure public safety. That includes you.' The young man shifted uncomfortably, 'I know, I wasn't...'

Bernard strutted back and forth examining the work in detail. 'I've seen worse, I'll grant you that. He pointed to the ceiling, 'I trust the insulation is as specified on the plan? Thermal values are the thing of today. If we are to save this planet from global warming it behoves us to ensure we use the minimum of energy.'

'Actually,' beamed the young man, 'I've put in more than was specified. You're quite right; we need to do all we can...'

Bernard smiled and twirled his walrus moustache, 'I'm gladdened to hear you understand about global warming lad.' He examined the newly plastered ceiling. 'Are you a plasterer?

The young man said hesitantly, 'Yes?'

'Thought so. Very nice skim finish.'

He stopped at a pipe exiting the ground. 'What's this?' He consulted the plan. 'I don't recollect passing groundwork. Did you advise us it was ready for inspection?'

The young man blanched. 'Yes. I was told on the phone that if you didn't come, to go ahead and fill it in.'

With careful deliberation Bernard folded the plan. 'I'll not go so far as to say you haven't completed the work successfully, and to the local authority requirements, but I must be satisfied that it has been done to standards and requirements of the Building Regulations, as recently amended. You can't cover up drainage and expect us to accept your word for it. Were only a week ago a two-story extension had to be demolished because builder had skimped on't drainage and scuppered foundations. You'll have to dig an access hole to facilitate an examination of the work.'

The young man gulped, 'But I was told to go ahead. I'll have to dig out the concrete I've just put down. I can assure you I have...'

Bernard headed toward the front door. 'Inform me when it is ready for inspection, thank you, good day.'

The young man slumped against the ladder, deflated. Bernard reappeared. 'And you'll have to remove enough ceiling for inspection of insulation. Good day.'

Back in his car Bernard checked his next visit muttering, 'Chilvers, bloody cowboy if ever I saw one.' As he pulled away the young woman appeared on the doorstep clutching her enormously swollen belly. Her husband had his arm around her; she was dabbing tears away. Bernard glimpsed the anxious tableau in his rear-view mirror, twirled his moustache and accelerated; the tiny traces of a satisfied smile twitched his lips.

Bernard turned on radio four which he considered the only one worth listening to: the others full of banal chatter and a poor excuse for music. He maintained a steady thirty miles per hour (despite the speed limit) which he believed a necessary requirement of a local council representative. With a magnanimous gesture he allowed an AA van out from a side road, accelerating enough to close the gap and prevent a woman in a four by four to pull out. Bernard talked out loud to himself more often than he would admit - something Margaret often threw at him during their regular "disagreements". He did so now peering into the rear-view mirror. 'You want to drive bloody big vehicle like that using up precious world resources then go ahead, but I'll not be condoning it by letting you out'.

He settled back and listened to woman's hour. The compare was in discussion with a guest who was describing how natural birth should be encouraged more at home.

He shouted at the radio, 'Do what! not in my bloody house! Only place for all that mess is bloody hospital. Woman nowadays, they want it all.' His cheeks flushed, moustache twitching he snarled with indignation, 'Bout time they realised it's a man's world and always will be.'

With disgust he punched the radio off. Grunting with the exertion of having to lean over, he grabbed a CD jewel case and fiddled with one hand to get the CD out. It was resolutely refusing. He glanced down to see why, noted it was upside down and.... a blare of a car hooter brought his attention back to the road as a car headed toward him, the driver wildly gesticulating at him to get back to his own side. Bernard snatched at the wheel, snarling into the rear-view mirror. 'Bloody idiot! Eh, how do these people ever pass bloody driving test.' He put in a cd and pressed play. Tammy Wynette filled the car with soothing country music. 'Now that's proper music.' He relaxed into the gentle soft voice.

It began to rain. The road he was looking for came into view and he turned into it peering past his windscreen wipers and muttering, 'Yes, thought so, trying it on again Chilvers are we? Well we'll see who has bloody power round here.' He pulled up outside a small building site on which was being constructed a four-bedroom house, with scaffolding, rubble, cement mixer grinding away and two men working on a half-finished wall. He snatched a plan from his brief case and got out mumbling, 'Bloody cowboys.'

The two men stopped working as he marched toward them, ill concealing their satisfaction as he tripped on a brick half buried in the remains of what was once a lawn. He made a quick hop and step to cover himself.

The older of the two men raised his trowel as if preparing for combat. Bernard clutched his plan tighter in response as he drew closer. 'I recall you were to send amended plan before proceeding Mr Chilvers.' He looked around, 'That wall was further over if I remember correctly, which is why I required an amended plan. Any variance from the original...'

With no attempt to hide his dislike Mr Chilvers snarled in a wide Yorkshire accent, 'Wouldn't matter if plan had been fuckin gold plated, you'd still find something to moan about. There's nowt wrong with position of wall and you know it. Come round ere with your airs an graces! I knew you when you were lad with socks round ankles, and you know what?' he leant forward menacingly, 'You were twat then an all.'

Bernard puffed himself up. 'You can't address a representative of local authority in such a manner. Fact is, we are required to ensure compliance with building regulations as amended...'

'You can shove it up where sun don't shine lad. I've been at this game long enough to know what works and what doesn't. The nearest you've come to building anything is fuckin leggo!' The younger man chortled eying Bernard with a contemptuous smile.

Bernard consulted the plan then checked the wall. 'Cavity insulation seems up to specification anyway.' He moved over to exposed pipes deep within a hole, water covering any detail. 'Groundworks need inspecting. You'll have to pump water out for me to check connection.'

Mr Chilvers put down his trowel and stood beside Bernard. 'So now its bloody drains is it? Listen you little tin pot wanker, when time is right you will be notified so that you can do a pressure test. Now if you want to get down there and splash about in shitty water, I'll be pleased to give you a shove. Otherwise,' he gestured to Bernard's car, 'Fuck off.' He turned to his colleague with a sly grin. 'At least you've got yer trousers on!'

Bernard rolled up the plan and snorted, 'I shall return to inspect groundworks.' He turned and stomped off, careful to avoid the half-buried brick. He ignored Chilvers singing loudly, 'Fly me to the moon, ha!'

***

Bernard was still smarting from losing the verbal battle with Chilvers. After all there was not much he could say about the carpark incident given it was spread over the national press. But his steadfast arrogance had reappeared and now he hummed "My way" (grossly off tune) to himself as he stood before the mirror in his living room preening his large walrus moustache with a pair of scissors. Being a fastidious, albeit a careless man, copious clippings from the moustache were forming a hairy covering on a collection of ornamental fish on the mantelpiece giving the impression that they were swimming in a sea from some strange mythical hirsute world. Oblivious, he drew in his enormous belly and puffed out his chest admiring himself.

His chest deflated, and his oversized belly relaxed back into its normal position hanging over his trousers as he heard the crunch of tyres on gravel announcing the arrival of Margaret. He often reflected upon the unfairness of life and for how long must a man be punished for a few minutes of pleasure at a time when such young man had needs beyond his control? He paused, sighed heavily then returned to the last few seconds of his private party, aware that forces beyond his control were about to be unleashed which would inevitably lead to an argument that he knew deep down he would lose. He always did. Why was it he would ask himself, he could win any argument at the golf club committee meetings and yet at home...

There was a rattle of keys in the front door and a few seconds later Margaret appeared. 'Bernard! How many times have I-'

'And hello to you too.'

'Those are my kitchen scissors.'

He glanced at them mid snip and sniffed them with distaste, 'Haddock,' he waved them at her, 'Bout time yer improved washing up skills then...' She snatched them away and he yelped, 'Be careful Margaret nearly had me finger off.'

Margaret disappeared into the kitchen muttering to herself, 'Look at the mess you've made...it mystifies me why you don't use the mirror in the bathroom.' She reappeared with a dustpan and brush and began – at first delicately then with gusto fired by many years of frustration, to remove the hairy trimmings, tutting furiously to herself.

Bernard realised his recent suspicions were correct; her moods were getting worse. In fact, today she seemed very prickly. Better tread carefully if he wanted his tea tonight, on a plate and not sliding down the wall like last week.... Talk about an over-reaction to what he considered an innocent comment about brussels being like snooker balls.

She sighed loudly and went into the hall to return with a vacuum cleaner. She plugged it in and switched it on just as he said, 'Had a good day at-'

She furiously sucked up the hair from between the figures and shouted over it (it was a very old and noisy machine) 'What?'

He shouted, 'I said had-'

She switched it off. 'What?'

With forced cheerfulness he asked, 'I asked did you have a good day at the vineyard?'

She brandished the hose at him. 'Don't pretend you have anything but contempt for my job.'

He smiled condescendingly, 'Come on, a vineyard. In Bolton?'

'At least he tries to make it a success.'

He twirled his moustache. 'I have a wealth of knowledge he could use but no he refuses to-'

She switched it back on and pushed him out of the way to get at some stubborn trimmings hiding amongst a tableau of goldfish. He watched her furiously vacuuming and wondered how he had ended up married to-

She switched it off and glared at him. 'Go on say it.'

He puffed himself up. 'I accept the wine tasting event was successful in finding an investor but I'm afraid Tom is not cut out for wine growing,' he couldn't resist it (although he realised he was suddenly on dangerous ground but it was too late) 'nor his useless father, Arthur isn't it?'

Margaret stopped, turned and with an even more aggressive flourish of the hose, far too close to his face in his opinion, muttered, 'After your escapade in the carpark two weeks ago and absence of any explanation, you have the audacity to-' She huffed and returned to her task in removing the hair from the mantelpiece with a duster and inadvertently caught a fish's tail knocking it off the mantelpiece to shatter on the fireplace surround. 'Now look what you've made me do! Just...just go away!'

Huffily he replied as he left, 'Obviously not. I'll be in't shed.'

She shouted after him, 'Don't forget we're meeting Frank and Diane this weekend. Frank doesn't want to go to France unless everything is working alright. The caravan needs checking, and you need to sort your clothes out.'

As Bernard slammed the backdoor, Julien, came in slamming the front door and slung his bag on the sofa, following it arms crossed in a sulk. Margaret wondered how long the door frames would withstand such treatment but decided it was not worth consideration. She donned her diplomat's hat and asked casually as she breezed past him, 'Bad day?' Julien grunted. She fussed around in the kitchen patiently waiting for him to enter. Two minutes later he appeared and asked grumpily, 'What's for tea?'

Margaret smiled sweetly, 'Spaghetti. Your Dad hates it.'

'Great!' He sighed dramatically. 'Sebastian thinks we should get a flat.' He stroked Tiger who purred contentedly.

Margaret sipped her tea, 'Sounds easy when you say it like that, but you need an income. Anyway. You're not old enough. There's no rush. He can come here any time he wants...' Julien glanced in the direction of the shed and pulled a face. Margaret stroked his arm, 'I know dear. Your father's problem is that he is an ignorant pig.'

They both laughed. Bernard entered and without a word went to the kettle and switched it on. He got out a mug and popped in a teabag.

Margaret said innocently, 'Julien's home Bernard.'

Bernard looked round. 'I can see that. Bout time an all. Where you been? Wait up, I know, at that KFC or should I call it, "kids fattening centre".'

Julien stood. 'I'm going out Mum. Won't be long.' The front door shut with a bang.

Margaret sighed and focused on the enormous belly in front of her as he busied himself with his tea making. 'People in glass houses...'

Bernard looked over to her as he put the kettle down. 'What?' He picked up his mug and sneered, 'I was against bloody name from word go, but you had to have your way, and now look at im. Who would ave thought I would end up wi bloody-.'

She stood and glared at him. 'I should have listened to my mother-'

'Ere we go again-'

'She warned me, and she was right. She said you were a bigoted git...'

Tiger began moving slowly toward him as if hunting its prey. Bernard decided to retreat to the shed again.

A few minutes later, the shed door opened, and Margaret poked her head in. 'Sorry to disturb your vital work Bernard but we have visitors. I'll let you deal with them.'

He noted a slight movement out of the corner of his eye, on the second shelf behind a tin of creosote, and eyed an aerosol spray. It was getting too bold. He could put up with most creatures but a spider gave him the creeps.

Margaret's dulcet tones made him jump. 'Bernard!'

He went into the kitchen as Margaret was drawing the living room curtains. Puzzled, because it was only early afternoon, he said, 'What the hell are you doing now?'

She stopped and stood with arms folded and nodded toward the street.

Bernard did a double take. 'Bloody hell!'

The street was packed with journalists jostling to see into the house. Neighbours were tooting to get into their drives.

'You caused it Bernard; you sort it out.' She went into the kitchen and shut the door.

He peered around one of the curtains and was immediately spotted.

'There he is! Mr Grimshaw!'

A bang on the front door brought a shout from the kitchen. 'Go out there and get rid of them. Now!'

Reluctantly Bernard opened the front door to be met with a clamour of eager reporters thrusting microphones in his face and camera flashes blinding him. 'Mr Grimshaw!'

A young female reporter eager to beat the competition thrust a microphone at him. 'What charity is this for?'

Bernard gasped, 'What?'

She jostled to maintain her position. 'Like, did it really happen or is this a fund raiser?'

Bernard leaned into the microphone. 'How dare you. Do you think I wanted to be in't carpark like that?'

She pushed back against the other clamouring reporters. 'Were you abducted?'

Bernard sighed. 'I don't know what happened. It wasn't me said anything about flying saucers.'

'You disappeared for five days. Were you treated well?'

How many times do I have to say that I remember nowt?'

Another female reporter managed to push her microphone in front of the other reporter and asked in an urgent tone, 'Were you tortured? Did they anally probe you? Was it scary Mr Grimshaw? What was-'

Bernard put up his hands for silence. 'For goodness sake I don't remember anything-'

A barrage of questions fired at him. 'Was your memory wiped Bernard? Did they take you off planet? Do they come in peace?'

Bernard looked at the baying crowd and shook his head. What was the point of speaking to them, they would only distort anything he said. He began to close the door as a loud male voice shouted, 'Have you got a message for us?'

Angrily he snatched the door open and yelled, 'Yes!' The crowd fell silent in expectation.

'Piss off!' He slammed the door and snatched the curtains closed.

Margaret appeared and sighed. 'You really have a way with people don't you Bernard.'

He shrugged and marched back to the shed.

Margaret sat in the kitchen and tried to ignore the shouting outside and breathed a sigh of relief when it subsided. She sipped her tea contemplating a more pressing matter concerning Bernard's mother Ingrid. Margaret had been putting off dealing with the phone call from social services that morning. Ingrid was not her favourite person but being Bernard's mother, she felt some responsibility. Well, if there was no option other than her living with them until other accommodation could be found, so be it. She sipped her tea staring out of the window; there was no good time to break the news to Bernard about his estranged mother, she just had to light the fuse and stand back.

She finished her tea and wondered what life was going to be like, when there was another knock on the front door. She hesitated, deciding whether it was worth shouting to Bernard but decided that would just make matters worse. Taking the less damaging route she opened the door to find two men staring at her. They were identical in height (well over six feet) dressed in black suits, black fedora hats and wearing dark glasses. One of them said with an impassive tone, 'We need to speak to Mr Grimshaw.'

Margaret looked from one to the other. 'Who the hell are you?'

The same one simply repeated, 'We need to speak Mr Grimshaw.'

She said, 'Wait there.' Shaking her head, she went to the shed. 'There are two American weirdos at the door wanting to speak to you.'

He sighed as he doodled on a writing pad. 'Tel em to go away Margaret I'm not in the mood.'

'That might be so Bernard, but I don't think they will.'

He jumped up. 'Right!' He stomped into the house and snatched open the front door. 'What is it, I'm busy.'

They pushed past him into the lounge. The one that spoke sat on the sofa while the other opened draws in a sideboard. On the sideboard Tiger was comfortably nesting on the broadband router (a warm spot he returned to whenever Bernard brushed him carelessly off) and watched the interlopers with disdain, considering whether it was worth launching an attack. He decided to give a cursory hiss as the man opened a drawer.

Bernard followed them and stood in front of the man sitting down. 'Who the hell do you think-'

'The press was here.'

Bernard was watching the one poking about in the cupboard. 'Hey you what the-'

The man sitting down said, 'Sit down Mr Grimshaw.' The veiled threat in his voice convinced Bernard to do as he said. 'What do you know?'

Bernard was beyond being frustrated. 'Well now let me think. I know it is 2020, I know the interest rate is two percent, which in my opinion should be lower-'

The same impassive voice cut him off. 'Don't play games Mr Grimshaw. We know what happened.'

'Well in that case what the hell are you asking me for?'

'We need to be sure you do not speak about it.'

Bernard gritted his teeth. 'How can I talk about something I don't remember?' He looked from one to the other. 'Who the hell are you anyway?'

'You don't want to know. You are involved in matters beyond your comprehension. It is important that you do not speak to anyone.'

'How many times-' The silent one came back in the room carrying Julien's laptop. Bernard stood up and shouted, 'Oi, leave that alone.'

The vocal man said, 'Hacking is a serious offence.'

Bernard slumped down again white faced. 'Hacking? I only use it for me bank statement. And anyway, it's my son's not mine. I think you'd better go.'

'You have missing time. What do you remember?'

He jumped up again. 'I've had enough of this. I don't remember nowt.'

The men exchanged glances. The one sitting said, 'You will not talk to the media.'

'And what if I do?'

'You won't.' They exchanged glances again and he said, 'If you want your family to be safe.' Without a sound they left.

Margaret came in. 'Who the hell were they?'

'No idea. Bloody cheek threatening me! If they come again don't open the door.' He marched out to the shed.

Bernard's mind was reeling. He desperately needed some peace which the shed provided although this haven was slightly marred by the presence of a large and cunning spider.

Being well practiced at retreating, the spider darted for cover as Bernard entered swearing to himself as he slammed the shed door with sufficient force to rattle tins and plastic containers on the many shelves the spider considered its kingdom. Perhaps as a reaction to being threatened, Bernard decided to attack the resident in the shed. It watched as he crashed around looking for something. On a shelf he found what he was looking for and stood brandishing an aerosol. The spider knew it would be curtains if it got sprayed with *that* and retreated deep into the cover of the tins.

'Where are you, you little bastard.' He sprayed indiscriminately until he realised he couldn't breathe and staggered outside coughing.

Margaret came to the backdoor to shake out a duster. 'Not that spider again, what's the poor little bugger done to you eh? Grown man afraid of a tiny spider...should be ashamed of yerself.'

'You've not seen the size of it! Eyes like dinner plates!'

'Oh, get over yerself...'

Bernard stopped coughing. 'If the bloody cat was allowed out it might get these monsters.' He paused. 'And might stop attacking me.'

'He is a rescue cat and deserves love and care. We don't know what happened to him before he came to us.'

Bernard grunted. 'It's only a bloody cat.'

The front doorbell rang. Bernard peeked into the shed to see if the coast was clear.

Margaret sighed. 'I'll just go and see who that is shall I?' He grunted as he peered around the shed door with a hand over his mouth.

She re-appeared. 'Somebody here to see you.' She went back into the kitchen and he heard her ask the visitor 'cup of tea?' A young woman's voice replied that she would. Bernard immediately straightened himself and tossed the aerosol into the shed - like a grenade into a bunker - closing the door with a slam. Relieved it was not *them* again he hurried into the kitchen, sucking in his large belly.

A young woman was talking to Julien about school and stroking Tiger. She turned to Bernard as he entered. 'Mr Ramsbottom? I'm Felicity Fielding. Social Services. I am here to speak to you about your mother, Ingrid Kazakof.'

Julien barked at Bernard. 'Where's my laptop?'

Bernard sat down. 'Some weirdos took it. Said something about hacking.'

Julien welled up with anger, 'You have no right to-'

Margaret intervened. 'Don't worry luv, we'll sort it out. We've had all sorts here today.' She glared at Bernard, 'Since the carpark incident. Now we have to talk to the social worker about something.'

Bernard turned to the social worker, 'What's the daft bat done now.'

Margaret said quietly, 'She has nowhere to live Bernard. She will have to come here.'

***

Zac Childersberger furiously scribbled in his journal and snapped it shut. If his suspicions were right, then he was onto something big. Very big. The enchiladas. Whatever, the expression was, this could be it. He had been following such cases as Bernard's and knew this one was different. The two strange men clinched it as far as he was concerned; their interest indicating that he would be taken seriously.

Zac had wanted to be taken seriously for most of his thirty-two years. Most people he knew considered him to be on the fringes of living in a fantasy land - one consisting of far-off worlds and strange beings. He spent much of his time daydreaming and working and there was not too much space for friends; hence he was a loner. He was conscious of his American accent, living in the north of England.

He dialled his mobile and spoke. 'I have an update. He's up to something.'

An American male voice answered. 'Keep up surveillance. It's a hell of a theory Zac, but if you're right, we have to shut him down.'

THE PAST

Bernard entered Ramsbottom police station and stood at the reception counter staring at the bald pate of Sergeant Turner. He noted a spot on it and wondered if it was a bite of some sort or maybe-'.

Sergeant Turner stopped writing and looked up. 'Yes Sir.' A spark of recognition as he said, 'Mr Grimshaw isn't it? Of carpark fame?'

Bernard ignored the reference. 'I want to report a theft.'

Sergeant Turner smiled. 'Would it be a few items of clothing?'

Bernard blushed. 'No. A laptop.'

'I see.' He began to write and said as he did so, 'A laptop.' He looked up. 'Was this your laptop?'

'No, my son's.'

He wrote carefully speaking as he did so, 'My son's. Where was it when it was stolen?'

'In't house.'

'Your house?'

'Yes.'

'Was anything else stolen?'

'No.'

'Was this a break in?'

'No.'

He stopped writing and scratched his head. 'So, a laptop was taken from your house but there was no forced entry. Can I assume the house was empty then when the laptop was stolen?'

'No. I was there. And my wife.'

'Hmm. Logically then, it must be that you knew the individual, or of course individuals, who took it?'

'They were strangers.'

'But you let them in. Was there a struggle? I'm assuming because you are reporting this as a theft that the laptop was taken without your, or your wife's permission?'

'Yes.'

Sergeant Turner noticed blood under his fingernail and took out a large extremely white handkerchief. 'Why were they in your house?'

Bernard sighed realising this was going to be difficult. 'I opened the front door and they barged in and sat down, asking me stupid questions about... you know.'

Sergeant Turner suppressed a smile as he put away the handkerchief. 'The carpark incident?' Bernard nodded. Sergeant Turner said, 'I see.' He picked up his pen. 'Can you describe them?'

'They looked identical; about six four high, both dressed in black suits, black fedoras type hats and wearing dark glasses.'

'This time of the year? Interesting.'

Bernard said, 'Only one of em spoke and he sounded weird, sort of like an American computer voice, know what I mean?'

Sergeant Turner put his pen down. Deep in thought. 'Yes, sadly I do. My nephew bought me a device that I could ask questions, give simple instructions to etc. Half the time I think I would have had a better conversation with the sofa.'

'They went on about hacking. Don't really understand much about it.'

Sergeant Turner looked thoughtful. 'The Americans are overly sensitive about such matters since the infamous case of Gary Mckinnon in,' he scratched his head in thought and flinched, 'yes, 2002. He hacked into the American security computer system and discovered details pertaining to secret military operations off planet. UFO buffs thought Christmas had come early, confirming their beliefs that the Americans were working with Aliens.'

Bernard was beginning to think too much sun had – over the years – done something to Sergeant Turner's brain. He considered leaving.

Sergeant Turner was deep in thought. 'He was later diagnosed with Asperger's and the Home secretary at the time, Terresa May, successfully fought to stop him being extradited to face an inevitable lengthy prison sentence for the rest of his life. I could think of a few individuals I would gladly see receive such a sentence, but that's bye the bye.'

Bernard sighed. 'Yes, very interesting, but what about my son's computer?'

'Hmm. I would think the chance of getting that back is about as likely as me winning the lottery, and considering I don't partake in it, therefore zero.' He looked over Bernard's shoulder to the world outside. 'Why people need more than they have has always seemed folly to me.' He looked back to Bernard who was gritting his teeth, 'Of course if your son has been attempting to hack into their system…'

Bernard leant closer, 'Is Asperger's the same as being,' he pulled a face, 'gay?'

Sergeant Turner shook his head. 'I suppose you could have Asperger's and be gay, but they are not mutually inclusive.' He noted Bernard's bemused expression. 'Asperger's has nothing to do with being gay.'

'I want to report it anyway.'

'Your son being gay?'

Bernard gritted his teeth, 'The laptop.'

'Of course, Mr Grimshaw. Perhaps your house insurance might cover it?'

Bernard knew he was getting nowhere fast and grunted as he turned to leave.

'Just one other matter Mr Grimshaw.'

Bernard stopped and turned. 'What?'
'Can we have our blanket back please?'

***

Bernard sat in his shed feeling sorry for himself. Competing memories were joining forces to depress him: the most recent ones beyond his conscious mind overlaying repressed memories of childhood. As he absently decanted wine from one bottle to another he thought of that day; the day his world was turned upside down. He stopped decanting and sat down. Why did his Dad disappear? Who was the big foreign man who arrived shortly after and moved in? His head began to spin as emotions welled up. He remembered the fear as he was bustled onto a bus to a friend of his father and left there with his belongings and told by his tearful mother she would come back soon. Well, she didn't did she? He felt a deep swell of anger rise. Then the children's home and those horrible bullies. His things taken or broken, horrible food, constant feelings of fear.

He was disturbed from his nightmarish reverie by Margaret. 'If we're going then we need to do it soon or we'll get rush hour traffic.' She paused, unsure. 'You hear me Bernard? We need to go.' He nodded. She sighed. 'I don't know what gets into you sometimes. You sit out here getting yourself in a state.'

'Give it a rest ok? I'll not be long.'

She shrugged and over her shoulder said, 'You're the one who moans about the traffic Bernard.'

He tidied up the bench mumbling to himself, 'Aye and it's me with bloody dodgy family to put up with an all.'

Bernard drove slightly below the speed limit occasionally checking the sat nav. Margaret was trying to read a magazine but she couldn't concentrate. She sighed, 'Why did she have to appear now? Couldn't have been at a worse time if she'd tried.'

Bernard gripped the wheel tightly — his knuckles white beneath his leather driving gloves – trying to control his temper.

'I mean we're not exactly spring chickens are we? Working hard for retirement for what? To look after a doddering old woman who probably needs lots of care. I'll tell you this for nowt, I won't be spending all my time doing it. She's your mother.'

He pulled into the hospital car park looking for a space. 'An I've worked long bloody hours to put a roof over yer head so we're quits.'

Ingrid sat on the edge of her bed with her plastered leg resting on a stool. A nurse was sitting with her. 'So big day then Ingrid! Are you nervous?'

Ingrid looked out of the window and shrugged.

'If the visit becomes stressful just ring the bell.'

Ingrid sighed as the nurse left wondering what on earth she was going to say. Hello Bernard, how are you? Lovely day. She picked at the edge of her plaster cast.

The nurse knocked gently and stuck her head in. 'Ingrid, you have some visitors.' The door opened and Margaret entered pulling Bernard by his arm followed by Felicity. The nurse stood aside for them. 'Here we are Ingrid, your son Bernard, and his wife Margaret. I'll leave you to get acquainted.' The door shut silently.

Ingrid studied them. Felicity fussed around with Ingrid's bedding. 'So here we are then!' She looked from one stony face to another wishing she was somewhere else. 'Bernard looks like you Ingrid, doesn't he Margaret?'

Margaret stood stiffly, clasping her handbag. 'Hmm.'

Felicity looked to Bernard. 'I know you have a few issues to get off your chest but perhaps we can start with saying hello?'

Bernard stood stiffly his moustache seeming to quiver with anger. He tensely waved a hand in Ingrid's direction. He turned to look out of the window.

Felicity said. 'Ingrid, perhaps you could say-'

Bernard blurted. 'Thirty-seven bloody years!'

Felicity drew a deep breath, 'Pardon?'

Bernard stood with his hands clasped behind him, fingers fidgeting between themselves as he stared out of the window. 'Ask her why. Ask her why she dumped me.'

Ingrid stirred. 'I do not remember. I have lost memory.'

Bernard murmured. 'How convenient for you.'

Margaret said, 'Do you remember what happened to your flat Ingrid?'

'Is pile of rubble. No I do not remember.'

Felicity stood. 'Anyway, we've made a start. Perhaps we can discuss when your mother will move in with you.'

Margaret spoke directly to Ingrid. 'Seems we have no choice but for you to come and live with us. I've no grudge.' She nodded at Bernard, 'I can't speak for him.'

She turned to Felicity. 'Let us know when Ingrid will be discharged, and we'll take it from there.'

Felicity smiled at her. 'Thank you Margaret, that's very helpful.'

***

The next morning, Bernard sat in his shed ruminating on the impending arrival of his mother. To say he was not looking forward to it would be an understatement: he had not spoken to her for thirty years, despite her being within easy travelling distance.

Margaret snatched the shed door open (Bernard believed to catch him out doing something she would disapprove of) and entered. To provide a reason for being in the shed he had the wine club minutes in front of him.

'You have a visitor.'

'Who?'

'Your mother.' She turned and left him to stew in the deafening silence of the shed. He sighed and wearily stood. Out of the corner of his eye he thought he sensed a fleeting movement near the white emulsion on the second shelf. 'Still alive you little bastard? Enjoy it while it lasts.' He gave an involuntary shiver and left.

As he opened the back door, he heard the unmistakable Russian/broken English of his mother Ingrid Kazakof. He took a deep breath and went into the lounge.

Felicity, the social worker welcomed him. 'Bernard. Your mother is here to see you.'

Bernard stood stiffly by the door. 'Right.'

Ingrid, looking totally at ease and sitting next to Margaret said, 'Hello Bernard.'

'Mother.'

Felicity said, 'So, Bernard, your wife tells me you work for the council as an architect.'

'Nope.' He sat down as a far away from Ingrid as possible. 'Building control. Planning permissions actually.'

Felicity smiled tightly knowing this was going to be difficult, but to meet her "targets of positive outcomes" drummed into her by her manager she had to persevere. 'Right. I understand you haven't seen each other for a while.'

Bernard snorted. 'Thirty years.'

Ingrid smiled sweetly. 'You were always welcome to visit Bernard, my tiny flat up in the sky.'

'You chose to live there, *mother*.'

Ingrid rearranged her coat. 'The bastard of your father left me little choice. Stranding me in this country, away from my home in,' she sniffled, wiping away an imaginary tear, 'Russia. He took all our money. What was I to do?'

Bernard bristled. 'All his fault then. What a surprise.'

'He cheated on me. In Russia my father would have cut off his-'

Felicity seeing her targets drifting away over the horizon interjected. 'Anyway, sadly your mother has lost her flat and is homeless. We must consider family before any other options.'

Bernard ignored her as he smiled evilly at his mother. 'What happened to your flat, *mother*?'

She sniffled into her handkerchief. 'There was terrible accident, big explosion.'

Bernard smiled smugly. 'And what was the cause?' He savoured the moment for a second as if in possession of secret knowledge. 'I'll tell you.' He turned to Felicity, 'See, I have contacts in't council Felicity. The explosion was caused by the storage of gas cylinders, poorly stored and maintained, which were being used in *her* flat to assist in the cultivation of cannabis.' He smiled at Ingrid. 'Isn't that right mother?'

Ingrid sniffled into her handkerchief. 'I was not aware bad man downstairs was using my spare room for such terrible thing.'

Bernard smiled at Felicity as he said, 'Do tell us mother what you thought he was doing in your spare room?'

'I trusted him. I thought he was growing medicine.'

Bernard sneered, 'According to my colleagues in the crime squad, there was enough high-grade cannabis to send most of Ramsbottom off on a trip for bloody days.'

Ingrid looked wounded. 'How can you accuse your poor–'

Felicity gave up trying to meet her targets. 'Anyway, Mr Grimshaw, the bottom line is your mother will have to come here at least until other accommodation can be found for her, although of course, should prosecution follow, that might be resolved.'

'An old weak lady like me in prison! All I was doing was helping a poor man downstairs.'

Margaret stood. 'Bernard, Ingrid is coming here, end of story, so get used to it. I have to go to work.'

Felicity opened a file. 'Just before you go Mrs Grimshaw, we need to finalise some paperwork. Mrs Kazakof is in bed and breakfast and we need to move her out as soon as possible, financial restraints on the council–'

Bernard leapt up. 'Spare us the sob story. Just get on wi it.' He stomped out to the shed.

Margaret sighed. 'I would like to say Ingrid, that he will soften, but unfortunately that won't happen. But as far as I am concerned you are welcome. Now I must go to work. Bernard is hiding in his shed Felicity. He will sign whatever you give him.' She wanted to say *or else* but stopped herself in time.

Bernard sat at his workbench and idly dug a chisel into the wooden top past caring about the damage it was doing. Felicity opened the door and peeked in.

'I have a couple of forms for you to sign Mr Grimshaw?'

He grunted and held out his hand. 'Signing my bloody life away. She won't leave once she gets her feet under table.' He scribbled a signature without reading the documents. 'Let's hope they put the old bat away.'

Felicity could not help her curiosity. 'What went wrong between you Mr Grimshaw?'

The chisel began to drive deep furrows in the worktop. Felicity felt behind her for the reassuring presence of the door.

'My mother is not what you think. She might give the impression of being old and weak, believe me she isn't. She's a tough old witch who thinks only of herself. She chucked my father out when I was ten and being an only child, I had to look after myself. Do you know why? Because she was out all hours up to her nefarious ways. A few years ago, I found links to the Russian mafia. Believe me or not.'

'Oh.'

'Hmm.'

'Have you not tried to reconcile your relationship?'

'I did once, against my better judgement I might add. I thought it was working for a few weeks until I discovered she was planning to use my house as a drop for her associates to collect their "gear".

The spider moved from the safety of the tin of emulsion to get a better view of the interloper. Bernard stiffened as he spotted it and reached for the aerosol.

Felicity saw it and gasped. 'Mr Grimshaw, please, you can't harm a helpless creature-'

'Bloody watch me!'

Felicity grabbed her paperwork and made a swift exit.

As she closed the door she heard Bernard exclaim, 'Take that you bastard!'

THE TEST TRIP

Bernard paced the kitchen, ranting. Margaret ignored it as usual. He stopped and sighed. 'Why? Why do we have to have her? Daft old cow.'

'Because Bernard, she has blown up her flat. Don't ask me how, that's up to the investigators.'

'I've told you how. She's a perishing drug dealer. Eighty years old and behaves like a teenager.' He slumped in a chair at the table. 'Why she didn't go back to Russia…'

'Well she hasn't, she's coming here, so get over it.'

'And what about this,' he was going to upgrade his expletives but checked himself, 'flipping trip to France? She won't be coming on that I can assure you.'

'Yes, she will Bernard and you will be civil to her, and Frank.' She smiled. 'And Tiger, we can't leave him here.'

He snorted and stood. 'I'm going in the shed.'

'Don't see why you don't get a bed in there.'

Something Bernard had considered many times. He slammed the backdoor and entered the haven of peace, the spider notwithstanding …

Bernard needed to think about the problem relating to his estranged mother but found it too stressful and instead ruminated on a more important problem concerning the wine club.

From a dark recess, the spider watched as Bernard leant on the workbench peering out between the copious cobwebs that were gradually reducing the area of the dusty window facing the road. The discomfort of having to share the shed with a spider (to say he had a phobia would be an understatement) constantly far outweighed the discomfort that awaited him indoors.

He spent many hours watching people come and go, like the "posh" at number 52 for instance. Now what would he have to earn to drive a car like that he thought as out of the corner of his eye he noticed the patch of rust getting worse beneath the driver's door of his modest Focus. He sighed, painfully aware that the car was grossly underpowered to tow a caravan. He tried to get a glimpse inside the house as the front door opened and a scantily clad woman waved to the driver. He had considered investing in a telescope...

The thought of telescopes stirred a sudden and profound anxiety prompting him to involuntarily crane his neck toward the sky.

The panic quickly subsided as his attention was drawn to a bottle of wine. 'Time for a little tipple I think,' he said as he picked up his finest waiting to be savoured and gently caressed it. 'Blackberry and garlic, who'd have thought such a combination would be so successful,' he said as he lovingly took in the deep colour. 'It'll be competition for you next year me lad.'

As he caressed the bottle, he noticed a stranger wander past and his suspicions were raised. Since the incident relating to the carpark, he had become wary of strangers – for all he knew he had been kidnapped – and at times he pondered who would want to, but too many candidates formed a list for him to think about. As Bernard opened the wine, he pondered about calling his neighbourhood watch rep but decided against it when he remembered that the organiser, Dave Shaw at number 23, would ask him round for a brew. He could tolerate Dave but not his elderly wife who had a propensity to fart - it seemed to him on demand - and at his age his lung capacity was not up to a long period of breath holding.

Bernard strained to see where the suspicious interloper had gone but there was no sign. The spider made a run – it seemed to Bernard directly at him with vicious intent - causing him to leap back and knock the bottle of wine over. 'No!' He shouted as he desperately tried to scoop up the growing puddles forming in the deep furrows he had carved into the worktop. 'Bloody typical!'

The spider decided a swim was not on the agenda and made a hasty retreat behind a can of Golden oak fence paint. With half an eye on the possibility of the spider reappearing, Bernard stared out of the window avoiding the red patches on the bench, but the potential kidnapper was gone.

His reverie was shattered as Margaret banged on the shed door and shouted, 'Bernard! Caravan.'

He mumbled mimicking her, 'Bernard Caravan...'

'Bernard!'

He sighed deeply and opened the door. 'What about it?'

She stood with arms crossed. 'We are going to France. Frank says he needs to-'

'Yes, yes I know all about his bloody flash motorhome. Why we have to go to bloody Lake District wi him-'

'Because Bernard, he needs to do a test run with their new motorhome and he is my future brother-in-law. Family might not mean much to you...' She sighed, 'Anyway, it needs sorting out.'

Bernard knew he would not escape checking the caravan and after enough delay to make his point he dragged himself out of the shed. He sullenly walked around the caravan noting the fibreglass was beginning to show its age. As part of his avoiding work at all times plan, he opened the bonnet of the car where he could pretend to be busy.

Margaret appeared with the first of the many boxes of items she considered necessary; most of which he did not. He quickly hid under the bonnet of the car pretending he was engaged in vital preparations whilst looking in total bemusement at the ducting, wires, pipes etc. He considered the coming trip. And Frank. Bernard wriggled on the horns of his dilemma; to get Frank onside to ensure he helped get him re-elected as chairman or punch the daylights out of him. The fact Frank was courting Margaret's sister, Diane, complicated matters.

Margaret knew Bernard didn't have a clue what went on under the bonnet of that car; a fact she ruminated on with every to and fro of boxes until the sight of his backside in the same position again, tipped her over the edge, 'Bernard!' she shouted with sufficient venom that he banged his head on the bonnet in shock. 'Stop pretending you have any idea what is under there and do something useful.' With indignation and rubbing his head he took a box from her. 'And don't drop it, there are eggs in there.'

Later, after much reluctant and sullen loading of boxes and bags containing what he considered as, "women's crap" Bernard was ready to hitch up. He sat in the driver's seat and strained to look over his shoulder as he reversed toward the caravan. Margaret stood astride the tow hitch - waving her arms as if directing an aircraft into land on an aircraft carrier - supposedly guiding him to the towing ball, most of which movements were above the rear window and out of his sight. Frustrated and anxious not to damage the car, he stamped on the brake and jumped out cricking his neck in the process.

'Argh!' He held his neck as the spasm locked in and he went around to the back of the car. 'Bloody miles yet woman! And too much to right.'

She snapped back, 'If you reversed properly like you're supposed to, I wouldn't need to be standing here. I've got more important things to do.'

'If I could do it without you, which I am basically doing because you're waving bloody arms in't air where I can't see em, I would.' With gritted teeth he got back in and tried again, watching in the side mirror to avoid the pain in his neck. Now all he could see was her right elbow as it moved back and forth as if she were furiously, but in slow motion, playing the violin. He muttered, 'What's that supposed to be...' A grating sound came from behind. He stamped on the brake. He took a deep breath.

'Stop' she shouted.

'What wer that?!' He leapt out aggravating the pain in his neck and hurried to the rear again.

Margaret was examining her nails. 'You went too fast.'

He looked down to the tow ball jammed into the bumper. 'Now look what you've done!'

Margaret gently delivered the coup de grace. 'You were driving Luv.'

Bernard could only respond with a weak splutter as he marched to the driver's door and gingerly got in holding his neck. With controlled anger he said quietly, 'I will pull forward. I will then reverse slowly when I want you to shout left, right, or stop, before I ram caravan in't back of car again.'

She appeared at his window. '… did you say-?'

He turned to see her lips moving and pressed the window switch. As the window hummed open, he heard her say, '...Something?'

'What?'

'Did you say something?'

He sighed deeply and said with deliberate calm, 'I will pull forward. I will then reverse slowly when I want you to shout left right or stop. Ok?'

'Why didn't you say so then?' She wandered back to the rear of the car.

He pulled forward and then slowly reversed estimating for himself how far he should go, ignoring the sporadic hand appearing in the side mirror.

'Stop!'

He sighed again, got out and went to the rear of the car which was a foot away from the tow ball. 'What did yer shout stop for? Bloody mile yet.'

'Look Bernard, I have better things to do than stand here all day. Now are you going to fix it or hitch it or whatever else you do with it, or not?'

With teeth clenched holding his neck he stomped back to the driver's door. 'You're no bloody use ere anyway.' He got back in.

'Please yerself.' She went back in the house.

Eventually with much grunting and groaning he hitched it up. Margaret appeared with Tiger in a cat carrier and with the cat protesting loudly, strapped the carrier onto the rear seat. He groaned. 'You're not serious. I'll not be driving with bloody cat making that row all the way.'

'You will Bernard. Poor little thing needs company and I can't trust Julien to feed him.' Tiger focused his attention on Bernard and hissed baring its claws.

A few minutes later with Margaret in the passenger seat filing her nails he jerkily pulled away, only too aware that the clutch was protesting. She picked up a newspaper.

'Have you set sat nav Margaret?'

Margaret studied the paper. 'No.'

'Well how can I find me way to a site I know nowt about wi out sat nav?'

She glared at him over the paper, 'So you want me to do it?'

'I'm driving Margaret.'

She mumbled getting the sat nav from the glove compartment, 'If that's what you call it...'

'What?'

She consulted the caravan site guidebook and tapped in the postcode, stuck the holder on the windscreen and fitted the sat nav to it. She sat back with her eyes closed. Bernard looked from her to the cat spitting at him keen to get its claws into him. Bernard let out a deep sigh thinking of the boredom the next two days promised. If he sings country roads again, I'll break the bloody guitar over his head. Pompous southern git thinks he's bloody hippie. His mood dropped lower and lower remembering that bloody awful singsong they all had to partake in, just so he could get Frank onside.

A TIGHT SQUEEZE

After driving for some time, he glanced over to Margaret who was now asleep; snoring loudly and making that puffering sound between her lips he detested as she exhaled. He hated that puffering, he noted her wrinkles, the way her hair...

The Sat nav broke into his thoughts, 'Take the next turn on the right, then bear right one hundred yards.' He looked at the screen. The road he was currently on was a major road taking them to the Lake District. Bernard was not familiar with the area they were heading for and although suspicious, reluctantly decided to trust it. He took the next turning which proved to be a narrow lane and immediately realised he was in trouble. Just those few seconds of trust in an inanimate object had now set a course for major problems because the narrow lane was becoming narrower by the yard. 'Ayup' he exclaimed, 'this int' right road!' He pulled up before a sign which read "unsuitable for vehicles". The high grass verge was now tight up to the wheels of the caravan. The sat nav announced, 'Turn around when possible'. Bernard took a deep breath and switched off the engine.

'Margaret?'

She puffered loudly.

'Margaret!'

She jumped awake fearing an impact. 'What?'

He pointed to the road sign. With a satisfying satisfaction – a rarity to the norm and for once being in the right – he nodded at it.

She checked the sat nav. 'Says bear right up there.' She gestured to the dead straight dirt lane vanishing toward the horizon.

Bernard felt the flush of victory creep into his bones, 'What did you put into sat nav Margaret?'

'The postcode.'

The winning post was coming into view, the cheering crowds ready to yell, "Bernard was right!" 'And did you mess about with any other settings Margaret?'

'I put the shortest route.'

Gently, with the careful precision of a surgeon he asked, 'And pray tell why?'

Huffily she replied, 'Because you'd made us late.'

The knife began its incision. 'But we're towing a caravan Margaret, length nineteen feet, width,' he wound down his window, 'Bout the same as this lane. Not only is this the wrong lane it's also too narrow. What do you suggest we do now? You see, by selecting the shortest route the computer has chosen this lane, not of course being aware that we are towing a caravan.'

'Turn around. You always boast you can manoeuvre it so well, so manoeuvre it.'

Bernard angrily started the engine and tried to pull forward but only managed to drag the caravan wheels deeper into the verges. An ominous smell rose from the innards of the car.

Margaret pulled a face, 'What's that horrible smell?'

Bernard knew full well it was the clutch overheating because (although he tried kidding himself otherwise) the car was underpowered for towing. He got out and slammed the door. 'Probably cat shit in't carrier.' His feet began to sink into the soft grass verge. With a deep sigh he looked ahead to the narrow lane disappearing into the distance. He trudged to the road junction, glanced back at the caravan sitting defiantly between the high grass verges, and took out his mobile. He dialled and waited.

A recorded message instructed him to select one of five options. With another sigh he selected the third and was then instructed to select from a further three. He selected the second one, then another two options from which he selected the first. A warm, friendly recorded female voice told him that the call may be recorded for training purposes.

A tinny version of "Mama Mia" followed blasting his eardrum taking him by surprise. 'Bloody hell!'

The warm, friendly automated female voice informed him that his call was important to them and an advisor would be with him soon. However, they were experiencing a high volume of callers and alternatively, he could avail himself of their website. He irritably kicked at the grass verge mumbling, 'And what bloody good would that do?'

A jolly female voice answered, 'Hello? You are through to caravan support, my name is Delia, how can I help you today?'

'I need roadside assistance.'

'And what is the nature of your breakdown sir?'

'I've not broken down, I'm stuck in't verge on a narrow lane.'

'I'm sorry to hear that Sir. I'm afraid I cannot help; you have come through to the finances section.'

'I followed the endless bloody instructions that connected me to you.'

'I can transfer you?'

'Aye do that then.'

Mama Mia assailed his eardrum again. It abruptly stopped, and the recorded voice instructed him to select from five options assuring him that his call was important to them. He considered seeing how far he could throw his phone before going through the process again. "Mama Mia" blasted again. He began wandering back toward the caravan when a familiar voice said cheerily, "Hello? You are through to the finance section, my name is Susan, how can I help you today?'

'Bloody hell, not you again.'

The voice took on a less friendly, more business-like tone. 'What is the nature of your enquiry please?'

He sighed as he kicked the wheel of the caravan irritably. 'I need roadside assistance.'

'And your name please?'

'Grimshaw.'

'I can't assist you with roadside problems Sir, this is the finance section.'

'I followed the bloody instructions and it's connected me to you.'

'I can transfer you?'

'You said that last time.'

'It wasn't me Sir, it must have been my colleague. I'll transfer you.'

He pre-empted the pain to his eardrum by holding the phone away just in time as "Mama Mia" blasted out again.

From inside the car Margaret shouted irritably, 'What are you messing about at Bernard. It'll be dark by the time we get there.'

He resisted the urge to jump inside the car and...

The music ceased abruptly and a sing song female voice came on. 'My name is Sarika. How can I being of helpful to you today Sir?'

Bernard rolled his eyes. 'I need roadside assistance.'

'And your membership number?'

Bernard realised it was in his wallet in the car. 'Wait a moment.' He hurried to the car and leant inside.

Margaret looked up from her newspaper. 'What one earth are you doing? We should have been there ages ago.'

He gave her a withering look as he fumbled for his wallet and took out the membership card. 'Hello? I have it.'

Margaret shook her head in amazement and went back to her paper as Bernard slammed the car door.

'And what is it being the nature of your breaking down Sir?'

'I've not broken down, I'm stuck in't verge on a narrow lane.'

'Can you repeat that please Sir?'

'I said... I'm stuck in a lane!'

'You are being stucked in a lane? Is that correct Sir?'

'Close enough.'

'So what part of you is stucked in the lane Sir. Do you need medical assistance? If so I cannot-'

'I don't want bloody medical...' deep breath, 'I'm towing a caravan and its stuck.'

'Sorry this line is not good. What is hurting with your toe?'

'No!'

'I'm sorry Sir. Can you please be telling me the nature of your problem if it is not medical?'

Bernard spoke with exaggerated calm, 'My caravan is stuck in a narrow lane. I need to be tow...pulled out.'

'We are only be dealing with mechanical problems Sir.'

'Listen carefully you...' he took a deep breath, 'I need to be pulled out of a narrow lane.'

'Can you not just be driving further and turn around?'

Patience was becoming a rare commodity. 'I can't turn around because I've got bloody great caravan on't back.' He let out a deep breath, 'I need a tow.'

'I'm sorry Sir but we don't provide that sort of service.'

'Then what bloody good are...' He kicked the caravan wheel again and winced from a shooting pain up his big toe. Some might say instant karma.

'I can be arranging for a local garage to assist you.'

'Yes, fine.' He passed on the relevant information as he headed back to the car and got in.

Margaret sighed and looked up from her newspaper. 'I don't know what sort of mess you have got us into Bernard, but we will lose our plot-'

'The mess we are in was caused by your stupidity in selecting the short route thereby landing us in the position we now find ourselves, namely, stuck in't a narrow lane.'

She glared at him. 'It's always my fault isn't Bernard.'

Tiger hissed and made horrible feral cat noises at him.

His phone rang. 'Yes?'

'You need a tow I understand?'

'Yes.'

'Why did you try and take a caravan down that lane?'

'Because...look, can you please just tow me out?'

'Be there in about forty mins mate.' The line went dead.

Bernard decided he would commit an act of violence if he remained in the car having to listen to the inevitable tirade with which he would be subjected and decided to wait at the main road.

Bernard stood forlornly at the entrance to the lane. As he stood pondered on his misfortune of being married to Margaret and the impending forced cheerfulness she insisted he displayed toward Frank, he found himself looking toward the sky in dread fearing something (of what he had no idea but that anxious feeling was lurking again) would … would what? He had no idea - just that it would be horrible. It was a clear autumn sky just after midday and yet he could see a star hanging there as if it was watching him. He kicked a clod of earth. Probably a satellite. As he continued to ruminate on the impending two days with Frank, he glanced up to see it had not moved. With virtually no knowledge of stars he shrugged and wandered back and forth imagining what he could do to Frank. Roasting him on a spit perhaps.

Eventually, a tow truck pulled up and a man in his late fifties wearing a greasy boiler suit sporting a long grey beard and covered in tattoos jumped down. He nodded toward the caravan. 'That yours mate?'

Bernard felt bile rise but contained himself. 'Yes. Sat nav sent me the wrong way.'

The man stroked his beard. 'Technology, it's taking over if you ask me. Know what I mean?'

'Yes, look I'm very late and just need to get turned around.'

'Not there you won't mate. I can't reverse back onto the main road with the van, so I'll have to go around the other way. You unhitch the van and pull the car off onto the verge.' He was about to get back in his cab and paused giving Bernard a quizzical look. 'I recognize you from the paper. You the nutter who said he was taken by little green men? Blimey mate, get a life, know what I mean?' He got in and roared off leaving an acrid cloud of black sooty smoke.

Bernard sighed yet again and went about unhitching the caravan. Thirty minutes later the tow truck came down the lane and stopped in front of the caravan. The man jumped out and examined the problem then glanced at the car on the verge. 'Seriously mate, you shouldn't be towing this,' he nodded at the caravan, then toward the car, 'with that.'

Bernard was wondering if he could get something heavy and brain the … 'Right, yes ok. So, can you just please tow it to where I can get re-hitched?'

'There's a wider spot about a mile up the lane, I'll get it to there.' He burst out laughing. 'Couldn't your mates have towed you out with their flying saucer?' He rubbed his beard as he rolled about laughing back to his cab.

IT GETS WORSE

Eventually Bernard pulled into the caravan site.

Margaret waved at the reception block. 'There. Go in and tell them we're here. And apologise for being so late.' She got out and headed down the access road to the site looking for Frank and Diane. Far down the field amongst the rows of caravans a brand-new motorhome stood out. A young woman waved at her.

Margaret waved back, 'Coo-ee Diane!'

Bernard squelched up to the reception desk. A young woman looked up from her paperwork and wrinkled her nose at the smell of drying mud.

'Yes Sir? Booking in?'

'I am.' To explain his ruined clothes, he stated, 'Had to help a fellow caravanner who was stuck. You know how it is; they think it's easy...'

'Registration number?'

He fumbled for his wallet and took out his club card with the registration scribbled on the back.

She gingerly took it and copied his details. She consulted her site plan. 'You were on plot eighteen, but we had to let it go, busy weekend you see. Sorry. Luckily, we have plot thirteen available.' She pointed it out on the map. 'Far corner, you'll find it under the beech trees.' She held back a laugh as she said, 'We don't often get celebrities here...'

Margaret took the luxury camping chair offered by Frank and sat down. 'Phew! What a nightmare. Talk about making a fuss!'

Diane sat next to her. 'Lovely to see you sweetie. You ok?'

Margaret watched as Bernard slowly drove past toward the bottom of the field. He gave a cursory wave to Frank who touched his peaked cap in recognition as he exited the massive inflatable awning.

Margaret looked back to the gleaming motorhome and sighed.

Frank chuckled as he joined the two women, nodding at the plot next to them with a motor home on it. 'We had booked that for you. Tried to stall them but...anyway you've got a plot, although to be honest, I wouldn't like to get on it.' He smirked, 'Still, easier with a caravan than a flying saucer eh?'

Diane nudged him. 'Frank, you said wouldn't-'

Margaret sighed. 'Don't worry, I'm getting used to it. Can't walk down the high street without somebody saying summat.'

Frank glanced down the field to see Bernard stop beneath the beech trees, settled into his luxury chair and opened the news of the world. He chuckled as he muttered to himself, 'Tesco's carpark in underpants...'

Diane hugged Margaret. 'Good to see you sis. How are you coping?'

Margaret swiped away a tear. 'He's gone too far this time Diane.'

'Is it worth getting someone to look at him... you know one of them...'

'Psychiatrist? No, he'd never go. And anyway, they don't deserve to have to look too close into his head. I know I wouldn't.'

Bernard hoped stopping at this point would allow him to reverse the caravan onto the plot of grass. He got out and tested the grass with his foot realizing it was waterlogged and, he noted with ill-disguised horror, sloped down toward a thick evil looking hawthorn hedge. Not wanting to appear a beginner (which he was this was only the third tow) he attempted to look as if he knew what he was doing –being aware of Frank watching from his executive chair outside his very expensive mobile home – and looked at the caravan and back to the slope as if gauging a long putt. From within the car, Tiger made it clear he was ready to do serious damage to Bernard as he hissed and spat at him.

Frank poured a glass of red wine for Margaret and one for himself. 'I wandered down there earlier, nasty slope and a newly planted conifer in just the wrong place where you need to turn in. But I'm sure Bernard will be up to it.' He sipped his wine. 'How's Julien?' She glanced accusingly at Diane who furiously read her magazine.

'Julien's fine thanks Frank. He's hoping to get into A level violin next year.'

Under his breath he muttered, 'Or the girls' basketball...'

The sound of rending tree branches and wheels spinning in mud caused Diane to look up from her magazine. She piped up, 'Oh! I think Bernard's...oh dear...Frank go and give him a hand.'

Frank eased himself out of his luxury camping chair, 'Ok.' He wandered nonchalantly, with hands in pockets, down toward Bernard desperately trying to pull the remains of a conifer tree out from under the front offside wing. 'Want a hand?'

Bernard leapt up ripping the shoulder of his sport coat on a stiff piece of tree sticking out and snapped irritably, 'If I wanted any...' he realised it was Frank, 'Oh Frank! Well if you could perhaps lift...'

Frank took over and with a hefty pull extricated the tree together with some of its roots. His gaze wavered over the mud patches on Bernard's trousers. 'Looks like you've been in a scrum! Always thought my rugger days would come in handy! You ever play the game Bernard? Margaret was telling us you took a wrong turning. Easily done. Do you want me to reverse the old girl in for you?'

Bernard tightened his grip on the branch of the conifer he still held, 'No problems thank you; I can manage. You go and keep the girls entertained.'

'If you're sure? Got some great new songs Bernard. We can give them a bash after tea and the vino has kicked in.' He smiled condescendingly, 'Perhaps we could try "fly me to the moon"? Frank strolled back to his mobile home.

Bernard got back into the car mumbling to himself, 'Fly you to the moon with my boot up your arse.' He glanced in the rear-view mirror and could see Frank join the women, sit down and pick up his glass of wine, legs crossed relaxed and waiting for the show. He also noted a few others pulling their chairs round for a better view. He wiped his brow, loosened his tie, started the engine and engaged first gear letting the clutch out causing the wheels to spin on the wet grass. Globs of mud spattered the car and front of the caravan.

Bernard felt sweat trickle down his neck as he tried in vain to get the wheels to grip. Bernard was not remotely religious but as we all do in times of disaster, he desperately prayed for the wheels to grip and save him from humiliation. He slowly let the clutch out only to splatter more mud this time onto the windscreen. In a desperate attempt to salvage the last shreds of his pride he put it in reverse and with elation felt the wheels grip. The caravan swung slowly round, its rear pointing toward the hedge. Bernard let out his breath with relief and gently applied the brake so that he could get out and check progress. He put it in neutral, applied the handbrake and opened the door. With horror he saw the car and caravan were now the guests of gravity and sliding down the slope at increasing speed. In panic he jammed it into first gear and let out the clutch inadvertently catching the windscreen wipers which ground and screeched throwing mud in all directions. The front wheels spun spattering mud to add to that already all over the front of the car. He frantically slipped the clutch but despite his best efforts the clutch was overheating giving off an acrid burning smell.

Frank appeared at his window. 'I can smell the clutch from up there old mate. Want me to do it?'

Bernard wanted to punch him in the face but...he forced a smile, 'It's no problem, nearly got it. Grass is a bit slippery that's all.' Frank sauntered back to his caravan.

Diane stood, 'Well?'

'Says he can do it himself.'

Margaret joined her, 'He would.'

Frank sat down again, crossed his legs and picked up his wine. 'You see Margaret the thing to remember when reversing...'

The sound of screaming revs, blue smoke and a muffled, 'Nonoo,' came from plot thirteen as the caravan gathered speed and slid backwards into the hawthorn hedge.

Diane nudged Frank, 'For goodness sake, go and put him out of his misery!'

Frank stood beside Bernard who was looking glumly at the caravan buried in the hedge at an impossible angle having slid sideways dragging the car with it which was now jack-knifed front end into the hedge. 'Beyond me old mate. Need a tractor. I'll go and see if the site organiser can help.' Bernard swallowed the weight of injured pride and nodded. A drop of sweat dripped from his nose onto the wing of the car and slid over its contour through the coating of mashed grass and mud.

He trudged back up the hill behind Frank to their gleaming, enormous mobile home complete with full width awning, gas fired BBQ, full outside furniture suite - in addition to the luxury camping seats – solar panel and of course state of the art satellite dish. Frank continued to the office whilst Bernard joined Margaret and Diane.

'Bernard, poor dear,' soothed Diane with open arms and almost a hug until she saw the glistening fresh mud. She could see he was about to sit down on one of her expensive chairs and exclaimed in horror, 'Just a minute dear, I'll get you a towel to...' She waved vaguely at the seat as she hurried inside the caravan.

Margaret gave him a scathing stare. 'Look at state of you Bernard! Showing me up int' public.' She looked him up and down in disgust. 'Again.'

He was about to retort when Diane scurried back with a towel. 'It's the dog's but I've brushed most of the hair off.' She spread it over the seat.

'There!' She exclaimed. Bernard was about to sit down when Margaret whispered, 'We need luggage out of the car Bernard,' she smiled a little, 'And Tiger needs to be let out in caravan.'

Diane added anxiously, 'When you get settled Bernard, perhaps if you don't move too much?'

Eventually the caravan was towed out of the hedge and Bernard tried to remove the cat carrier from the car, doing his best to avoid being seriously injured. Later, after they had finished eating - and Bernard had prised himself out of the rigid blanket cast of his backside caused by solidified mud and doghair - he managed to get Frank on his own. 'So, as you know the election for club president is coming up shortly...'

Frank poured some wine for them, 'What do you think then? Not too acidic?'

Bernard took a sip, 'Seems fine. As I were saying, chairman is coming up soon...'

Frank finished the sentence for him, 'And you want me to second you. Sorry old mate no can do.'

Bernard was dumbfounded. 'But....'

Frank said smugly, 'I would old chap but I'm standing myself you see?'

Bernard spluttered his wine, 'You are standing for my position?'

'Not actually yours old mate though is it? No. I think it is time for new blood. There seems to be good indications that I will be elected actually.'

Bernard fought to contain himself, 'Of course. The club comes first.'

Frank jumped up as the two women returned from the loo, 'At last. Now we are all here I have some special songs, Norwegian folk songs...' He went to the car for his guitar. Bernard inwardly groaned.

Margaret moved close to him and whispered, 'Grinding your teeth is not very attractive Bernard.'

He whispered back, 'We're going early tomorrow. I can't stand this idiot anymore.'

She smiled sweetly. 'Oh, so he told you he is standing did he?'

Bernard groaned again as Frank reappeared clutching his guitar. 'You knew?'

Margaret said smugly, 'Of course. I thought you did.'

THE ARRIVAL

Bernard was stinging from Margaret's obvious enjoyment at his predicament over re-election. To repay her he ensured she bore the brunt of Ingrid's arrival and stayed late at work.

Margaret was also at work when Ingrid arrived in an ambulance with her suitcases and wheelchair, but Julien was home from school early and greeted her. 'Gran!' He ran out and grabbed her cases as she slowly followed grunting at the exertion of using a wheelchair. 'Julien turned to her concerned. 'You alright Gran?'

She winked at him and whispered, 'Have to put on show for ambulance man.'

He showed her into the lounge and sat close to her. 'I didn't know about you until the other day.'

'Your father is not good at communication. In Russia we speak what we mean. We do not waste time arguing.' She looked thoughtful. 'My first husband Boris, he was big Russian man, would use gun to sort out problems.'

Julien was spellbound. 'Wow.'

'He was real man not like English second husband.' She took out a tobacco pouch and began rolling a cigarette. 'That is your Dad's father. He was pig.' She took out another small bag and took out some cannabis leaf. 'I think your father has his genes.'

Julien watched in wonder. 'Gran, is that…'

'It is for stiff joints.' She nudged him, 'That is what they all need to believe anyway.'

'So is it… you know?'

'Is good stuff. Blow socks off.'

'How do you get it?''

'You look like good boy, so I tell you. But do not pass this onto your parents.' She leaned in and whispered, 'I grow it in flat. My neighbour helps me.' She paused. 'Used to anyway.' She smiled conspiratorially, 'Until I find new site.'

Julien looked solemn. 'I won't tell anyone Gran.' He picked at his fingers, 'What's it like?'

She smiled and offered the completed roll-up to him. 'Have couple of puffs. Better do it outside.'

He stood outside the backdoor and Ingrid lit it for him. He took a deep drag and collapsed in a fit of coughing.

'Another drag Julien, you will feel better.'

'Wow, this is brill.'

She took it from him, had a couple of drags and handed it back to him. After a few more puffs Julien leaned against the wall and began laughing.

She did the same. 'What do you think huh?'

'I've been too scared to try it.'

'This is our little secret Julien. When they are out, I give you more. It is not a problem.'

He began giggling.

'Yes, is good to laugh.'

'But I don't know why!'

She smiled. 'Just enjoy.' She studied him. 'You have problems, I can tell these things. You tell your Granny Ingrid.'

He moved a stone around with the toe of his shoe. 'I get bullied sometimes.'

'Uhuh.'

'So does my friend Sebastian.'

'Ah. And is he good friend?'

'Very.'

'A very, very good friend?'
He blushed. 'Hmm.'
'But he is not yet your lover I think?'
'Gran!'
'You get to my age is not time to pussyfoot around. You love him?'
'I think so.'
'This is good.'
There was a comfortable silence as they enjoyed the spliff.
'There is no rush Julien. Enjoy time together.' She considered for a moment, 'But I don't think your father is approving?'
'Huh. He's horrible to me.'
'I do not know what went wrong with him. We must try and do something about him.'
The front door opening made them both jump. Ingrid took the roll-up and looked nonchalant as Margaret appeared.
'Sorry Ingrid, I thought you were coming later.'
'Your son has been looking after me, do not worry.' She smiled at Julien who was trying not to giggle.
Margaret took off her coat and said, 'I'll sort out tea.' She noticed Julien was grinning.
'You're in good mood young man.'
'Gran has been making me laugh.'
Bernard entered and grunted as he took off his coat. He said coldly. 'Mother.'
Ingrid said, 'Ah here he is. I have been talking to my grandson. I think he is great person Bernard.'
'Do you now. I'd wait till you know about im.'
'I've learnt all I need to know. He has been confused but not anymore'. She gave Julien a sly wink. 'Is that not so?'
Julien kissed her cheek and went inside.
'He is lovely boy.'

'He's bloody gay.'

'And you are a bigot. I did not bring you up to-'

'You didn't bring me up full stop.' He stood and went to his shed.

Ingrid smiled to herself.

Margaret returned and sat beside her. 'Well here we are then Ingrid. I've made a bed up in the dining room until you can get around better. We have a downstairs loo so that's alright.'

Ingrid looked around the room. 'Where has Bernard gone?'

'In his bloody shed. He goes in there to sulk. No doubt he'll be back through in a moment.

Doesn't like to miss anything you see. Would you like a brew?'

Ingrid nodded. 'You have nice house.'

'Thank you.'

Bernard came back in and looked uncomfortable not sure where to sit other than as far away from his mother as possible.

Ingrid smiled sweetly at him. 'Bernard, you have nice house.'

'Aye, happen we do. Just right size for us.'

Julian sidled in and sat near to Ingrid. They exchanged smiles. Julian asked, 'Are you really Russian?'

'From Leningrad. Now you know as St Petersburg.'

'Wow!'

Bernard huffed and stomped out. Margaret brought a tray with the teas which she placed on a coffee table in front of the sofa where Ingrid could reach.

'I am sorry to be problem Margaret. I will sort it out when this plaster goes.'

Margaret sipped her tea. 'I know you are. I can only apologise for,' she nodded in the direction of the shed, 'him. Don't take any notice, I don't. When we've finished our brew I'll show you where you're staying. Like I said, I've made up the dining room for you.'

The next Day Margaret left shortly after Bernard had gone to work. Julian had a rest period at school and didn't need to go in at the usual time. Ingrid was in the lounge when he came in. He asked her if she wanted a cup of tea and she nodded. She wheeled herself after him into the kitchen. 'So how is school for you?'

He shrugged as he filled the kettle. 'Ok. Exams and shit,' he realised what he had said. 'Sorry, I mean —'

Ingrid laughed. 'Is not a problem if you swear in front of me. You must be yourself.'

He switched on the kettle. 'I didn't know anything about you. They never told me. I don't blame Mum.'

Ingrid watched him. 'And your father?' He blushed. She continued. 'He is not happy man I am here I think.'

Julian retorted. 'He's not happy full stop.'

Ingrid smiled. 'And you. Are you happy person?'

Julian got down two mugs and tea bags. 'Suppose so.'

Ingrid studied him for a few seconds and laughed. 'It is good to be gay person. And to have boyfriend.'

Julian felt himself redden as it spread down his neck. He poured the tea.

Ingrid laughed again. 'I tried it once but was not for me. I prefer good man. Like you do!'

Julian was surprised that he didn't feel in any way insulted or put down; on the contrary he felt elated. 'His name is Sebastian.'

'And he is same age as you?'

He nodded. 'We both enjoy the same music and films and all sorts of stuff.' He passed the mug to her. 'Do you want any sugar?'

She studied him. 'No thanks. And do your parents know?'

He sighed. 'Mum sort of does but we don't talk about it.'

'And your father?'

Julian looked awkward. 'He says nasty things.'

'That is sad. You must be strong, do what is right for you. Be proud you are gay!'

Julian laughed. 'You're really cool!'

Ingrid wheeled herself into the lounge. 'Are there betting shops in this town?'

Julian followed her. 'I suppose so. In the precinct probably.'

The next morning Ingrid gathered a coat and blanket which she draped around her. She maneuvered herself toward the front door. 'Ok. I go to betting shop and win some money. Then I give you some to buy present for your lover!'

Julian said awkwardly, 'We don't you know...'

She opened the front door and said over her shoulder, 'Is good to experiment. Just be careful!' She rolled out onto the pavement. A few minutes later a taxi arrived and bundled her in. The driver asked. 'Where to?'

'Take me to town centre. Is there betting shop in town centre?'

'Three I think.'

'Take me to biggest one.'

Later that day Bernard arrived home from work to discover a mobility scooter in the hall which he had to squeeze past to get in. He shouted to Margaret as he struggled. 'Margaret! What's this bloody thing doing here?'

Margaret appeared. 'Ask your Mother Bernard. It's hers.'

Ingrid wheeled herself in. 'I bought scooter. I need to get outside, get fresh air.'

Bernard bristled as he squeezed free. 'Oh really. So now we can't get int bloody house! Thank you very much. And another thing, I don't want bloody fag ends in't garden.'

Ingrid smiled sweetly. 'Then put bucket by door. Also give me door key.'

He stooped down to her level and said evilly, 'No.'

Margaret sighed. 'I can't be doing with you two arguing all the time. Bernard, go and get that old bucket from the shed and fill it with sand.'

He began to take a deep breath – a sure indicator a rant was on its way.

'Now!'

He stomped out.

Ingrid smiled. 'I see where trousers are in house. He is English wimp, no Russian blood.'

Bernard stormed back in. 'I thought you were on benefits. How did you afford that?'

Julian bounded down the stairs. 'Gran won! On the horses! An accumulator. Really hard to get one of them isn't Gran?'

Ingrid smiled serenely. 'I am good gambler. I go back tomorrow win more, perhaps on roulette or blackjack. I have many things to buy.'

Bernard spluttered, looked at Margaret who shrugged as she turned to leave as if to say, 'Doesn't surprise me.' She went into the kitchen and he hurriedly followed her.

He strutted back and forth. 'She's bloody potty! Gambling? How old is she? Eighty odd? Ok so she's been lucky, but what happens when she gets into debt? Well, I'll tell you who won't be bailing her out that's for sure!'

Margaret was thoughtful. 'If she does have some money, she might be able to find her own place to live.'

'Can't see that happening. Mark my words she'll lose bloody lot.'

Julian sat with Ingrid. 'Can you show me how to bet Gran?'

Bernard threw up his hands. 'See! She's nothing but bloody trouble. Next thing we know she'll be encouraging him in his —'

Margaret strangled the scream inside which escaped as a rasping whisper. 'Don't you dare...'

Bernard went into the lounge and studied his profile in the mirror mumbling to himself then caught sight of the mobility scooter blocking the front door. He joined Julian and Ingrid by the back door. 'That bloody scooter is blocking door. You'll have to get rid of it.'

Ingrid was rolling a cigarette, licked the paper then lit it. 'Is problem getting over front door bottom. You will have to get ramp or build a house for it.'

Bernard began glow to bright red as his irritation grew into fury. 'I'll —'

Margaret appeared. 'Bernard! Not now!' He strutted off toward the shed.

Ingrid pointed to the shed. 'There is good home for scooter, we put it there.'

Margaret smiled. 'Yes good idea, the perfect place.' Julian laughed.

The next day the same taxi driver arrived for Ingrid who was waiting outside. 'Same place?'

As he helped her in she nodded then thought a little. 'No take me to casino. Not good to win all time in same place.'

***

Bernard stared at an extension to his shed trying to ignore the condescending grin on Chilver's face who rolled a cigarette and handed it to Ingrid. 'This is my bloody house! I demand to know what —'

Ingrid lit it and blew a smoke ring at his back. 'I look in book, get number. You said get house for scooter. There is house.'

Bernard looked closer at the alterations. 'You don't need to make it that big for bloody scooter.'

Chilvers smiled knowingly at Bernard. 'That's true but,' he glanced at Ingrid. 'Not if you want to incorporate a kennel.'

Bernard looked from her to him and back. 'Kennel?'

Ingrid said innocently. 'Is for Alsatian.'

Bernard swallowed. 'Alsatian?'

'I see such dogs have bad time, so I adopt.' She blew a cloud of smoke into the air. 'I have another win today.'

Chilvers smiled sweetly at Bernard and hummed, 'Fly me to the moon.'

Bernard threw up his hands and went inside to Margaret sitting at the kitchen table reading a newspaper sipping a cup of tea. 'Have you seen what's happening out there?'

She carried on reading. 'What the alterations to the shed? Good idea if you ask me. Didn't serve much purpose anyway.'

'Didn't serve much purpose?'

She turned a page. 'Fancy Mr Chilvers being the builder.'

Bernard growled. 'Aargh! I'll not listen to you harping on. I'm going to shed.'

She slowly turned a page. 'Don't think so.'

***

The next morning Bernard sat in his revamped shed looking ruefully at the extended area thinking it would have been perfect for expanding his wine making but sighed looking at - what seemed in the confined space - the massive mobility scooter. And of course the partially constructed kennel area. He could insist she … not worth considering, the fall out would be unbearable. It was time to leave for work and he went inside to get his coat. Margaret sat at the kitchen table drumming her fingers looking out of the kitchen window. She looked up as he entered and thrust a newspaper at him. He took it from her. She sighed. 'Page two. Full page article.' She stood and glared at him. 'Well. That's the knit and natter finished. I can't show me face there anymore after…' she nodded at the newspaper, 'that.'

He opened the paper and sat down heavily as he read; ABDUCTIONS, HOW MANY ARE THERE. WHAT HAPPENED TO UNDERPANTS MAN? WAS HE PROBED?

'I'll bloody sue them.'

'Good luck with that Bernard.' She flounced out and left for work. He dragged himself from the chair and reluctantly left for work hoping to escape more derogatory comments. Sadly, that was not to be the case.

As he pulled out of the drive a neighbour slowed down and opened his car window. 'You should be ashamed of yerself.' Before Bernard could reply the neighbour roared off. He stopped at the end of the road ready to pull out when Mrs Reed from number 33 motioned for him to wind down his window as she crossed the road toward him. 'Poor Margaret. How could you Mr Grimshaw?' She waddled off.

He sat dazed wondering when it would end. He'd never liked her; too fat and nosey he thought. And then to complete his misery a white van with "Chilver's builders, all jobs undertaken" turned into his road. He pulled up opposite Bernard.

Chilvers leaned out of his window and smiled. 'Morning underpants man. Just popping round to finish the kennel.' He laughed, 'Hope you've got clean cacks on, just in case, ha!' He pulled away laughing hysterically. Bernard groaned as he pulled out.

***

Bernard returned from work that evening and despondently- on autopilot – threw his coat onto the sofa and went out to the safe haven of his shed completely forgetting anything had changed. He opened the door to be met by a low growl, deep and guttural. He leapt back in shock and slammed the door shut. Either the spider had developed considerably or... He marched indoors into what was, in more civilised times, the lounge but had been commandeered into Ingrid's bedroom.

Ingrid was reading the racing news. 'Hello Bernard.'
'There's a dog in my shed.'
'Of course, to go with the kennel. It is Alsatian, retired.'
'Scared bloody daylights out of me.' He postured. 'It will have to go.'
'No.'
'What do you–'
'It is rescued dog. I give it good home.'

With a grunt of frustration, he turned and stomped back to the shed contemplating the best course of action. He found a broom and tentatively opened the door enough to peek in. Two white eyes stood out like organ stops in the dark of the shed. He pushed the door open and took a step in. With a sigh of relief, he realised the dog was in a wooden enclosure, but it still scared him as it smashed against the chicken wire door snarling and baring its teeth. 'Fuck me!' He backed out and shut the door. A safe haven it certainly was not anymore. His appetite gone he contemplated going indoors but decided it was too toxic and instead walked down the road to the dog and kettle. (He often pondered in better times how these pubs got their names) but tonight he was seething. His one place of escape had gone. He entered the pub and ordered a pint and bag of cheese and onion crisps. He looked around relieved to find there were only a few people in. He was about to find a table when Chilvers strolled in. 'Mr Grimshaw!'

Bernard groaned and headed for a table in the corner. Chilvers ordered a pint and joined him.

'Bernard Grimshaw, underpants man.'

Bernard hunched over his pint and muttered.' Not now.'

Chilvers leaned over to him. 'I thought you would be out there buzzing around planets or whatever it these little green-'

Bernard looked up and glared at him. 'You've had yer fun now piss off.'

'What do think of the kennel?'

'Just leave me alone.' His mind desperately searched for a weapon – any weapon - he could use to defend himself. 'I'll be round to check drainage, hope it is up to standard. Be a pity to dig it all up.' He gave Chilvers a defiant smile.

Chilvers stood and smiled. 'You can take that to the bank mate. Solid work.' He hummed "fly me to the moon" as he moved to another table.

Bernard crunched his crisps as he sipped his beer contemplating his future, It was not rosy. In fact, it was as choppy as the impending ferry crossing to France.

THE JOURNEY

Bernard had tried to find ways of avoiding the impending trip but knew from the start he was doomed to spend fourteen days with Frank and his mother (the latter becoming a very large and painful thorn in his side). With nowhere else to retreat to he had forced himself to enter the shed, having to sidle between the scooter and wooden cage erected by Chilvers. His very presence in the shed seemed to bring on a furious bout of barking and snarling from an animal (he thought Alsatians were relatively passive dogs, apparently not) hell bent on ripping him to pieces. Despite his hatred for Chilvers, he had to admit the cage/kennel was built securely. He flinched as the monster launched itself against the chicken wire door snarling and baring very nasty teeth. He made it to the bench and looked around the remains of his safe place – now a storage facility for an enormous mobility scooter and vicious animal. He caught movement out of the corner of his eye near the white emulsion and shuddered, feeling caught between a rock and a hard place.

Margaret poked her head around the door. 'You can't stay in there all-day Bernard; we have to get going if we're to meet Frank and Diane at the ferry.'

He grunted and ran his fingers over the deep gouges made in the ply worktop from earlier ruminations with his chisel. Is this what his life had come to?

'Bernard, Now!'

'Alright, alright.' He dragged himself from the bench and made the perilous journey out of the shed trying to ignore the crashing snarling commotion from the darkness of the kennel. With one last attempt to scupper the journey he said,

'What about the bloody thing in there? We can't leave it for two weeks. Best she stays behind and looks after it. And the cat an all.'

'Julien can feed it and take it for walks.' She smiled, 'it seems to like him,' she stifled a laugh, 'and your mother. It's just you really. And Tiger comes with us.'

'Why can't Julien look after him an all?'

'Because Bernard, I enjoy his company.'

***

Bernard was concerned by the number of boxes and – in his view unnecessary – bits and pieces filling the caravan despite his repeated warning that as little weight as possible should be in it and anything heavy for the back of the car. Clearly that warning had fallen on deaf ears. The wheelchair was no lightweight and there was no room in the car for it given Ingrid was in the back together with too many suitcases belonging to her and Margaret.

As he pulled away, he knew the car would struggle. One steep hill and … he realised with horror that ferries have ramps, steep ramps. Men waving on, other drivers waiting… His stomach was tying itself in knots. The only good thing was Tiger seemed to be pacified by Ingrid's attention.

Margaret peered over the newspaper at him. 'Can't we go any faster? Ferry will have gone by the time we get there.' He ignored her. 'At least underpants man is not mentioned today.'

He turned on her. 'Give it a bloody rest will yer. Wasn't my fault.'

She shook the paper. 'Never is.'

Ingrid poked his shoulder and chuckled. 'I remember when you were little boy and pooped your pants!'

Margaret said over her shoulder, 'At least he didn't this time, although exactly why he was in't carpark that time of night is beyond me.'

Ingrid poked him again. 'What happened huh?'

He growled, 'I keep tellin yer, I don't know.'

Margaret resumed reading the paper. 'So you say.'

He changed gear trying to keep up with traffic on a slight incline. 'Ask yerself, why would I choose to be in't carpark… like that?'

Margaret huffed. 'I have no idea.' She looked up at the car in front gradually pulling away as the car slowed down struggling to maintain speed. 'Can't you go any faster?'

He snarled. 'Not wi half bloody house in back, no.'

***

Eventually the port came into view and Margaret pointed to Frank standing outside his massive motorhome nonchalantly smoking a cigarette. 'There they are.'

Bernard ignored her and pulled up to the end of the queue.

She sighed. 'Can't we join them?'

'Not unless you want me to ram my way through,' he did a quick estimation, 'Fourteen vehicles, so no Margaret I can't.'

'You have to make things difficult don't you. If we had left earlier…'

He sighed deeply. 'And if you hadn't loaded so much crap in't caravan we would have made better time.'

She turned to Ingrid. 'See, always my fault.'

Ingrid nodded. 'They don't understand Margaret. His father was just the same.'

Bernard snarled, 'Was he now.'

'Uhuh. Must be in your… what is word Margaret?'

'Genes.'

'Yes. He was pig headed chauvinist too.'

Bernard got out and slammed the door, trying to ignore the rusting flakes falling to the asphalt. He peered ahead at the ferry and groaned. It had ramps as he feared, only they were much longer and steeper than he had imagined.

Frank wandered over to him. 'Made it then.' He gave the focus a pitying look. 'Bit of a struggle I would imagine old mate.' He laughed. 'Hopefully we won't need to get you towed out of a hedge this trip!' He went around to Margaret's side. 'All set?'

She tried to open her window, but the ignition was off. 'Bernard!'

'What?'

'I can't open the window.'

He leant in and turned on the ignition. Ingrid poked him. Cheer up, we have good trip.'

***

Bernard had never, and would never, like boats. He liked to feel solid land beneath his feet. To be standing on the deck of a ferry to Santander was therefore not something he was enjoying, made worse by Frank seeming to relish the cold wind and spray. Bernard clung to the rail with white knuckles.

Frank shouted over the wind, 'Wonderful don't you think old boy?'

Now that Bernard no longer needed Frank's support for re-election, he saw no point in being civil to him; he was after all, a traitor. He mumbled a strong expletive.

'Didn't hear old mate.'

Bernard was about to shout it when Margaret and her sister appeared and leant against the rail taking in the bracing air.

Frank laughed. 'Didn't think you were going to make it up that ramp old mate. Clutch certainly took a beating.'

Bernard balled his fist wanting to shut him up.

Frank put his arm around Diane's shoulders. 'Wonderful don't you think?'

Diane pulled her coat tight and braced herself against the elements. To Bernard she appeared more concerned about her dishevelled hair than Frank's attentions. He considered his marriage aware of invisible waves of "don't touch me" emanating from Margaret.

Diane turned to Bernard and shouted over the wind. 'What's it like being famous? You must like the attention. I mean those people in that carpark. What were they shouting Frank, I couldn't make it out.'

'Underpants man, Diane.'

'Oh yes that's right.' She snuggled up to Frank. 'I wouldn't want to be famous.'

He laughed. 'Not like he is for sure!'

Margaret shouted above the wind, 'Where's your mother Bernard?'

He would have shrugged but preferred to keep both hands firmly on the rail as the ferry bucked the rolling waves. 'No idea.'

'Well go and look for her. She's a frail old lady Bernard.'

'Frail my arse.' Reluctantly he staggered against the pitching of the ferry and made his way down two flights of stairs to the bar. He wasn't surprised to find Ingrid ensconced in a corner with a shady looking man in his mid-thirties. The man who called himself Mike, had befriended them not long after boarding, on the pretext that he was lonely, had never done this before and was anxious. Bernard had decided after a lengthy consideration of one millisecond that Mike was anything but anxious. More likely to be a con man. Given that Ingrid had been around more blocks than the average taxi, he thought it would be Mike who was in for a fleecing. Bernard was about to leave when Ingrid shouted to him.

'Bernard! Come meet my friend Mike.'

He reluctantly joined them eying Mike with suspicion. Mike gave him a big smile. 'How you doin mate.'

Bernard ignored him and glared at Ingrid. 'Margaret was concerned where you were.'

'I am here with my good friend.'

Mike said, 'Me and me mates having a little trip abroad, know what I mean? Tell you what, your mother's a real laugh.'

Bernard was distracted as out of the lounge window he saw three lights in formation following alongside the ferry. The same lights he had seen at home. He jumped up and ran up the stairs to the deck.

He went to Margaret and gasped, 'Did you see them?'

'See what?'

'Lights, three of them following us.'

Frank winked at the two women. 'Must be an aeroplane old mate.'

Bernard held onto the rail. 'There were three of them, in a line.'

Frank said, 'Ok. Three aeroplanes then.'

'You don't understand. 'They were the…' He realised they knew nothing of the lights that have been bugging him. He ran along the deck to see if they were on the other side.

Margaret sighed. 'He's been right odd since we found im in bloody carpark.'

Diane whispered, 'Do you think he was-'

Margaret gritted her teeth. 'That cow? Better not have been.'

'Are you sure though Margaret, I mean…'

'That he's a fat git who no woman in her right mind would -'

Diane put her arm round her sister's shoulder. 'You have been married a long time.'

'Don't bloody remind me.' She turned to her sister. 'In some ways I would prefer it if he had been taken by… you know.'

'You don't really think-'

Margaret pulled away. 'I don't know what to think.'

Bernard felt misunderstood as he staggered along gripping the rail for dear life heading toward the bar where he could lose himself in a few beers. No good trying the wine; it was too expensive and of poor quality compared to his own. The lights came into view again in the distance and he stopped to peer at them. He looked around for someone to verify them but he was alone. One of the lights glowed brighter than the others and suddenly seemed to be very close. He felt a buzzing surge through his body and a sensation of floating into a tunnel of light then – nothing.

Margaret sipped her wine as her sister sat cuddling with Frank. A couple of tables away, Ingrid was howling with laughter with her new friend. Margaret looked away with disdain. And where was Bernard anyway? She checked her watch; he had not been seen for two hours. She finished her wine and decided to see what he was up to, maybe having secret chats with… her. She braced herself against the breeze and made her way to the back of the boat, she accepted she had no idea about boat terminology. She gasped as she saw a figure huddled under a lifeboat. It was him. She knelt down. 'What the hell are you doing under there?'

He didn't answer. She poked him. 'I said-'

He came round with a jolt and looked around in panic. 'Where am I?'

'On a bloody boat. Where the hell do you think you are?' She poked him again. 'You been under here for the past two hours? What the hell is wrong with you?' She stood and stretched her back. 'I'm going to bed. If you're not in our bedroom or whatever the hell you call it, I'm locking bloody door.' She stomped off.

He dragged himself out and welcomed the breeze as it brought him round. He didn't fancy sleeping outside and hurried after her his mind racing to make sense of the missing two hours. As he gripped the rail he checked the sky and shuddered.

INGRID'S NEW FRIEND

Bernard awoke with a start, the prodding in his side stirring a panic reaction to … a dream? of lying in blackness, bright lights, pain! He sat up gasping for air. Margaret put down the fly swat. 'You are going to flaming sleep clinic when we get back, snoring like bloody beached walrus. I've not had a wink of sleep all night.'

He looked at the plastic fly swat. 'You been digging at me wi that? What's wrong with yer?'

'What's wrong… I'll tell you what's wrong. Your bloody snoring because you are a fat git.'

He snorted and adopted a superior pose. 'I do not snore. It's your imagination.'

'Hmm so you keep insisting.' She pulled out her phone and tapped an icon, holding it up for him to hear. A deafening example of the worst sort of snoring possible emanated. She smiled sweetly. 'I rest my case.' She brandished the fly swat in his face, 'Soon as we get back.' She got dressed, pulled on her coat and left in a wave of indignant fury.

He sat back and rubbed his side where a small red wheal was evident from her prodding. He noticed another on his left forearm, assumed it had been her prodding again and sighed. But an unease flowed over him and seemed to focus on the mark on his arm which he examined again. It was triangular.

He sighed again and realised he was hungry. Far more important than trying to make sense of these odd feelings of unease. Probably bloody Frank. Traitor. Well, no need to pussy foot around him anymore was there. Tell it how it is and Diane can sob all she likes to her sister. As long as she does it out of his sight.

Bernard wished the cat was out of sight – preferably overboard. Tiger had taken over the cabin as his own and eyed Bernard with contempt as it scratched in the litter tray producing an horrific stink. Bernard had considered whether he could encourage him to take a stroll on the deck, but the fall out would be off the scale, and things were bad enough as it was.

Bernard entered the breakfast area and selected cereal and milk. He put a slice of toast in the conveyor belt toaster and watched as it hardly seemed to move under the element. He shrugged and joined the others at a table where Frank was telling one of his boring "funny" stories. Margaret looked up from her cereal and gave Bernard a thunderous look of disapproval, frustration, anger, even pity. He mused to himself at times how she managed to incorporate so many emotions in one single look. Practice he supposed. There were a few families dotted around and he spied a small child. Not his favourite animal at the best of times, but even worse when he was feeling so horrible. If it got too noisy he would shout at it – obviously out of sight of the parents.

Frank finished his story and they all – except Bernard- laughed. 'Frank winked at him. Morning old chap. Sleep well?'

Bernard ignored him spotting out of the corner of his eye a family loading up the toaster. He stood and headed over to it as his slice of toast exited which was picked up a tall woman in her thirties who then proceeded to smear it with jam.

Bernard drew in his fat belly and snatched it away from her. She looked up in horror. 'What the- how dare you -'

'That was mine, wait for yer own.'

A thickset man in his forties grabbed Bernard by the arm. 'Oi mate, who the fuck do you think you are? He took the toast from him and handed back to the woman. 'Here you go babes.'

Bernard eyed him with venom and grabbed the next piece to appear. The man lent across him and snatched it away. 'And that's mine.'

Bernard knew when he was up against a foe he could not take on and mumbled, 'Hope you choke on it.'

'What you say?'

'Nothing.' Bernard made a quick exit back to the table to be greeted by a group of eyes observing him as if he was an alien. 'It was my bloody toast.'

Frank sipped his coffee. 'Bit over the top though mate?'

Bernard sat forward and snarled at Frank. 'You are such a stuck-up git.' He noticed glare number two appear on his wife's face, one which caried a severe health warning to anyone stupid enough to ignore it. but he continued. 'You think your so clever and better than us. Well news" mate" you're not.' Frank's smile tightened a little, but he covered well. Bernard felt a trifle uneasy as Margaret's face contorted into glare number three; the equivalent to DEF COM THREE in the Armageddon films as the world heads for disaster. But his bile was up and all the recent events culminated in the final comment that slipped out, sealing his fate forever. 'If you dare to take my position as chairman of winemakers club you'll... you'll,' he leapt to his feet blustering, 'you'll rot in bloody hell!' He turned and marched out trying to ignore the sea of breakfasters watching him exit.

Margaret stood and turned to Frank. 'Ahem. I apologise for my husband; I think he's lost his marbles.' She hurried out.

Bernard gripped the rail as if it would discharge his anger as Margaret stood beside him. She said softly, 'You have over the years Bernard, attempted to make a fool of me in many ways, but this, this was the final straw. Frank is my sister's fiancé, and she deserves to be happy. If your pathetic ego can't deal with him then that's your problem.' She turned to leave and whispered above the wind. 'And you can find somewhere else to sleep tonight.' She hurried off.

***

Bernard groaned and tried to stretch but found something stopping his arms from extending. He became aware of seagulls and the sound of waves pounding something metal. He began to panic as terrifying memories overwhelmed him; of being in a dark place enclosed in some sort of envelope… Panic took control, and he thrashed around until he tumbled out of the lifeboat onto the deck. He breathed in the cold morning air and welcomed the wind striking his face. 'Bloody hell. What wer that about?' He looked around as reality returned. And the memory of Margaret telling him sweetly to sleep somewhere else. He tensed as a shadow crept over him.

'You look rough old mate.'

Bernard looked up at Frank in jogging gear. 'Just fu'-

'Thing is old chap you're making a bit of a chump of yourself.'

Bernard struggled to his feet. 'I've never liked you Frank. Your stuck up. You're jealous of my position in't wine club an all.'

Frank roared with laughter. 'Believe what you like mate. By the way, seen any little green men lately? I mean if you want to impress the committee keep on with that rubbish.'

Being on the edge of a breakdown Bernard's self-control was now in the minus territory. He lunged for Frank and pinned him against the lifeboat. Margaret and Diane appeared. Margaret grabbed Bernard's jacket collar and pulled him away. 'What is the matter with you? Scrapping like bloody school kid. Grow up and accept Frank will be the new chairman.'

Bernard pulled free and gasped, 'Never.' He staggered away.

Frank adjusted his jogging top. 'Sorry to be the bearer of bad news Margaret, but your husband has lost the plot.'

Ingrid appeared with her new friend pushing her wheelchair. 'This is Mike, Margaret. He is new friend.' She hugged his arm. 'He travels with us because he is scared of boat.'

Margaret eyed him with suspicion. 'Is that right?'

Ingrid smiled. 'He covers it well.'

A young woman appeared clearly concerned and addressed Margaret. 'I think your husband has fallen over.'

Margaret sighed. 'What a surprise.'

Ingrid signalled to Mike who willingly pushed her after the woman. Margaret turned to Frank. 'I don't know what's got into him Frank. He's always been weird, but this?'

Frank smiled and took her by the arm. 'Come on.'

Near the entrance to the bar a small crowd was gathered obviously around Bernard prone on the ground. Somebody had put him in the recovery position and Ingrid was leaning over the edge of her wheelchair directing Mike to help him up. Mike did so and brushed him down. Mike was very attentive. 'You alright mate? Got just the thing for shock.' He searched his pockets and produced a small tinfoil package which he unwrapped and handed the contents – a small cake - to Bernard. 'Eat this mate, it'll settle you down fine.' He turned to Ingrid and smiled. 'Good stuff this is.'

Ingrid nodded and turned to Margaret. 'It will do him good, calm him down Margaret.'

Margaret eyed Mike suspiciously. 'Hmm.'

Mike smiled and turned to Ingrid. 'Tell you what. Let's take him to my cabin and I'll look after him.' He gave Ingrid a wink.

The next morning Margaret woke up to find the bed empty. She hurried to Ingrid's cabin and banged on the door. Mike opened it and smiled. 'Morning. Bernard's fine, just sleeping it off.' Margaret entered and saw Ingrid sitting in her wheelchair and Bernard comatose on the bed.

'What's up wi' him?'

Ingrid looked up from a crossword. 'He was in shock, but Mike's medicine makes him better. He slept well.'

Margaret's eyes closed to suspicious slits. 'And what's in the *medicine*?'

Mike said. 'Nothing special. Just something to calm him down like.'

'What sort of something?' She poked Bernard who stirred a little and began to snore. 'I hope it's not drugs. I'll not be having drugs.'

He smiled slyly. 'CBD. It has great healing properties but without the hallucinations.'

Ingrid said, 'Is natural substance. Mike is clever boy; he has been researching Cannabis oil.'

Margaret snorted. 'Hmm. Well don't give him anymore.' She left and stood in the doorway. 'He'll lay and there and snore all day if you don't get him up. Don't forget we land in an hour, and he's got a lot of driving to do.'

After the door shut, Ingrid laughed. 'I think we have way to get good stuff over.'

Mike looked to Bernard snoring like a beached walrus. 'Him?'

'Who would suspect such a person?'

Mike smiled. 'You are clever Ingrid.'

'I know. On streets of Russia in war we had to be to survive.' She winked. 'I get caravan key and put,' she looked puzzled, 'what is word?'

Mike smiled knowingly. 'A decoy.'

'Yes. A decoy. Will be insurance.'

ARRESTED

The exit from the ferry was not straightforward, made worse by Bernard seemingly half asleep, at least to Margaret's way of thinking. The truth is he was stoned from cannabis administer by Mike by way of the cakes - of which Bernard had consumed a great deal. And so, what would usually set Bernard off on a rant, only made him smile benignly. Margaret found that disturbing. Very disturbing. And driving on the opposite of the road didn't appear to concern him in the slightest. Even more disturbing, because normally he would have been over the top, obnoxious. Ranting.

Margaret was not comfortable going the other way round a roundabout and was worried Bernard was not concentrating. Ingrid poked him. 'Do you want more cake?'

He nodded. Margaret watched concerned as Ingrid passed him one. 'What's in those Ingrid? I hope they're not illegal.'

Ingrid smiled. 'They are herbal. Nothing special.'

Margaret watched Bernard scoff the cake. He was definitely different. Definitely not himself. (However much she disliked that version of him). The paper drifted out of focus as she reflected on his recent behaviour. When he had been *involved* with that whore Penelope Smythe, he had acted weirdly, but not like this. If he was messing around with her, why would he go to such lengths as to be found in his underpants in a carpark? And not just any carpark, but the one she used every week. Did use, she had to go elsewhere now for fear of being stopped and asked stupid questions about flying saucers.

She needed to get to his phone and see if he had been in contact again. If he had... she snorted and shut the paper.

'Don't give him anymore Ingrid, it's not good for him. He'll be asleep and then what will we do?' She folded the newspaper and prodded him in the ribs. 'Don't fall asleep you hear?'

He turned to her and smiled. 'Good idea.' He glanced in the rearview mirror and pulled over onto the verge, switched off the engine and settled back. He immediately began snoring.

In her side mirror Margaret saw Frank pull up behind them. She turned to Ingrid. 'I rest my case.' She got and made her way along the grass verge.

Diane got out and met her. 'Why has he stopped?'

'He's bloody fallen asleep that's what,' she nodded back at the car, 'she, has been giving him cakes and they've made fall asleep.'

'Cakes? I thought you had banned him from-'

Margaret pulled her coat tight, 'These are not just cakes. They have something dodgy, in them.'

'Like what?'

Margaret rolled her eyes. 'Really Diane?'

'Oh.'

'Hmm. Snoring like bloody walrus.'

Frank got out and joined them. 'Problems?'

Diane put her arm around Margarets shoulders. 'Bernard is asleep Frank.'

'Asleep? We have two hundred miles to go yet, and the speed he's going it'll take three flippin days.'

Margaret nodded at the caravan. 'He's out cold. Ingrid has given him,' she glanced at Diane, 'something.'

Frank lit a cigarette. 'I thought the bloke she met up with looked a bit dodgy.'

Margaret sighed. 'He's not the only one.' She thought of the whore and realised this would be an opportunity to check his phone. 'Give me a few minutes, I'll wake him up.'

She got back in the car and noted that Ingrid was dozing. And snoring. Loudly. Bernard had left his phone on the tray under the console. She quickly opened it to check his messages. And jumped as it rang (Tammy Wynette took her by surprise singing "Stand by your man") making her almost drop the phone. She stared at it for a few seconds and steeled herself in case it was *her*.

The male voice sounded vaguely familiar. 'Mr Grimshaw?'

'This is Mrs Grimshaw.' She glanced over at the comatose heap snoring behind the steering wheel. 'He's not available.'

'Sergeant Turner here, Ramsbottom police. I thought I would ring you myself given the sensitive nature of my call.'

She held the phone closer. 'Sensitive nature?'

'It's your son, Julien. He's been arrested for possession and of smoking cannabis in a public place. Also, I'm sorry to add to your problems, but he was also in the possession of a ferocious animal that tried to attack three people in the local park. Actually it did successfully inflict sufficient damage for a man to require a few stitches. I don't question the owning of pets Mrs Grimshaw, but I can't see much to be gained by owning a dog that's sole purpose – it appears – is to try and tear people limb from limb. I understand the victim needed twenty stitches, which sounds quite a few now I think about it.'

Margaret stared at the phone in disbelief. 'Julien?'

'He is your son?'

'Yes but…'

'We need a responsible adult to be present whist he is questioned.'

'We're in France.'

'Ah. Never liked the French. Can't trust anyone who would eat snails. We can provide an appropriate adult from Social Services, but if he has nowhere to go we have to consider his safety.' He seemed to go quiet. 'I don't know, nanny state but there you are. We can't release him home because of his age you see.'

'We won't be back until tomorrow at the earliest Sergeant.'

'Then we will have no alternative but to place him in a children's home until such time as-'

'Children's home? They'll bloody eat him alive.'

'Unless you have family he can go to, we have no choice.'

'We'll get back as soon as we can.' She disconnected and poked Bernard with the newspaper again, only this time with sufficient force to rock him causing him to snort in the middle of a snore. She was not in the mood to be gentle (She rarely was with him) and poking was not enough so she hit him over the head. Twice. He stirred and she poked him with venom in the ribs.

He came to and looked at her. 'What the bloody hell-'

'We've got to go back, now. Julien has been arrested.'

That brought him awake. 'Arrested? What for, mincing-'

'Shut up and listen. He's been arrested for possession of cannabis and,' she nodded back toward Ingrid, 'you mother's bloody dog attacking someone.'

'I told yer she'd be trouble.'

'They need us there to be appropriate adults (the irony was not lost on her as she watched him begin to build for a rant) and because of his age they can't send him home. So he'll have to go to a kid's home.'

'Kid's home? He'll get-' The enormity of it struck him. The overload of information had blown a fuse in his brain and pictures of gay men *doing things to each other* was too much. 'I should never have agreed to calling him-'

Margaret exploded. 'Shut up Bernard and turn bloody thing round. We've got to go back. Children's home! My God, I thought you had shamed me enough but how can I face knit and natter after this.'

'You insisted on the name Margaret. I knew-'

'Just… bloody drive!' She rang Diane. 'We've got to back, now. Family emergency.'

***

The cannabis had ceased to affect him now as the port came into view and his anxiety began to build as the ferry, with its long, steep ramps came into view. Even before he had pulled up, Margaret was out of the car heading toward the booking office. Bernard grunted and turned to Ingrid. 'You haven't changed have you *mother*. I'll not be having any more of those cakes. I intend to be in control of meself thank you very much.'

Ingrid smiled. 'You need to relax.'

'And you need to-'

'Is not good to be so angry my son. Have cake.'

'I don't want your cake. And I don't consider you my mother.'

She sighed. 'Such anger is not good for heart.' She picked at a nail. 'Especially when you are such fat person.'

He sucked in his belly automatically but could only sustain it for a few seconds. 'I want you out of my house.'

'Of course. But police are difficult persons to me.'

Margaret got back in breathless and gasped, 'Told em we had an emergency. We can get on this one.' She struggled back out and told Diane.

Bernard groaned. The situation was a mixed blessing, no more trip to France with Frank but a cart load of trouble at home. And all *her* doing. It was obvious Julien had been given the drugs by *her* (he couldn't bring himself to call her mother anymore) as was the dog. It didn't surprise him it had attacked someone; it had almost done the same to him. Perhaps he can now get rid of it and regain the sanctity of his shed. Hopefully she will get caught at customs carrying her drugs and get locked up, just sooner than she will for blowing up her flat. That raised his mood a trifle and he got out for a stretch. He saw Margaret talking to Diane and Frank and decided to go in the opposite direction.

Frank spotted him and caught him up. 'Bit of a disappointment old mate but I've decided we will carry on, no point everyone's holiday being spoilt is it?' He lit a cigarette. 'Big surprise about Julien though. Didn't think he had it in him.' He gave Benard a sly dig in the ribs. 'Dark horse eh?'

Bernard ignored him. 'I can't say I will miss your company Frank because I won't.' He drew in his big belly, 'And we'll see about election an all.'

Frank laughed as turned to go. 'Dream on mate. You're out.'

The queue began to move and Bernard headed back to the car. Margaret was already back in. 'Made friends with Frank now have we?'

'No.'

'Thought it was too good to be true.'

'I'll try to be civil to him because she is your sister.'

'Yes you will.'

He started the car and began to move toward the ferry. And those ramps. As they drew closer he noticed it was a different ferry to the one they had crossed in. This one had different ramps. Much longer ones. He groaned. But not as much as the car did trying to haul the caravan up the ramps on the outward trip. His stomach cramped as he remembered the acrid smell from the clutch as he did his best to negotiate the ramps without stalling. But of course being underpowered it was inevitable that it would. And so it did. Twice. The second time was worse of course because he was overwhelmed by ferry operatives yelling for him to move forward, the driver behind tooting as the caravan began to drift back as Bernard fought to get traction and of Margaret shouting something he ignored as sweat trickled down his neck. He couldn't face that again.

'I hope you make a better job of getting on than last time.'

He turned to her; his mouth tried to start a rant but sort of flopped open and shut then gave up. He didn't have the energy; the remains of the cannabis having dulled his senses.

***

The ramps proved to be much - if not more challenging - than before. He knew the clutch was on its last legs and vowed never to try that again. He sighed with relief as they left the ferry and headed toward passport control. He smiled inwardly hoping Ingrid would get searched and at least one thorn in his side removed. They were signalled to pull into a bay and get out of the car. All three stood as passport officers searched beneath the caravan with a mirror.

Confident he had nothing to hide Bernard relaxed a little as they finished. 'Thorough job lads, very good.' His smile dropped realising they were conducting a full search as one of them said in a friendly but firm way, 'Keys please Sir?'

Bernard bristled. 'Keys?'

'For the external lockers Sir.'

He reluctantly handed them over and the two men went about opening and closing small access doors such as the front locker, battery compartment, gas bottle storage and elsan toilet cassette. They seemed to confer about something and turned to Bernard. 'Please take out the cassette Sir.'

'Do what? It's full of… you know.' They stood aside and nodded to it.

Margaret said impatiently, 'For goodness sake just get bloody thing out or we'll be all day.'

He snarled, 'You notice it's me what has to empty it. You ought to try sometime.' He pulled the cassette out and stood back. They shone a torch inside and looked at each other knowingly as one of them withdrew a bag of pills, which he held up for his partner to photograph.

Bernard leaned close to inspect it. 'What the hell is that?'

One of the passport officers smiled. 'We were hoping you would tell us Sir.' He turned to his colleague. 'Ecstasy?'

'Probably.' He motioned to Bernard, 'Come with us please Sir.' His tone and demeanour suggested he had no choice. As he was taken away he looked back in shock at Margaret and saw Ingrid having a little chuckle to herself.

He was taken to an interview room where he sat at a small table. The officers sat opposite him. He was not in a good mood. 'This is a bloody mistake. I am,' he drew in his belly and unconsciously twirled his moustache, 'an official of Bolton Council, namely a building control officer. Those,' he nodded at the bag of pills on the table between him and the officers, 'whatever they are, have nowt to do wi me. So I'll be on my way.' He began to stand.

'Sit down Sir. Smuggling is a serious offence.'

'Smuggling? Now listen up–'

The officers looked at each other and smiled. For once the boot was on the other foot so speak as someone – and not Bernard - exercised their authority. 'We will have to thoroughly search the caravan and car. We will also have to search you.'

***

Margaret sat in the car filing her nails as Bernard appeared. He did not look happy. But then as far as she was concerned, he never did. He got in and started the car. He sighed as he checked his watch. 'Four hours. Four bloody hours.'

She glared at him. 'You don't have to tell me.' She furiously filed a nail.' While you were in there chatting, they took everything out of the car and caravan.' She huffed indignantly, 'Even searched my bags. I had to put everything back in the caravan and car. I don't like things out of -'

He sighed and switched off the engine. A spring boinged in his seat as he turned and said softly, 'Searched your bags you say. That must have been traumatic for you Margaret.' He took a duster from the door pocket and idly wiped it over the steering wheel. 'Very traumatic.'
She stopped filing and prepared herself for a rant.

'It's been a trying time for me recently Margaret, what with the media etc, but I've just realised there is always something worse around the corner. Something I never imagined in my wildest nightmares would happen.' He asked softly, 'Have you ever been searched Margaret?' She was about to speak but he put a finger up to silence her. 'It's not something you would forget.' He sighed and looked out of the window with a thousand-yard stare. 'What about a full body cavity examination?' He pinched his eyes and looked back at her. 'Well, I just have, and I wouldn't recommend it.' He gazed out of the window and sighed.

'As we both know, our son is not normal.' Margaret opened her mouth but stopped as he put up his finger again. 'I've not wanted to think what these gay people get up to, it's not my concern.' He grimaced and moved as if to avoid a discomfort making the seat spring boing again. 'However, while they were poking about up my arse, I did have the opportunity. It seemed to take a very long time,' he sighed and almost looked wistful, 'like an eternity you know?' He gazed out of the window. 'As they seemed to explore most of my colon, I realised that it might be for *your* son but I don't think it's for me.' Margaret went to speak but he again put up his finger and shook his head. 'I thought at first he was using a torch,' he smiled ruefully, 'but it felt more like a bloody truncheon. Mind you I suppose it's dark up there so probably not a truncheon as I was beginning to suspect after all.'

Margaret decided this was not a time to argue. When he was loud and ranting he was harmless, but quietly angry was unsettling.

He started the car and pulled away. 'It just gets better doesn't it. I have to report to court and get a hearing date.' He turned to Ingrid who was feigning sleep. 'Might end up in same prison as *her*.'

Margaret decided it was not the time to tell him that Ingrid had not been searched because she made such a fuss about being elderly and in the wrong country, they decided the real perp was already in their custody. Ironic when in fact she had ten times the number of pills stashed away.

Three lights in the sky hovered at a distance and then flicked out.

OUT OF THIS WORLD

It is true that most of us do not glance up at the sky in wonder and certainly do not consider there to be other races outside of this little planet. Bernard certainly never did. He would have been the first to lambaste such beliefs. It is ironic then that he should be the victim of the very thing he would ridicule. Even more ironic was that although everyone thought Bernard was bonkers there was in fact a spacecraft following him and the creatures aboard had been taking him for examination.

Aboard the space craft the occupants were - at a telepathic level (having evolved way past the need for the clumsy communication of speech) discussing their next move. It is believed that many races visit earth, but this race of aliens are perhaps the least evolved and concerned with pleasure more than the spiritual elements virtually all the other races pursue.

They undertook regular abductions around the world and the latest specimen was currently laid out on an examination table. They were gathered around commenting (telepathically of course) on the strange shape and especially interested in the large hairy growth beneath the subject's nose. Some conjectured it was for sensing odours, others that it was a filter. One suggested it might for adornment but the lengths sticking outward and twisted into a point was beyond him. Being extremely tall and thin they found the overextended mid-riff somewhat of a challenge to understand.

Many human subjects were being taken but this one intrigued them because it was carrying an object that was a puzzlement to them and tests had so far proved inconclusive. It was agreed that another tracking device be implanted beside the first (in the subject's arm) to monitor in more detail it's habits and to determine what purpose the object served, mindful they could use whatever it was to their advantage and add to their already enormous collection of pleasure devices. They also needed to implant a false memory so that the subject will not be aware of being taken. The less bright of the bunch – one described him as being one galaxy short of a planet - suggested making the subject believe he had been taken by a race eighteen feet high who had four arms. He was confident nobody would believe the subject. The group had to admit it was a brilliant idea, despite it coming from the equivalent of the village idiot.

***

Similar discussions were also being conducted within a highly secret location somewhere - being secret the whereabouts are of course unknown to us lesser mortals and of course they were verbal, given that we are millions of years behind the occupants of the space craft. Two middle aged men resplendent in American military uniform — both heavily medalled — sat in a luxurious lounge high up in a New York apartment building smoking cigars and sipping brandy. Subtle lighting filled the room and highlighted many expensive artefacts scattered around. Outside, thirty floors below lay the Hudson River and the city of New York.

One of the men, William Sheft, blew a plume of smoke into the air and watched as the air conditioning wafted it toward an air vent as he said, 'So what's the problem?'

The other man, Doug Hammel, studied the end of his cigar. 'These are magnificent William.'

Sheft replied, 'King of Denmark. Made to order.'

'And the brandy?' Sheft said smugly, 'Remy Martin Black Pearl.'

Hammel blew a cloud of smoke into the air. 'I'm impressed.' Deep in thought he knocked the ash off the cigar into a silver ashtray. 'It looks like our off-world friends are developing a interest in alcohol.'

'Alcohol?'

'Hmm. Blackberry and garlic wine to be precise.'

Sheft looked concerned, 'It was agreed in 1950 by the president that we would allow them to take samples in exchange for their technology. We don't have a problem with that, but booze?'

Hammel drew on the cigar. 'I know. Who would have thought.'

Sheft sipped his brandy. 'Of course, our source might be wrong. But the subject has been taken more than once I believe.'

'Really?'

'He was taken from a ship and arrested for drugs.'

Hammel blew a cloud of smoke into the air and watched as it quickly swirled out of the air vent. 'We need to find out. Can't afford to go off half cock.'

Sheft nodded. 'What would they want with wine?' He studied his cigar. 'We don't want a repeat of the native Americans.'

Hammel smiled. 'True. Dread to think what an advanced species could do if pissed.'

'Perhaps not so advanced as we assumed?'

'It's one race, the Perturbians I understand. Late comers to the party so to speak and a law unto themselves.'

'Not spiritual then.'

'Far from it. Pleasure seekers.'

'At least they're not like the reptilians. We 're having enough trouble with them as it is.'

'Quite.' Hammel sat forward. 'Get surveillance on the subject and monitor closely. What do we know about him?'

'According to my sources the subject is... odd.'

'Who is your source? Is he reliable?'

'Zac Childersberger, failed entrance to CIA but is a solid informant. Carries out surveillance for us when needed in the UK.'

'Ok So in what way is the subject odd.'

'A little man, council official. Not the type I would associate with having any understanding of what is happening to him. Makes his own wine which he was carrying when taken.'

'We might have to shut them down from our end, so to speak.'

Sheft blanched. 'Shut them down?' He looked alarmed, 'You mean kill -'

'Neutralize is the term I prefer.'

'Well, if it comes to it, we can call in a drone and drop a reaper on the house. Maybe all of them in this wine club. Sod the collateral damage, we own the media anyway.'

BACK HOME

Bernard was strangely quiet which Margaret found concerning. Quiet with Bernard was usually the calm before the storm. He finished parking the caravan and the car and sat morosely on the sofa. Margaret had finished sorting the washing and stood arms folded in front of him. 'You're very quiet. What's up with you now? I know you didn't like being searched; I don't like being prodded about but I have to get on with it.' 'I can't go to kid's home Margaret. Too many memories.' She sat beside him. 'You've never talked about it, was it bad?' 'Aye, it wer horrible. Bullying from breakfast to bloody teatime.' 'I'll go then.' 'Thank you, Margaret.' It was a rare moment of honesty; there weren't many. After Margaret left he sat thinking about his childhood and decided it was not doing him any good and he would be better off in the shed. As he opened the backdoor reality struck home with a vengeance as he couldn't ignore the large extension to the shed and what it represented – namely, the takeover by his mother of his life. He gingerly opened the shed door to be met by loud barking and snarling as the monster inside crashed against the chicken wire cage door. What the hell has she been feeding him thought as he reached in and turned on the light. This only served to increase the ferocity of the barrage within. The only way to the workbench was to squeeze between the cage and the enormous scooter - which was a journey fraught with hazards as far as he was concerned. He decided it was not worth the risk and instead wheeled the scooter out of the second door especially built for access into the shed extension and onto the garden patio. He felt a few drops of rain and smiled to himself. 'Serve you right you old bat, hope it bloody rusts.' He went back into the shed and now there was more space to manoeuvre felt less intimidated by the caged monster - it felt to him – set on ripping him apart. The back door opened and Ingrid appeared in her wheelchair. 'Ah, thank you Bernard I am going out. You save me time.'

He gave her an evil look. 'Don't get too comfortable *mother* you'll not be here long.'

'Oh Bernard. Why don't we get along huh? Life is too short.'

He ignored her and went back into the shed setting off a tirade of snarling and growling from the dog – if that's what it was – because something that evil must surely be connected to the devil. From the safety of his workbench he shouted, 'What is your bloody problem?' He turned to the bench and ruefully ran his fingers over the deep furrows made by the chisel in what had been a decent work surface, now more like a ploughed field. 'This is bloody nightmare.' He looked up as Ingrid passed the window on her scooter. 'Hope you bloody fall off.'

He felt - more that saw – movement near the white emulsion and leapt up as the spider decided to see what was going on in it's shed. 'Right!' He crashed around and found the aerosol spray blasting it wildly in the direction of the white emulsion. The atmosphere quickly became toxic and he made a quick exit, giving the monster a blast as he passed. Saturday, usually a day of peaceful contemplation in the shed, his only refuge, now lost, he wandered into the kitchen and slumped down at the kitchen table. The phone rang and he picked it up.

'Hello. Mr Grimshaw. My name is Angela from Tanklin, Tanklin and Heywood solicitors. Rebecca Thatcher asked me to make an appointment pending you court appearance.'

He answered despondently. 'Aye.'
'Would Wednesday at four fifteen be ok?'
He shrugged. 'Aye.'
'See you then Mr Grimshaw, I'll send a confirmation letter with details of how to find us.'
He disconnected and sighed knowing full well what the media would make of it. Would he ever get his life back to before? He muttered as he filled the kettle, 'Nope.'

***

Margaret glanced at Julien as she pulled away from the children's home. 'Let's get you home.'

He sniffled. 'Didn't like it in there, mum. They were worse than the boys at school.'

'I'm sure dear.' She looked over to him again. 'What the hell did you think you were doing?' She shook her head. 'How I'll ever show me face at darts club what with your father's nonsense and now this. Whatever possessed you to smoke bloody drugs? And in public? Eh, I thought I'd brought you up better than that.'

Julien was torn – on the one hand he wanted understanding from his family, well his mother anyway - but also loyalty to his grandmother who had been the only person to really understand how it was for him. 'Just a stupid mistake Mum, that's all.'

'And what about the dog?'

'Grandma Ingrid asked me to walk him. He seemed alright with me.'

She gave him a stern look. 'He wasn't with the poor man in the park.'

'He just went mad. I couldn't hold him.'

Margaret considered his slight build and the latent power in an Alsatian, especially an angry Alsatian. 'I'll go to court with you, best we keep your father out of it.'

Julien looked out of the window at the countryside passing by. 'Thanks.'

She parked on the drive, and they entered the kitchen to find Bernard asleep in the chair, head back, mouth wide open snoring for the world record. She poked him. 'We're back.'

He awoke with a start. 'Ah. Just… so what the hell you been doing? Bringing shame on't family drug dealing.'

Margaret sighed as she took off her coat. 'He wasn't dealing, Bernard.'

'Ok, then, smoking drugs in't public. And letting a ferocious wild animal loose to maul someone half to bloody death. God knows how much that's going to cost me.'

Julien exploded. 'I didn't let it off it just-'

Margaret stroked his head. 'Don't fret luv. Go and sort your room out.'

He stomped off. She glared at Bernard. 'You can't help yerself can you. The blame lies with your mother and don't forget that.'

'I'm not bloody likely to am I.' He was about to announce he was going to the shed but instead grunted, 'I'm going for a walk.'

Ingrid entered in her wheelchair. Margaret picked up the kettle. 'Sure that's wise?'

'What do you mean?'

'Well.' She raised her eyes skyward. 'You never know.'

Ingrid joined in, 'Poor boy Margaret. He is upset at being in horrible place huh?'

Bernard sneered, 'Seeing as it's your fault, *mother*, that's a bit rich.'

'Why you blame your poor mother?'

'Because you gave him drugs.'

She laughed. 'Was a little something to make him feel better.'

'Well, he doesn't feel better now does he?' He threw on his coat.

Ingrid said, 'You don't go to shed anymore?'
He snarled as he opened the front door, 'Not since you took it over *mother*.'

COURT

Bernard stood outside the solicitor's office and hesitated, wondering whether he could just pretend and it would all go away. But he knew that was not reality. While he waited, he looked around the plush office with disdain; fancy paintings by pretentious dickheads did not impress *him*. As for the deep pile carpets and...

Rebecca Thatcher came out of her office and approached him. 'Mr Grimshaw?'

He stood. 'Aye, that's me.'

She showed him into her office. He noticed how business like it was, the desk minimal, furnishings just sufficient. No pictures on the walls. One photograph in a frame of her and a young man. He could see it was her and judged her to be in her late thirties. And he had to admit, very pretty.

She sat and noticed him looking at the photo. 'That's Tom.' She smiled. 'He runs the winery with his father.'

'Aye I know. My wife works there.'

'I assumed by your surname it was Margaret.' She frowned. 'If that's a problem-'

'No. Margaret doesn't say much about it and I don't ask.'

She sat forward. 'So you are bailed to next week to answer a charge of attempted smuggling?'

'It's all down to my mother.'

'Please explain Mr Grimshaw.'

'We had to take her in after she lost her flat,' he smiled grimly, 'by blowing it up growing cannabis.'

'I see.'

'She said she had nowhere to live, and we had no choice.'

'And why do you consider her to be responsible for your predicament?'

'Because it was her wi bloody drugs and some bloke she met on't boat tried to smuggle pills out in my caravan toilet.' He felt his anger building. 'Just cos she's Russian she thinks she is entitled to do what she wants.'

'Russian?'

'Aye.'

Rebecca looked thoughtful. 'What's her name Mr Grimshaw?'

He almost spat out the words. 'Ingrid Kazakof.'

'I know Ingrid. She owns shares in the farm and owns a large house nearby. It's a long story I won't bore you with.'

'Large house? Next winery?'

She noted his colour suggesting he might be having a heart attack.'

'Mr Grimshaw, are you alright? Should I call-'

He took a deep breath and waved a hand at her. 'No, I'm fine. Just a shock that's all.'

'I can understand why. She is acting illegally, claiming she has nowhere to live.'

'Cunning old bat. The trouble she has caused me...' He sat deep in thought. 'I need to know how to get her out.'

'Yes, I understand but we need to get this matter of smuggling out of the way first.'

'Aye and then we get rid.'

***

Bernard left the court shocked at having to stand in the dock and be charged with smuggling. As he left the building he was faced with a barrage of reporters.

'Mr Grimshaw, what was it like to be caught smuggling? Why did you do it? Was it the aliens made you do it? I understand you had to undergo and full body search. Did the aliens do that to you as well?'

He waved his arms at them and bellowed, 'Leave me alone.' He forced his way past them to his car.

He drove home breaking the speed limit and not caring. Inside Margaret had just got home
from work.

As he opened the door she greeted him with arms folded and a scowl.' Well done Bernard.'

'I'm not in mood.' He took off his coat and threw it onto the sofa.

'That's as maybe.' She turned on the tv and selected Sky news. A young women was talking earnestly to the camera. 'It appears underpants man has struck again. Despite insisting he didn't want any publicity he has just left court on drug smuggling charges. He refused to-'

'Turn bloody thing off.'

'It just gets better all the time doesn't it Bernard.'

'You talk like it's my fault. I didn't chose to be in't carpark.'

'So you say. But then you haven't explained why you were there in't first place.'

'How many times-'

'Have you been seeing *her* again?'

'Who again?'

'That whore, Penelope Smythe.'

'Penelope... That wer five years ago. You're not still-'

'Going on about it? Is that what you were going to say? I mean why would I worry after finding my husband had been knocking off some other woman?'

'It wasn't like that. Just a bit of flirting, that's all. And I apologised.'

'Hmm. So you say. How do I know you haven't been seeing her?'

'Because I haven't. I told you; she was using me to get her husband onto golf committee.'

'So have you?'

He threw his arms in the air. 'No!'

Julien came down the stairs. 'What's all the shouting Mum?'

'Nothing dear. Going out?'

'Granny said I could go with her to walk Fluffy.'

Bernard looked at Margaret, 'Fluffy?'

'Her dog.'

'The one that tries to rip me apart when I go in't shed? The one that mauled a man so bad he had twenty bloody stitches. Fluffy?' He grabbed his coat. 'I give up. Bloody thing should have been shot.'

Julien went into Ingrid's room and said over his shoulder, 'He's alright with me.'

Bernard struggled to get his coat on. 'I wonder why.'

Margaret went into the kitchen and shouted as she got some ironing out. 'Can't help yourself can you Bernard.'

Ingrid was sorting some clothes when Julien entered. 'Ah, you ready to walk Fluffy?'

'Yes Gran. Don't see what all the fuss is about.'

It's your father. He is stupid man.' She put a blanket over her shoulders and stuffed a bottle of vodka down the side of the wheelchair. 'I give this some thought. Man in park. Did he have moustache?'

Julien pondered for a few moments. 'Yeah, he did. Big one.'

'Like your father's.'

'Yes it was.'

'I think that is why he go mad at the man in the park. He thought it was your father. He is not kind man to animals.'

'You're right Gran!'

Bernard was about to leave as he saw Julien enter the shed. He waited for the barrage of barking and snarling only to see Julien reappear with the dog perfectly happy on its lead with him. Bernard shook his head and got in his car. 'Whole bloody worlds up creek.' He pulled away and was stopped leaving his drive by Margaret's friend Doris, who motioned to him to open his passenger window.

As soon as it was open she stuck her head inside. 'You should be ashamed of yourself Mr Grimshaw. What has that poor woman ever done to deserve what you are putting her through.' She stuttered with indignation. 'You, you grhhh, cruel man.'

'And a pleasant day to you.' He wound the window up hoping it would drag her head up with it and he could drive off dragging her along. She extricated herself in time and waved her fists at him as he pulled away.

Margaret switched on the iron and waved to Julien as he waited for Ingrid to get out her scooter. The phone rang.

A breathless voice said, 'Margaret.'

'Doris? Are you alright? You sound-'

'He's a monster Margaret.'

'Who dear?'

'Your husband.'

Margaret tested the iron with a finger and winced being distracted by the phone. 'Oh I know that.'

'I've just spoken to him outside. He was horrible Margaret, and,' she took a deep breath, 'he nearly had me head off.'

'Oh. Well I wouldn't put anything past him.'

'What's up wi him Margaret?'

'Buggered if I know Doris. These past few weeks have been hell what with him being found in't carpark and now this court thing.'

'I saw it on the news and in the paper. Who would have thought him to be a drug dealer?'

'To be honest I don't think he is.' She considered whether to confide in her. 'It's complicated. I think his mother has some explaining to do.'

'Ah. Never could trust these foreigners. What is she?'

'Russian.'

'Hmm. Reds under the bed do you remember that?'

'Yes. But I think they're more into money than we are now.'

'Probably.' She was silent for a few seconds. 'He looked shifty Margaret. I hope he's not; you know…'

'Penelope Smythe? Hope for his sake he isn't, that's all I can say.'

'Eh you can't trust em can you. I was thinking after we spoke outside police station, about Gerald. What happened to him in't end?'

'He eloped with Fanny Price.'

'He never! Well, you know I always wondered how she would end up. I mean she wasn't backward in coming forward if you know what I mean.'

Margaret switched off the iron and sat down. 'No.'

'The church was never the same was it?'

'No.'

'Especially after the vicar admitted to all his goings on. With little boys. Eh, what is about men Margaret?'

'Don't know. All I can say is he's got worse every year. I mean he wasn't George Clooney at his best but at least he didn't get himself into bother like now.'

'I always fancied Graham. You remember him? Played for the local team. I thought he would make it big in football, but the accident put paid to that as we all knew it would.'

'You know Doris, I never could understand what he was doing wi vacuum cleaner in't bedroom in't middle of the night.'

'Nor me Margaret. Very suspicious. He never convinced me he fell backwards onto it.'

'Hmm. I recall it was the same model me mother had, and there's no way he could have fallen onto it, after all the nozzle was part of a long hose.'

'How long was he in A and E?'

'I think it were about four hours for them to get it out.'

'And how is you son?'

Margaret didn't appreciate the vague connection to her son's possible predilection and decided Doris was getting too nosey. 'Just a misunderstanding. All sorted.'

'He won't be going to prison then?'

'Oh no.'

'Not like his father then?'

'Got to go Doris, lot of ironing to do.'

'Ok. Anytime you need to chat.'

'Thanks luv, bye.' In your dreams she thought as she turned the iron back on.

***

Julien was walking with Fluffy alongside Ingrid on her scooter. 'What are going to do Nan. I don't think Dad wants you to stay with us. But he can't throw you out, can he?'

'No, he cannot throw me on street.' She stopped and leaned close to him. 'I tell you secret, our secret huh?' he nodded. 'I have big house near winery. And I have money in winery also. But nobody knows this.'

'I won't tell anyone nan.'

'You are good boy. They do not understand how it is to be Russian in foreign country without husband.' She started the scooter. 'Perhaps home is not good place for you huh? Why not you go to friend's house?'

'Sebastian's?'

'Yes, he is your boyfriend, no?'

'Sort of.'

'Ah yes, you have not made love yet, I remember. You go to live there and see what happens.'

'I'll think it about Nan. Thanks. We do want to get a flat but mum thinks we should wait.'

'She is parent, will worry too much about her child.' She stopped the scooter again. 'I have another secret also. I have another big win. I keep this safe and with one more I can get flat, rent out house, make little profit.'

'Sounds cool. Can you show me how to bet?'

'Of course but first you must learn how to grow cannabis in secret. I show you, then you make plenty money for you and boyfriend. I have little spot at vineyard, they let me go there no questions asked.' She winked at him. 'Do not worry, I teach you good life lessons.'

Her mobile rang. She motioned to Julien. 'Go run with dog, I have business to deal here.'

He ran on.

'Yes?'

'Hello Ingrid, it's Mike, from the boat?'

'Ah.'

'It's been a few days and I want my gear; I've got a buyer. I saw the decoy at customs worked. Nice one.' He laughed. 'Now he's up for smuggling, classic!'

'Yes, but they took mine also.'

His voice became suspicious. 'Why weren't you arrested then?'

'They took them but could not prove they were mine.'

'But you still owe me. So pay up.'

She shouted, 'No you got to hell nasty drug dealer. I am old person do not need this strain. Goodbye.'

Mike disconnected and sat fuming, deep in thought. He dialled. 'Hello? Yeah put me through to Ramsbottom police station please.' He waited biting his nails.

'Ramsbottom police station.'

'Yeah. I want to report a drug dealer in the town.'

'Just one moment please.' Silence for a few seconds.

'DI Query.'
'I know of a big drug dealer in your town.'
'Do you have a name?'
'Yeah, Bernard Grimshaw.'
'Ok. Got an address?'
'No but he's been in the papers an that. You lot know him.'
'And your name Sir?' The line went dead.

DI Query sat back and sucked his ball point pen deep in thought. He possessed an active mind and an even more active imagination, hence his interest – more a deep passion – in UFOs. He closed the UFO magazine on his desk, which was extremely dogeared given it was published in 1981. (Magazines were a thing of the past and most information was on the internet) He checked his watch to see it was lunch time and picked up a tin foil pack for his lunch.

Sitting at a small coffee table in the lunch area, Sergeant Turner was taking a second bite of his ham sandwich. His Tupperware box was open containing the other half of the sandwich and positioned in such a way that he could simply drop his hand to pick it up. This was important to Sergeant Turner because to enjoy his break - from having to face the public at reception - he liked to immerse himself in the racing times. He had no intention of wasting money on betting he just liked to pretend he had betted and observe the outcome, a sort of participating voyeur. A cup of coffee was positioned next to the Tupperware – far enough away to avoid an accident, but close enough to facilitate picking up. Sergeant Turner applied the same obsessive, fastidious attention to his lunch as he did his work - in fact everything in his life.

He lived alone.

DI Query entered and sat opposite him at the coffee table. DI Query was also obsessive but differed from Sergeant Turner in that his was focused on one thing. UFO's. He jogged the table as he opened a tinfoil wrapping containing an egg sandwich. The abrupt arrival of DI Query together with the pungent smell from the egg sandwich disturbed Sergeant Turner's concentration and he looked up. Sergeant Turner was a decent human being and tried to consider other's feelings even if they had upset his. He was therefore a very polite and well-mannered man. However, he did smile inwardly from noticing blue ink on the Detective's lips. He deduced (a policeman is never off duty they say) that it was from sucking a ball point pen. Something DI Query did a lot. He nodded as he swallowed the bite of his sandwich. 'DI Query.'

'Sergeant Turner.'

Sergeant Turner took another bite assuming he could carry on with the racing times but feared he would not.

His fears were proven correct when DI Query said, 'Got a tip off today. Sergeant. Big drug dealer, here in the town.'

Sergeant Turner smiled tightly as he swallowed the second bite knowing that would be his last for a little while, being too polite to eat when his colleague was talking to him. 'Is that so?'

'Uhuh.' DI Query bit into the egg sandwich releasing a copious amount of - what Sergeant Turner would describe in private as – an awful pong like being too near a volcano. 'Name of Grimshaw.'

Sergeant Turner watched the blue ink mix with the yellow of the egg and form a green smear on his colleague's upper lip. 'Yes, I know the name. Of underpants fame.' He put the half-eaten sandwich back into the Tupperware container and picked up his coffee. 'Also, of UFO fame.' He realised with horror too late that that statement would bring forth a series of Einstein quotes. Something DI Query was infamous for within the station – and most likely, outside of it.

'The very one.' DI Query licked egg from his fingers struggling to contain the contents as the sandwich overflowed. 'And I must correct you there, Sergeant. It's not UFOs anymore.' He noticed green on his finger and studied it for a second then looked up.

Sergeant Turner smiled. 'Is it not?'

It's UAP - Unidentified Anomalous Phenomena.'

'Bit of a mouthful?'

'I agree but more accurate.'

'Yes of course.'

'Once you stop learning, you start dying.'

Sergeant Turner sighed. 'Albert Einstein?'

DI Query smiled. 'You are an educated man, Sergeant Turner.'

'Thank you.'

'I've been researching UAP for a long time now. I think there's something to the Grimshaw case, apart from the drugs of course.' He smiled. 'The only source of knowledge is experience. Know who said that?'

Sergeant Turner glanced down at the ham sandwich beginning to curl in the heat of the room. 'At a wild guess - Albert Einstein?'

'Correct.' The sarcasm was of course lost on DI Query, who was a serious person too busy being obsessed to get the bigger picture. 'Of course, I will be investigating the anonymous tip off, but my real interest is in his experiences with the UAP.'

'Naturally.'

DI Query finished off the sandwich and licked his fingers. 'Truth is what stands the test of experience.' Albert-'

'Don't tell me, Albert Einstein.' Sergeant Turner watched as his arrow tipped with sarcasm flew off into space wasted as DI Query fussed about with his tinfoil.

'It could be the breakthrough I've been searching for Sergeant.' He stood.

Sergeant Turner sensed a possible break in the conversation and reached for the curling sandwich. He managed a bite watching in horror as DI Query pulled an odd face.

'That's better, bit of wind.' He sat down again. 'What did you make of the man?'

Sergeant Turner cautiously sniffed the air and quickly replaced the sandwich in the Tupper ware. He hastily put the lid on. 'Loud, ill tempered, impatient, opinionated not untypical of the type of person who crosses our threshold I suppose.'

'I'll be on my guard then.'

Sergeant Turner waited for the inevitable quote, but it didn't arrive. 'Always the best course of action in our line of work.' He inwardly groaned as the second half of the egg sandwich appeared from the tinfoil. He idly wondered if DI Query wore it on his head at night. The tin foil not the sandwich…

As if he had heard Sergeant Turner's thoughts he laughed and poked the tinfoil. 'Don't worry, I'm not one of the tin foil hat brigade. At least not yet, although with all this 5G I might consider it.'

Sergeant Turner, although a kind and polite man, did resort to poking fun if it was required to alleviate his personal suffering in the presence of an individual he might consider an idiot. He used it a lot. Not because he felt superior, simply for the fun of it and because of his kind nature he could get away with it. 'I would have thought you used it a lot, DI Query. Keep all those nasty EMF waves out.'

DI Query bit into the sandwich and again egg overflowed, this time dropping in his lap. He tutted and quickly put the soggy sandwich down snatching out a handkerchief to wipe his trousers. 'Can't be too careful with this new technology Sergeant.' He smiled as he crammed the yellowed handkerchief back into his trousers. 'So, no I haven't used tin foil – other than for my lunch wrapping. However, as the great man said, "A clever person solves a problem. A wise person avoids it."'

Sergeant Turner gave him a quizzical look.

'Let me explain. I'm following research into 5G and will adapt as required to protect myself.' He took out his handkerchief again and rubbed at the green stain on his finger but with little success other than to make his handkerchief green as well as yellow. He could not work out why…

Sergeant Turner smiled and nodded to the ball point pen in DI Query's shirt pocket, which also had a feint blue stain. 'It's your pen, Detective.'

'Damn thing. Why can't they make them leak proof. We can go to the moon, 'he smiled knowingly, 'Although a lot of evidence suggests we didn't.'

Sergeant Turner pondered whether to explain the cause of the leak but decided it was more fun to watch. 'We didn't?'

'The jury's out as far as I'm concerned but it's odd, we have not been back for fifty odd years.' He took his pen from his pocket and examined it noting a few teeth marks. He shrugged. 'You've surprised me, Sergeant. Tell me what you know of EMF?'

Sergeant Turner eyed his sandwich considering it will soon be beyond what he would consider being eatable. 'Electromagnetic waves, such as that from a microwave or tv?'

'Spot on and very harmful if of sufficient intensity, hence my concern with 5G.'

'Hmm.' The sandwich drifted further toward the horizon.

'Obviously, you're an intelligent man Sergeant are you not also interested in the questions of where we come from and why are we here?'

The Sergeant nodded with a little smile. 'Thank you. No not really. I have enough trouble dealing with everyday life.'

'Fair play. Each to his own. Me, I like to learn. He wrapped up the remains of the egg sandwich and stood. Sergeant Turner prepared himself for the inevitable quote. 'Education is what remains after one has forgotten what one has learned in school.'

'Don't tell me. Einstein.'

'You're very perceptive Sergeant.'

'I know.'

DI query took out his handkerchief and wiped the remains of the egg off the coffee table. 'Grimshaw. Let's see what we can find.' He left.

Sergeant Turner took off the lid and reached for the sandwich. He smiled to himself and muttered as he bit into it. 'Best put on your tin foil hat Detective.'

REVELATIONS

DI Query preferred to work alone, and so it was that he sat in his Robin Reliant, three-wheeler car, parked in the shadows of a tree near to Bernard's house on what he liked to describe as a stake out. There was a strong American influence that coloured his life – mainly because a large proportion of UAP investigations and videos emanated from there. He considered the English to be far too reserved to have sufficiently open minds to accept the possibility of life outside of our little planet. Except his small circle of friends of course - a very small one; three in fact. Some less kind folks at the station described him as a nerd. Sergeant Turner did not join in these character assassinations – preferring to describe him as an individual. And so, DI Query settled down to a few hours of observation.

Half an hour into the stake out and approaching coco time for many in the street, Dave Shaw at number 23, tapped on the passenger window indicating to wind it down. DI Query gave him a scowl and returned to his dogeared UFO magazine. Dave Shaw at number 23, knocked harder, obviously with no intention of leaving. DI Query half expected it and adopted his PR smile as he leant over to wind down the window as Dave Shaw at number 23, was mouthing something.

'… There?'

DI Query smiled. 'Can I help you?'

'My name is Dave Shaw at number 23, I am the neighbourhood watch representative. Can I ask why you are sitting there?'

DI Query – although considered by many to be too serious – did have a mischievous side, something he couldn't always resist. This was just such a situation. He replied with a straight face, 'You may.'

Dave Shaw at number 23, was fazed. 'I may what?'

'Ask me why I am sitting here,' he checked his watch, 'At twenty-two - thirty-three.'

The hackles began to stir as Dave Shaw at number 23, sensed he had a possible felon on his patch. (He watched far too many American police crime documentaries according to his friends) I have the right to enquire why you are sitting there. I also have the right to contact the police.'

DI Query grew tired of the game and produced his ID. He smiled sweetly and said as he wound up the window. 'So no need mate.'

Dave Shaw at number 23, was not satisfied and banged on the window.

DI Query sighed and wound it down again. 'Look mate. I'm on duty. Now go away or I'll have to arrest you for obstruction. Ok?' He wound the window up again and returned to his magazine.

Dave Shaw at number 23, was a tenacious individual and took his role as neighbourhood watch rep very seriously. He would argue that the trauma of having one's house violated by burglars to be something he was determined to stop. He walked round to the driver's side and banged on the window.

DI Query sighed and wound it down. 'You're on dangerous ground my friend.' Being a detective, he quickly noted that Dave Shaw at number 23, was wearing slippers and on closer examination, pyjamas. 'You'll get chilblains mate.'

Dave Shaw at number 23, looked down at his feet and smiled. 'That's as maybe. I have the right to ask what you are up to.'

DI Query put down his magazine and looked up. 'Ok. I applaud your efforts to protect yourself and your neighbours. Just accept I'm doing my job and it's in your interest to let me get on with it.'

Dave Shaw at number 23, nodded. 'Ok got you. Don't want to get off on the wrong foot, so I apologise for disturbing you.' Of course, his interest was sparked. 'So, who is it? I know everyone in the – ah! Mr Grimshaw, got to be. What's he done now? I mean some of the things-'

DI Query noticed movement near to Bernard's house. 'I must ask you to go.' He pinned him with a severe look of *enough is enough mate*. 'Now.'

Dave Shaw at number 23, got the message as he looked up the road. 'Good luck detective.' He went to move away as DI Query wound the window up and returned motioning him to open it again. 'Be careful, I think he's a slippery customer. Won't pop in for a chat. Always made me suspicious of him. Who doesn't like a cup of tea and a chat?' He handed him a card. 'Call me if you need anything.'

DI Query ignored him and concentrated on the trees opposite Bernard's house as Dave Shaw at number 23, shuffled back to his house, hoping to see something interesting.

DI Query observed a certain individual well known to him and his colleagues, namely one, Darren Skint, well know drug dealer. He watched as Darren furtively – he wondered if he did everything furtively – went around to the rear of the house. He checked his watch and wrote it down.

Ingrid wheeled herself to the backdoor and opened it. 'You are Darren Skint?'

He nodded as he pulled his hoody tighter. 'I want a hundred.'

Ingrid pulled back a blanket and counted out one hundred green pills. 'These are dog's bollocks as you say here.' He took them and handed her a wad of cash, leaving with a nod.

She shut the door and deftly tucked the money under the blanket as Bernard appeared. 'Who was that?'

'Someone asking for directions.' She wheeled past him to her bedroom. 'Night Bernard.'

He followed her. 'Bloody liar. Who would be asking for directions at bloody back door?'

She shut the door. He went into the garden and peered around the corner. Eagle eyed DI Query saw him. 'Gotcha.' He was about to radio in that Darren Skint was acting suspiciously and needed pulling up but paused. This could prove to be a big case and he didn't want to act too soon. Let the little fish escape and go for the big one. Bernard Grimshaw.

***

The next morning Dave Shaw knocked at Bernard's front door. Margaret opened it and waited.

'Ah. Morning, Dave Shaw from number 23, I am your neighbourhood watch representative.'

'And?'

'I er, is Mr Grimshaw in by any chance?'

'No.' She shut the door and watched as he left their drive. She muttered, 'Nosey so and so.'

Ingrid appeared in her wheelchair. 'Morning Margaret.'

'Who was it came to the door last night?'

'A man asking for directions.'

'That might wash with Bernard, but not wi me.'

Ingrid shrugged. 'What can I say, if you call poor old woman a liar.'

Margaret leant down to Ingrid. 'You're up to something. We have enough trouble in this house at the moment, I don't want you making it worse.'

Ingrid continued to the back door. 'See you later.'

Dave Shaw watched her trundle up the road on her scooter and decided to follow her. He knew something was going on in that house and it was his job to find out what. He hurried out and followed her. After a mile or so she pulled into the entrance to a park and stopped. He hid and waited. After a few minutes two suspicious looking youths in hoodies approached her. An exchange was made, and they hurried off. She remained parked. Another youth appeared and again a brief exchange took place. Dave knew it had to be drugs, despite the dealer being an apparent helpless old lady. Was she working for Bernard?' He got out his mobile and rang DI Query.

'Yes?'

'Morning. Dave Shaw from number 23, the neighbourhood watch representative who spoke to you last night.'

'And?'

'I have some information that might be germane to your investigation.'

'Go on.'

'I followed an old lady on a mobility scooter from the Grimshaw house and observed her acting suspiciously.'

'How so?'

'She waited in the entrance to the park and some shady individuals approached her. Clearly there was an exchange of some kind going on, I suspect drugs.'

'Leave the detecting to me Sir if you don't mind. Anything else?'

'Er, no.'

The phone disconnected. Dave Shaw felt a bit short changed – some small amount of gratitude would not have gone amiss – as he wandered back home intent on keeping a keen eye on the Grimshaws.

DI Query doodled a flying saucer deep in thought. More little fish by the sounds of it. He decided a visit was necessary.

Margaret was late for work as was Julien for school. She shouted up to him. 'Julien! School.'

He bounded down the stairs. 'Is Grandma Ingrid here?'

'No.'

'Ok. I'll see her tonight.'

Margaret stopped him as he passed her and adjusted his coat. 'Mum, don't like it right up.'

'It's cold out there. Listen, it's good you help out your Gran, but be careful.'

'Careful about what?'

'I don't know. Just … look you've got court coming up soon. I know you won't say where you got the weed from. But I think we all know.'

'Whatever. Got to go.'

As he exited the front door she wondered where the innocent child had gone. She glanced toward Ingrid's room and asked herself, 'Whatever it is you are up to you cunning old bat, I'll find out.'

Bernard arrived at work and sat in his car steeling himself - for what was becoming a regular morning event – namely running the gauntlet of flying saucer related comments. He had adopted the *laugh it off* strategy, but his patience was wearing thin. Mavis at reception was subtle but hurtful, Steve in planning the worst. Bernard took a deep breath and got out of the car. William his colleague from building control caught up with him as Bernard walked away from his car.

'Bet that feels slow after being in a warp drive space vehicle, doesn't it Bernard?'

'I wouldn't know. Leave me alone.' He quickened his pace, but William caught up with him.

'When's the big reveal then?'

Bernard stopped and sighed. 'What?'

'Oh come on. Is it for a secret tv show about to be aired? Something like that, or a charity thing?'

'No. Go away.' Once inside the building he did his best to ignore a pair of underpants strung up over the door to the building control office. He ignored the banner bearing roughly drawn flying saucers but he couldn't ignore his Manager standing at Bernard's desk, looking perturbed. 'Drop your things off and come to my office please, Mr Grimshaw.'

Bernard sighed and followed him down the corridor to the Manager's office. He entered and the manager closed the door and sat behind his desk. 'We need to talk Bernard.'

That evening, Bernard got home carelessly depositing his coat onto the sofa and went into the kitchen, where Margaret was making a cup of tea. 'Knowles got me in his office today.'

'That was nice for you.'

'Not really. He gave me a written warning for being absent from work.'

'Not a great surprise though is it Bernard. I mean you disappear for five days then turn up in't carpark in underpants and expect no notice to be taken? Then we have the media and police...'

'You think I made it all up?' Why?'

'I have my suspicions.'

'Not that again. I'm going in't shed, call me when tea is ready.' He stormed out to the shed but took a deep breath before opening the door. He cracked it open a little and peered in to see the whites of two eyes in the darkness. He reached in and switched on the light. All hell broke loose as he entered, the caged monster seeming to launch itself at the chicken wire door in a frenzy to rip him to pieces. He realised the scooter was not there and although its presence was too much to accept, it did provide a barrier between it and the workbench. He sat down and idly moved tools around wondering what had become of his life. Out of the corner of his eye he detected movement near to the white emulsion. Torn between the two opposing enemies he froze looking back and forth. The spider made a dash for the golden oak can and paused as Bernard turned back to the shelves. It had come to the notice of the spider that the interloper was becoming too fond of that murderous spray - it had so far managed to avoid by extreme cunning – and if it did not take more evasive action it might be curtains. It considered moving house to the other side of the shed.

However, Bernard's attention was on the larger and noisier monster repeatedly launched itself at the door barking and snarling.

The door opened and Julien entered. He said in a sweet gentle loving tone, 'Hello Fluffy.'

The bedlam instantly ceased and Julien reached to open the cage door. Bernard leapt to his feet. 'Don't let that bloody thing loose!'

Julien ignored him as he unlatched the gate and reached in to snap on the dog's lead. 'There you glo Fluffy. Walkies.' Fluffy followed him out obediently. Bernard slumped down shaking his head.

A knock at the front door caught Margaret in the middle of buttering some bread and she tutted, wiping her hands as she opened it. 'Yes? What is it, I'm busy.'

'Detective Inspector Query. I wonder if I may have a moment of your time?'

'Margaret did not like talking to the police (recently, the Penelope incident was never too far from her thinking) but she knew it was no good ignoring them. She was shocked to think she expected it could be related either male of the house. She chose her words carefully. 'What's he done now?'

'Perhaps I could come in?'

She stood aside and shut the door as he sat on the sofa. 'So?'

'I'll come straight to the point Mrs Grimshaw. My job is to catch drug dealers. Now, I understand there is a charge against your husband, and also your son. However, I also have an interest in what has been happening to your husband, namely the odd experiences he has been subject to recently.'

She crossed her arms and glared at him. 'The carpark and underpants? What about it?'

'I believe he was taken by …beings.'

'Beings?'

'Not from this planet Mrs Grimshaw.'

'Are you in on whatever it is he's playing at, if so you can sling bloody hook out of my-'

'Trust me, I'm serious. I've been investigating UFOs (he decided it was not necessary to use the correct terminology) for a number of years and I do believe he was taken.'

'Who would want to take him?'

'We don't know why, although it is widely accepted that they take us for examination, even experiments, implanting devices in people.' He could see she was about to throw him out and he put up his hand. 'Please. Just hear me out. I want to help your husband Mrs Grimshaw.'

'Can they not implant a better personality then? Make him more bloody human?'

Di Query silently blessed his inability to make relationships, autism had its advantages perhaps, although the need to wash his hands over and over again… 'I don't think… anyway, understanding what is happening can only be of benefit.'

'Like to you lot you mean.'

'To you both.'

'So, what do you want?'

'To talk to your husband.'

'He's sulking, as usual in't shed. Help yerself.' She went into the kitchen. 'I've got tea to make. So don't be long.'

Bernard looked up as DI Query poked his head around the door. 'DI Query. Can we have a chat?'

'What's he done now?'

'I wanted to talk to you actually. Can I come in?'

Bernard nodded to a folding chair against the bench. 'Help yerself.' He said despondently. 'I've got nothing to add to me statement.'

'It's actually about the experiences you've been having?'

'Oh yes?'

'Look I understand it is a sensitive issue Mr Grimshaw.'

'Aye could say that.' He looked at him suspiciously. 'You got some connection wi bloody newspapers? If so, you can sod off, I've had it up to me-'

'I can assure you my intentions are genuine.'

'Hmm. We'll see about that.'

'Thing is Mr Grimshaw, as I was telling your wife, I've been investigating cases like yours and I believe you.'

'Do you now.'

'Yes. I believe you have been abducted.'

'By little green men no doubt?'

'That is a stupid term ignorant people use because they have no understanding of the subject.' He sighed. 'There might be green ones, I don't know, there are many races that visit here. Some friendly, some not so much. I think it is the latter that have taken you.'

'And what would they want wi me?'

'Don't know. But there is a way to find out.'

'Ah, thought there might be. And what will it cost me?'

'Hopefully nothing because I would refer you to a person I trust.'

'For what?'

'To be hypnotised in order to find out what happened to you. I know a very trustworthy woman who-'

Bernard leapt up. 'On yer bloody bike. I'll not be having some half-baked idiot poking around (a horrifying memory of the passport control popped up) in my bloody head, so let me put this to you as politely as possible, SOD OFF!' He nodded at the door.

DI Query stood and folded up the chair. 'I understand Mr Grimshaw. Just think about it please.'

'I have. Now on yer bike.'

He looked around the shed reminiscing about how it used to be a safe haven. Well it certainly wasn't now. However, he refused to be beaten and began reading the minutes of the last wine making club meeting when Julien entered with Fluffy and put him back in his cage, quiet and well behaved. Julien glanced over at Bernard and said, 'Don't see what the problem is. Fluffy is fine. Night.' He left and pulled the door closed. Bernard looked up and saw two eyes staring at him from the shadows of the cage. He went back to his minutes only to be overwhelmed by snarling, growling, and barking as Fluffy launched himself at the chicken wire door. He looked up in horror to see the door flexing alarmingly as Fluffy snagged his teeth into the wire and pulled shaking his head as if ripping off a piece of flesh from a kill. 'Bloody hell!' He jumped up and dashed for the door.

Margaret was watching coronation street as Benard burst in. 'The monster in't shed is going to breakout Margaret, mark my words.'

She popped another Malteser in and shrugged. 'Your mother, her dog, not my problem.'

He threw his arms up in despair. 'And with that resounding support I shall go for a walk.'

He decided to go along the canal and was deep in self-pity when he saw a long reflection of himself on the water caused by a streetlight. He stopped and looked at the elongated figure of him on the gentle ripples made by the evening wind on the water. A feeling of dread followed by sheer panic overtook him as a vivid memory flooded his brain.
Eighteen feet tall monsters with four arms were examining him. It was them who were taking him.

Despite the discomfort and constant fear of being ripped apart he returned to the shed. Defiantly, he sat at the workbench glaring at the wild beast trying to savage him. He reached up to the second shelve for a bottle of Elderberry, a wine he went to for comfort. A wine he desperately needed now. The spider had returned to the shelves after finding the occupant the other side of the shed to be a stressful neighbour - best kept at a distance. The toxic spray used by the intruder it could avoid with cunning - something it possessed much of. Bernard's hand shocked it from a deep slumber and out of instinct it dashed behind the white emulsion, its go to place. Bernard caught a glimpse of it and jumped back causing Fluffy to change gear and go ballistic. All hell broke loose.

Margaret crashed the door open. 'For goodness sake! I'm trying to watch neighbours.' She gave him a pitying look. 'Drowning our sorrows are we. Poor Bernard. Keep bloody noise down.'

Bernard defiantly snatched down the bottle and opened it. He didn't bother with the refinements of a glass; he just swigged it. Then gulped it down. The effect was as he hoped, and he began to feel a little more human. And quickly a lot more human, in fact the old Bernard. He waved the bottle at the thrashing wild thing in the cage and glanced at his .22 airgun. 'Come an get me. I've got weapons you won't like. I'll be the one to tell the world. Power will all be mine.' He held the bottle up and shouted, 'Wine will rule.' He addressed the rows of bottles, 'I will be your spokesman my friends. The world will hear all about you and bow down to your perfection.' He was very drunk, after all it was fifteen percent, much higher that shop bought rubbish - in his opinion.

'You think you can beat me? I'll be the one. The spokesman. they'll have to listen to me. The power is mine. We will work together!' He stuck two fingers up at the spider which was peeping out behind the white emulsion to check what the hell was going on in its shed. He tried to squeeze the last drops of wine from the bottle and lurched toward the door. 'I'll not be intimidated! I'm coming for yer!'
He staggered toward the Goat and Badger pub and burst in.

SUSPICIONS

Margaret had been through her backlog of soaps, watched bake off and was getting ready for bed. It was 10.30 and Bernard had been out for almost five hours. She considered his physique unlikely to encourage a walk that would take that long. To confirm that she peeked out of the kitchen window and his car was gone. Of course he could be at the pub now that he spent less time in the shed. She rang the pub.

'Goat and badger.'

'Hello. Could you tell me if my husband is there, please, Bernard Grimshaw.'

'Nope.'

'Oh.'

Silence.

'Do you mean you won't tell me or that you can't?'

'Neither.'

'Sorry?'

'He's not here.'

'You sound very certain.'

'I am.'

'Have you looked?'

'Nope.'

Her patience was at a premium. 'Has he been there tonight?'

'Certainly hasn't. I banned him last night for a week.'

'Banned him?'

'Uhuh.'

'Why?'

'Because he poured a glass of my beer over one of my regulars.'

'Oh.'

'So I banned him. Had to after he started a fight with another regular. These people are my bread and butter you see. I can't let them be assaulted and not appear supportive.'

'I understand.'

'I wish your husband did Mrs Grimshaw. A little horseplay is par for the course in a local like mine. Your husband needs to accept friendly banter.'

'I think he has had his fair amount of that.'

'So you believe he was taken by little green men then?'

Margaret sighed, 'Thank you.' She put the phone down and went into the kitchen to make a cup of tea. If he wasn't at the pub then he must be… She switched the kettle on and realised she was biting her nails. She never bit her nails. That meant she was stressed and she knew why. He must be at Penelope Smyth's house.

She sat in her car (only a little fiesta but it served her needs and meant she was not dependent on Bernard) considering the risk she planned to undertake. Well she would only go to the house if his car was nearby confirming her suspicions and if that was the case then it didn't matter about the consequences, she would just confront them.

***

The next morning Margaret once again trudged up the steps to Ramsbottom police station. Once again, Sergeant Turner was on reception. She went straight to the desk and knew it was pointless saying anything until he stopped writing. She pulled her coat tight around her and looked around the foyer confirming it was empty.

Sergeant Turner looked up and straightened his back. 'Mrs Grimshaw.'

'I want to-'

He smiled kindly with perhaps a little twinkle in his eye as he put one finger up to interrupt her. 'Don't tell me, your husband has gone missing?'

'Yes.'

'When?'

'Last evening. His car was not there, I checked the pub and… went to see if he was at *her* place.'

'This would be the woman you suspected before?' She nodded. He began writing and asked as he did so, 'I presume he was not there, otherwise I suspect I would have heard from my patrol colleagues.'

'His car wasn't there so I didn't knock.'

'I see. Any idea where his car could be? Could he have left it at work perhaps?'

'No. I've checked.'

He stopped writing and straightened his back again. 'Do you think maybe…?'

'Flying saucer rubbish? Certainly not.' She fussed with her hair, 'He's up to something and I don't know what.'

His recent discussion with DI Query was still fresh in his mind, as was his disturbed lunch. 'We can't rule it out though, however daft it may sound.' He considered for a moment and asked softly, 'Could there possibly be another …?'

She gave him a pitying look. 'Really? Who would be interested in that fat git.'

'Hmm. Can't rule it out though.'

'I think we can.'

'Anyway, we have all the relevant information; I'll get it out to my fellow officers.'

'Right.'

He stopped writing and considered for a moment. 'There was an altercation at the Goat and Badger - how they arrive at such exotic and to my mind frivolous pub names is beyond me – to which two of my colleagues attended. Evidently, your husband caused quite a fracas requiring the landlord, one Tony Drakesmore, to call for our assistance.' He inspected his pen and frowned. 'He's not a man of many words-'

'I know, I've spoken to him.'

'Ah. When you confirmed he was not at the pub. Anyway, when my colleagues arrived the place was in an uproar, requiring the officers to take out their riot sticks to protect themselves when the crowd turned on them.'

Margaret sighed. 'I'm the first to admit that my husband can be a pain in the arse Sergeant, but he doesn't start fights in pubs.' She bit a nail and realised. 'Well, he did once a few years ago but it was a misunderstanding about wine or summat stupid.'

He gave her an understanding - bordering on condescending - smile. 'Given the media attention he has been subjected to, it is no surprise that he hit him.'

'Who hit who?'

'Whom.'

'Pardon. The correct grammar is who hit whom.'

She aggressively bit her nail again. 'Whatever.'

He noted her growing frustration, having to remind himself that he can be pedantic – not everyone's cup of tea. 'Your husband hit a reporter. It appears the media is keen to maintain the story and were looking for anything they could use.'

'Was he arrested?'

'It's his job to chase up a story-'

She snarled. 'My husband.'

'No just a verbal warning. Once they got him down from the table he calmed down.'

'Table?'

'Hmm. According to the officers, he was jumping up and down on a table waving a chair leg in a threatening manner screaming "they are eighteen feet tall monsters". Before they could reach him, he jumped down and grappled the reporter to the floor. That's when they took out their riot sticks.'

'This is Bernard Grimshaw we're talking about here? I wouldn't have thought he was able to get up on a table let alone jump up and down on it - must have been a bloody strong table.' She looked puzzled. 'Chair leg?'

'That's right.'

'But-'

'Evidently, it started when your husband began shouting at a Mr Chilvers, a local builder, and threw a chair at him. The chair narrowly missed Mr Chilvers and broke on contact with a table.'

'He's definitely lost the plot.'

'Yes quite.' He returned to his writing, paused and asked, 'Is there anything else I can help you with?'

'No. Thank you.'

He watched her leave thinking you never knew what was going to happen next in his job.

DI Query entered. 'Morning Sergeant.'

'DI Query.'

'Was that Mrs Grimshaw just leaving?'

'It was.' He couldn't resist a little dig. 'Your powers of observation are amazing.' With the sarcasm lost in the breeze, he sighed, 'Mr Grimshaw has gone missing again.'

DI Query muttered, 'Really? Interesting.'

'We can't jump to conclusions of course.'

DI Query smiled. 'I'd rather be an optimist and a fool than a pessimist and right.'

Sergeant Turner sighed. 'Einstein I presume.'

'The very man.' DI query checked his watch. 'Lunch break?'

Sergeant Turner desperately searched for an excuse but was scuppered as Sergeant Miller appeared. 'Lunch break. Off you go Sergeant.'

Sergeant Turner accepted defeat and nodded. 'All up to date Sergeant.'

Sergeant Miller nodded. 'I would expect nothing less from you Sergeant.'

At the coffee table Sergeant Turner prepared his Tupperware as usual as DI Query produced a tinfoil package and a bag of marmite crisps. Sergeant Turner felt a shiver of distaste on seeing the crisps having no idea why anyone in their right mind would choose to eat them. But being DI Query it seemed to make sense. He toyed with his Tupperware waiting to see what travesty of a sandwich DI Query would produce (he had accepted over the years that he was oversensitive to matters relating to food) and was relieved when a ham sandwich appeared. A straightforward and simple ham sandwich - accepted it was on white bread and not brown wholemeal as was his own - but he could live with that. He opened his Tupperware and reached for his chicken sandwich when in horror DI Query reached into his jacket pocket and produced a bottle of ketchup. Sergeant Turner groaned and dropped his back in the box. He opened the racing times hoping to find solace from the nightmare opposite him but could not resist glimpsing over the top to see. His worst nightmare was becoming a reality as DI Query opened the crisps, then opened his sandwich and splurted copious amounts of ketchup over the ham, tipped a handful of crisps onto the puddle of ketchup and put the top slice back. Sergeant Turner almost gagged as DI Query then squeezed it down with a hand. Sergeant Turner watched as the ketchup oozed out onto the table.

DI Query smiled. 'Nothing like a good sarnie eh sergeant?'

Sergeant Turner glanced down at his and sighed. 'Certainly isn't.'

'So what else do think happened to Mr Grimshaw then?'

'No idea.' He shook the paper and tried to concentrate but his eyes were drawn to DI Query as he lifted the sandwich and crunched into it. Bits of crisp fell to the table followed by overflowing ketchup.

'Sod it.' DI Query took another bite adding to the mess on the table. He got out a handkerchief and mopped it up. 'If you can't explain it simply, you don't understand it well enough.'

'Don't tell me let me guess.'

DI Query smiled, 'Albert of course, genius.' He licked a finger. 'Sometimes we search for prosaic reasons for something we don't understand in order to maintain our paradigm of the world which can't be challenged. In other words, Grimshaw being abducted by aliens is more likely than being kidnapped by villains.' He picked up the sandwich and tried again saying through a mouthful, 'Everything should be made as simple as possible, but not simpler.'

Sergeant Turner thought if he heard one more quote…

'Thoughts Sergeant?'

'Not possessing all the facts, we cannot jump to any conclusions. You might not be aware that Grimshaw was involved in a fracas at a local pub. It started when he claimed he had been abducted by eighteen feet high monsters.'

'Haven't seen that. Odd I must admit. Most races seem to be of a reasonable height, I've not heard of any being that tall.' More sandwich content slopped onto the table. 'Could be a false memory of course.'

'What's that?'

'Aliens often implant a false memory to prevent the subject remembering what happened to them.'

'Interesting.'

DI Query said, 'Think I'll have another go at speaking to her.' He mopped up the mess with his handkerchief, realised it was beyond redemption and stood (much to sergeant Turner's discomfort) looking around. He spotted the waste bin and deposited the handkerchief, returned and stuffed the rest of the sandwich into the crips bag and said to it, 'Have you later my friend.' He nodded to Sergeant Turner's Tupperware. 'Not hungry?'

'Not anymore.'

'Right. I'm off.' He left.

Sergeant Turner sighed and put the box back in his rucksack and returned to the front desk. An alert had come through of an escaped sex offender which needed to be circulated around the station as he could be in their area. Sergeant Turner studied the photograph and did a double take. DI Query was heading for the doors and Sergeant Turner called him over. 'Just had this in.'

DI Query licked the remainder of ketchup from his fingers, glanced at it and also did a double take. 'Is that-'

'Looks the spitting image to me.'

INVESTIGATION

On the way to his car, he reeled from the uncanny likeness of the photo. He also mused on how uptight Sergeant Turner seemed. It never ceased to amaze him how far people will go to avoid the simple fact that we are not alone. Perhaps the Grimshaw case could be the one to get public interest at last. But first he had to pursue the drug aspect. It seemed unlikely the man was a drug dealer but who knows what goes on behind closed doors. And of course, he was arrested at customs for having illicit pills on him. He checked his wallet and found the card from the neighbourhood rep, Dave Shaw. Much as he disliked the public getting involved, any information was helpful. Being retired he was most likely at home and worth a visit.

DI Query knocked on the door of number 23 and forced a smile as an elderly lady opened it. She studied him for a moment. 'Do you have my bag?'

'Sorry?'

'Are you from the WI?'

'Pardon?'

She smiled. 'The women's institute, my bag?' He looked blank. 'The one I left there yesterday, are you Cynthia's husband?'

'No, I'm-'

'Where is my bag then if you haven't got it?'

'I' err-'

She began to close the door. 'The bins don't emptying yet.'

Dave Shaw appeared. 'Hi detective.' To his wife he said, 'He's here to see me dear, neighbourhood watch business.'

She shook her head. 'Oh. I thought it was my fucking bag.' She turned and roughly pushed her husband aside. Being very observant DI Query couldn't ignore her passing wind as she left. Very noisily.

Dave Shaw beckoned DI Query inside. 'Hope I can be of help detective.'

DI Query nodded as he held his breath and entered the hallway. He noted every power socket had an air freshener plugged in to it. He understood why as the disappearing figure shuffled into the kitchen, emitting phutting noises with every step. It didn't require amazing investigative powers to conclude she had a wind problem. They entered the lounge and sat.

Dave Shaw said, 'So it seems I can be of assistance after all.'

'Hopefully yes. A few days ago you rang about an old lady you followed from the Grimshaws?'

'Yes. Acting very suspiciously in the park exchanging something with some youths.'

'And what do you know about her?'

Mrs Shaw entered with an empty cup smiling vacantly as she put it on a coffee table between them. 'And don't eat all the fucking biscuits.' She shuffled out – soft phutting sounds continuing.

DI Query peered into the empty cup. He gave Dave Shaw a quizzical look.

'Sorry, Dotty is having a few problems at the moment.'

'Right. So, the Grimshaws.' He could no longer hold his breath and had to let it go.

'I don't know much about them other than they have a son of fifteen - I think he's, you know…'

DI Query made a "don't know what you are talking about gesture". He also wondered how the man could survive in such a toxic atmosphere…

Dave Shaw whispered. 'Gay.' He continued on more solid ground, 'And recently the elderly lady I spoke about arrived in a wheelchair.' He leant over and said quietly, 'Two strange men entered and came out with a laptop. Very weird looking, tall with dark suits, hats and sunglasses.'

DI query muttered to himself. 'Men in black. This is more serious than I thought.'

'Sorry?'

'No matter. That's been very helpful.'

He escaped as fast as possible and breathed in fresh air muttering, 'A few problems? That's an understatement mate.'

***

That evening DI Query knocked at the Grimshaw's house. The door was opened by Margaret who sighed. 'What now? He's not here. You might be aware he's missing?'

'I came to speak to you actually.'

'I'm not interested in talking about bloody flying saucers. When he reappears – if – you can speak to him then.'

'I want to speak to you about an elderly lady who lives here?'

'Do you now. Then you'd best come in.' She ushered him into the lounge and sat down, indicating for him to do the same. 'That would be Ingrid, his mother who is staying with us until she is rehoused.'

'Right. What can you tell me about her?'

'She's Russian, cunning, smokes dope, gets her own way and is – how can I put it politely – a bitch.'

'I see. And why is she being rehoused?'

'Because she blew up her flat growing cannabis.'

'Interesting. Is she here now?'

'No. Out most of the time on her mobility scooter. Broke her leg in the explosion.'

'Do you know where she goes?'

'Gambling most of the time. Seems to be very good at it.'

'I see. That's very helpful.'

She showed him out. 'Very sneaky lady if you ask me.'

NIGHTMARE

PC May was hoping it would not be another shift like the previous evening. Having to drag PC Jones off the young man trying to give rescue breaths to an elderly lady suffering a heart attack had been the final straw. He had made it his purpose to protect the public from what could only be described as an overzealous, male hating female police officer, fresh out of training and determined to make a difference by arresting every male she came into professional contact with, regardless of their guilty or not guilty, status.

PC May drove carefully on the way to a shout and gave PC Jones a stern look. 'There will not, I repeat not, be a repeat of last night.'

She looked out of the window at houses whizzing by and shrugged. 'Looked dodgy to me.'

'If you recall, I said as we pulled into the shopping precinct, "don't jump to conclusions" but you disregarded me and attacked him anyway.'

'I thought he was-'

'Saving a woman's life? No, you didn't think, you over reacted. Do I need to remind you that you are on probation? And that my feedback on your performance is crucial if you want to remain in the police force?' He had his fingers metaphorically crossed, fervently hoping she didn't.

She glanced at him, deep in a sulk and said sullenly. 'Yeah, I know.' Her mind was elsewhere having seen the alert that had been circulated by Sergeant Turner. She had been shocked to see it was the same man they had picked up from the carpark in his underpants. Bernard Grimshaw. Now she had good reason to get him put away for good.

'So, we are on a call at twenty-three forty to an incident in an Aldi carpark. All we know is that a man has been found in a confused state, and it is our job to attend and assist.'

'Probably the creep reported near the school.'

'We don't know, so keep yourself in check.'

They pulled into the carpark, the car headlights picking out two staff members waving them over. They pointed to a line of wheelie bins. One of them said to PC May, 'We were just leaving and saw him behind a wheelie bin.'

PC Jones tumbled out, one hand on her riot stick, the other holding her torch as she marched toward the bins. PC May sighed. 'Thanks. We'll take it from here.' Wearily he got out and followed PC Jones who had disappeared behind the bins. As he rounded the end bin he heard PC Jones shouting, 'I won't warn you again, have you been drinking? What drugs have you taken. Do you have anything sharp in your pockets that could harm me?' He gasped as he saw her leaning over a figure huddled in the shadow of the bin. Before PC May could reach her, she poked the figure with her riot stick. 'Last chance or I will spray you.'

PC May shouted, 'NO! 'He ran to the impending assault and dragged her off the cowering figure. 'How can he have anything sharp on him, he's only wearing underpants.' He crouched down to the sad figure, 'It's Mr Grimshaw, again. Call for a medic.'

She strutted back and forth muttering. 'Escaped from the nick and a sex offender on our patch. Knew he was a perv. Look at the state of him.'

'Now! He's shivering.' He took off his jacket and put it around Bernard's shoulders. 'Come on mate let's get you up.' Bernard allowed himself to stand and stood in a daze.

'What happened to you?'

Bernard mumbled, 'Won't leave me alone. Eighteen feet tall, four arms.'

PC Jones strode up and poked him with her riot stick again. 'See! High on drugs. Told you.'

PC May helped him to their car. 'We need to have another chat PC Jones.'

DI Query smiled to himself as he heard the call from PC Jones on the radio. He redirected the ambulance to the police station. Bernard was taken to an interview room and checked over by the paramedics who pronounced him dehydrated but otherwise unharmed.

He sat - with the same multicoloured blanket he had been given before around his shoulders – staring vacantly into space.

PC May was getting himself a well-earned cup of tea, congratulating himself from saving Mr Grimshaw from being pepper sprayed and probably beaten up. He had missed the alert. He looked around for PC Jones, constantly aware she could be causing trouble somewhere – even in the safety of the police station – but she was nowhere to be seen.

In fact, she was heading for the interview room intent on forcing a confession from the obvious escaped child molester. Thoughts of the trauma her sister had suffered burned in her subconscious – out of conscious thought but driving her escalating violent, misguided behaviour nonetheless. She was well on the way to being psychotic which meant she was becoming dangerously out of control, unable to see the insanity of her belief that it couldn't possibly be Bernard.

She entered the interview room and sat opposite Bernard who was staring vacantly at the wall behind her. 'Won't wash with me mate. I know your sort. Admit you're a perve and we can get on with processing you for the court.' She picked at a nail. 'You're going down for a long stretch mate.' He continued to stare ahead as if he had not heard her.' She began drumming her fingers. 'Now look, I aint got all day.' She leant forward and said softly, 'I know ways to get you to confess mate. Know what I mean? See, I'm a new breed of officer, and I don't intend for you to play these fucking silent games crap. Right?'

Bernard mumbled. 'Won't leave me alone.'

'Bloody right mate. As far as I'm concerned, you aint got no rights once you're in here. I'll keep on till-'

Bernard's mind was reeling with memories and voices in his head of tall monsters, being poked about, something probing his mind, something about wine? He struggled to make sense of all the conflicting images and thoughts in his mind - but something was surfacing, a vague thought about wine – which seemed they were interested in. 'Want wine.'

She saw an opening. 'I can get you what you want mate, just confess it was you outside the school.'

He whispered, his eyes darting back and forth. 'Not nice.'

'Definitely not. And you selling to kids isn't either.'

He sighed and looked tearful. She got up and walked around behind him. 'Poor old you. Tell me all about it mate.' She rested her hands on his shoulders.

'Won't stop.'

She felt her anger begin. 'Really? Is that a threat?'

'I think they want it.'

Her fingers began to dig into the blanket. 'Do they now? Little kids wanting…' She leant down and whispered, 'You're goin to fry mate. I'll make sure of that.'

'Got to give it to them.'

'Not on my watch you perve!' She got him in a strangle hold with extreme prejudice, as the Americans say. 'Confess you bastard!' His face was turning purple. She was very strong from working out three times a day.

PC May burst in. 'Let him go!'

PC Jones was beyond reasoning as she tightened her grip. 'I'll get a confession out of-'

DI Query arrived and helped PC May drag her off the hapless victim. PC May hurried her out. 'I think we're beyond a chat now PC Jones.'

DI Query sat opposite Bernard now in shock.

'Mr Grimshaw?' No response. He leant over and gently nudged him. 'Hello, Mr Grimshaw?' He sat back studying the unresponsive figure. Definitely a case of the light being on but nobody in, he thought. Although given the treatment he had just been subjected to, it was no surprise. In his opinion definitely the behaviour of somebody having been abducted by beings not of this planet. This was gold dust. He leant over and prodded the inert figure. 'Mr Grimshaw. I know what you've been through. Can you hear me. It was them wasn't it?'

Bernard stirred but kept staring ahead wide eyed. He whispered, 'You do?'

'Yes.'

Bernard whispered again, 'It's wine.'

DI Query sat forward pen poised over his notebook. His main interest concerned the alien abduction but his investigation into the drug issue surrounding the Grimshaw house was a professional priority he had to pursue. Wine might be a way in. 'Uhuh. Yes, I'm aware.'

'Want it.'

It seemed either a confession was coming - then he could explore the abduction element - or the man was coming down off some and wanted more. 'Tell me what I need to know and we can help you.'

There was a flicker of annoyance from Bernard. 'No. They want it.'

'Who?'

'Them.'

'Give me names and I can put in a good word for you.'

'No names.'

'Too late to protect them. Think about saving yourself Bernard.'

'Not human.'

'I agree, they're scum, so let me get them and save yourself.'

Bernard came round and muttered. 'Spacemen.'

DI Query suddenly realised. 'You mean aliens?'

Bernard nodded. 'Big ones. Very tall. Won't leave me alone until they get it.'

'The aliens want our wine?' Bernard nodded. 'But what would they want with wine? They're millions of years ahead of us!'

Bernard glared at him. 'Not this bloody lot.'

***

Sergeant Turner smiled as he put a full stop to a sentence and straightened his back.

'Let me get this straight detective. You purport that we have an advanced alien race that want our wine for nothing more than pleasure?'

'In a nutshell, yes. Hard to believe I grant you.'

'Certainly is. Or he could be making it up of course.'

DI Query nodded. 'Of course, but I don't think being found in his underpants on two occasions in supermarket car parks is a particularly effective cover.'

'That's true detective. But then we both know the vagaries of the average punter who crosses our threshold.'

DI Query smiled. 'Insanity: doing the same thing over and over again and expecting different results. Albert Einstein.'

'You're referring to the underpants I presume.'

'I am.'

Margaret burst in looking flustered. 'Can't you tell those horrible newspaper people to clear off?'

Sergeant Turner and DI Query both turned as she approached the desk. Sergeant Turner smiled. 'Sadly we have no control over the media outside of the station. I assume you are here to collect you husband once again?'

DI Query said, 'I'm here if you need to talk about it Mrs Grimshaw.'

She tightened her coat. 'What use would that do?'

'Like I said, I think I know what is happening to him.'

Sergeant Turner picked up his pen and bent down to write. 'Two things are infinite: the universe and human stupidity; and I'm not sure about the universe.'

'Nice one Sergeant. Albert had a way of putting it so succinctly.'

Margaret drummed her fingers on the counter. 'Whatever. Where is the old fart?'

'He will be through in just a moment.'

DI Query checked his watch. 'Got to go. Don't forget Mrs Grimshaw, anytime.'

Bernard appeared once again in the multicoloured blanket - once again looking like an enormous Christmas pudding.

Margaret bristled. 'Look at the state of yer.' She nodded to the door. 'That lot are going to love this.' She hustled him out as Sergent Turner said as he wrote, 'Don't forget about the blanket.'

The media interest had been big before; now it was massive. TV vans, reporters clamouring to get in first, photographers standing on walls, it seemed the whole world press was here. And behind them, passersby waiting to what was going on. Even a double decker bus had stopped and the passengers clamouring to see.

Margaret bustled him down the steps not caring that he was bare footed. They were met by a barrage of questions such as, 'Why do they keep taking you? Is this a publicity stunt? Are they coming to take us over? Were you anally probed? Are you still smuggling?'

Margaret was forced to stop by the sheer number of microphones being thrust in Bernard's face. She held up her hand. 'Leave us alone!'

One of the reporters closest to Bernard asked urgently, 'Is this the end of the world? Are you their spokesperson?'

Bernard gave them a dazed look and tried to move forward tripping over the blanket causing Margaret to lose her balance on the steps and tumble onto the female reporter in front of her. The reporter fell to the ground and cameras frantically clicked. A voice from the back shouted, 'We need to know the truth!'

DI query appeared and helped them up. He shouted, 'Stand aside please!' He pushed through and bustled them into his car. 'Let's get you home.' He was aware as he drove that he was not alone as a convoy of vehicles followed him. He managed to get them inside before the mob arrived shortly after he shut the front door. Bernard stood in a daze. Margaret took off her coat and sighed. 'So here we are again, you standing in't middle of the room like some oversized Christmas pudding with no explanation.'

DI Query said softly, 'I can help.'

Margaret looked him up and down. 'Really? I don't think so. But thank you for getting us away from that lot.' She relented a little. 'Give me time to get him back to reality and perhaps I'll call you.'

***

The next morning Margaret drew the curtains to see the same media outside the house but which now included hastily erected tents on the front lawn and pavement. Neighbours trying to get to work were hooting their car horns and a fracas erupted outside number 43. Margaret snatched the curtains shut and shouted at Bernard. 'Come and see what you've done now.'

He rolled over and began snoring. She poked him with a slipper with no effect. 'Bernard, wake up! No use hiding.' No response. She grabbed a glass of water from the bedside and tipped it over his head.

'What the bloody hell!'

'You might well swear. I suggest you look outside.'

He staggered out of bed and threw the curtains open. All hell broke loose as cameras flashed and reporters surged over what remained of the lawn to the front door. He hastily drew them closed. 'What's that lot after?'

'Hmm, let me think. You've been voted playboy of the year? You've won the lottery? Or is it that for the second time you've been found in't carpark in bloody underpants!'

He looked from her to the window and whispered. 'What bloody hell is happening to me?'

She slumped down on the side of the bed. 'That's a very good question Bernard. I think it's time you told me the truth.'

'I keep telling you, I'm being taken by these … creatures.'

She broke down and sobbed, 'Or is just a way to hide seeing *her*.'

He peeked out of the curtains again distracted by a police riot van up the road. 'Who?'

'That whore.'

He said, 'Eh, Martin from number 43 is being arrested. I know he's a bit weird-'

She pounded the bed. 'Did you hear me?'

He shut the curtains as cameras flashed. 'Do what?'

She burst into tears and rushed out. 'Make yer own bloody breakfast.' She reappeared, 'Or get Penelope fucking Smythe to do it!'

He sat down with his head in his hands confused and feeling emotionally battered. One thing - and one thing only - was worse than the baying crowd outside, and that was one of Margaret's moods. And this one was a biggy. But his mind was becoming overwhelmed struggling to understand these weird memories of creatures talking to him without moving their lips. Not eighteen feet tall ones, much smaller. And not with four arms either. A vision of a bottle of wine? What was it about wine? It came back in a flash. He heard the front door slam and hurried to the window and peeked out to see Margaret storm through the crowd casting them aside like they were skittles. This was not good. Not good at all. He got dressed and decided against breakfast - his appetite had gone along with any hope of peace in the house. And he would have to go to work, given he was on a warning.

Ingrid wheeled herself out of her room and into the kitchen. 'You have many friends outside Bernard, why don't you go talk to them?'

He muttered to himself something about why she didn't go and …

She smiled as she rolled a cigarette. 'They won't go away.' She lit it and blew a cloud of smoke in his direction.

He growled. 'Smoke bloody thing outside. I've reluctantly allowed you here, least you can do is abide by rules.'

She wheeled herself over to the backdoor and opened it. 'Fluffy needs a walk, why don't you take him?'

Because bloody thing will rip me …' A thought occurred to him and he smiled evilly. 'Yes perhaps I will.'

He put on his coat and opened the shed door to be met by a snarling monster launching itself at the cage door. He got the lead off the hook by the cage and shook it in front of the cage door. 'Walkies?'

The rage instantly diminished to that off a deep suspicious growl as Bernard shook the lead again. 'Just as I thought, dumb animal. Eh man's intelligence is no match for stupid dog.' He opened the cage door and slipped the lead onto the collar. 'See, my little growling friend. Now let's see what you make of them outside shall we?' He pulled and Fluffy followed him out, giving a little cursory growl just to remind itself who was boss. Bernard led him out of the side gate and smiled as the media seemed to turn as one at the creak of the gate.

'Mr Grimshaw! Talk to us!'

He felt the lead tug as Fluffy moved toward them beginning to growl louder. A reporter with a moustache was nearby and Bernard noticed Fluffy seemed to be growling at him. Bernard smiled evilly and whispered, 'Oh, whoops, dropped the lead.' Fluffy launched himself at the reporter in what would later be reported as a frenzied attack. Chaos erupted as Fluffy went to work on the reporter dragging him to the ground. Not sure what was happening but fearing the worst, the crowd of reports scattered in all direction as Fluffy dragged the man into the bushes. Bernard got in his car and drove at them not bothered if he knocked anyone over. He smiled as he caught site of the man's feet disappearing into the bush.

***

Bernard sighed as the police car pulled into station carpark and he was led into the station in handcuffs. DI Query sat opposite Bernard in an interview room and switched on the tape recorder. 'It is ten thirty-two and I am DI Query interviewing Mr Bernard Grimshaw in the presence of his solicitor Ms Thatcher. Mr Grimshaw. Do you own a dog?'

'No.'

'Did you release a dog this morning outside your house?'

'No.'

'There are numerous witnesses and copious film evidence that you did.'

'It slipped out of my hand.'

'I see.'

Rebecca intervened. 'It was an unfortunate accident Detective, nothing more.'

'That's as maybe, but a number of witnesses said you were smiling as the man was dragged into a bush.' Bernard shrugged. DI Query sat forward. This is very serious Mr Grimshaw, you seem to be getting yourself into a lot of trouble; like smuggling, the current charge of being in possession of a wild animal to cause injury and … other matters we needed not go into here.'

Rebecca stood. 'Enough. My client is unfortunately suffering from mental exhaustion and needs to be released. I believe that the animal is back safely in its cage. My client needs to be released so that he can recover at home.'

DI Query said, 'Interview terminated at ten thirty-eight.' He switched off the recorder. 'Anytime you want to chat Mr Grimshaw, call me.'

***

Bernard groaned as the crowd outside his house seemed to have grown, although now it had been supervised by the police into designated areas - much to the chagrin of Bernard's neighbours. He veered recklessly at a few rogue reporters on his drive making them dart out of the way. He parked and headed toward his front door, glancing over his shoulder to see the crowd watching his every move. He opened the door to be confronted by Margaret, arms crossed and definitely not in a good mood.

'You'll not be coming in here Bernard until you explain yourself.' She looked over his shoulder and nodded at the expectant crowd. 'Go and talk to yer fans why don't yer. Tell them about your hussy.' She slammed the door in his face.

He felt the energy change in the crowd as they sensed a drama unfolding. He turned to get in his car as they surged forward surrounding him. 'What's happening Bernard? Is she divorcing you Bernard? Is it true you're having an affair?'

'How the hell do you know about that?'

'So you admit you are having an affair.' The buzz swept through the crowd as they all frantically made mobile calls.

Bernard got into his car and slammed the door. 'Right!' He pulled out of the drive turning to look at a multicoloured marquee erected on the triangle of grass near to his house. A large sign over it read, WE ARE NOT ALONE. Outside it sat a group of middle-aged hippies smoking dope and doing - to Bernard's mind - some sort of weird dance. He shook his head and drove on.

He strode into the police station and didn't wait for Sergeant Turner to look up. 'I want to make a complaint.'

Sergeant Turner stopped writing and stood straightening his back. 'Mr Grimshaw. We seem to be seeing a lot of you as late ... for a variety of reasons. Complaint you say.' He picked up his pen. 'And what is the nature of the complaint?'

'Bloody press outside my house. They must be spying on me.'

Sergeant Turner looked up. 'I don't understand.'

'They knew about the affair.'

'Affair?' He recalled Margaret mentioning it but thought it best to remain ignorant.

'Some wild airy-fairy idea me wife has got in't head.' He puffed himself up, 'Nothing to it of course – you know what they're like when they get suspicious.'

'Quite.'

'So I want to know how they knew. I think they must have one of these listening devices in my house.'

'Unlikely though.'

'So you explain it then.'

'Overheard conversations? Perhaps your wife has spoken to them, a neighbour with a grievance,' he smiled sadly, 'enough of those I would think.' He thought for a moment. 'Don't see how you can make a complaint Mr Grimshaw. Too many of them you see.'

Margaret listened to the voicemail on the home landline and slammed the phone down.

Bernard's mobile rang. 'Now what?' He moved away from Sergeant Turner and listened. His body seemed to deflate and he became smaller as he wandered out of the doors. 'Do what?'

Margaret shouted loud enough for Sergeant Turner to hear. 'I said your manager has left a message on't landline saying you're suspended.'

'But why...'

'I can think of a few like the spaceship nonsense, smuggling drugs, letting vicious dog maul a defenceless man and ... let me think, oh yes, being bloody cheat and having an affair with *her*.'

'Margaret I-'

'I've had enough, I'm going to me cousin's.'

He put his phone away and stood looking despondingly down the steps of the police station. 'Now I've been suspended from me job.'

As he went to leave, Sergeant Turner coughed. 'Er, Mr Grimshaw.'

Bernard turned his face gaunt from shock.

'Can we have our blanket back please?' He couldn't resist it and said with a straight face, 'You never know when it might be needed again.' He picked up his pen, 'After all you do seem to have a predilection of disappearing.'

A KIDNAPPING

DI query opened the door to his two up two down terraced house; enough for one person, and that's all he wanted. Relationships were something other people had. And any way he never knew when he might want to go abroad as part of his investigations into UAPs. That was his dream and it felt with the Grimshaw case that he might be getting closer to something big enough to go public with. What he needed was evidence, solid concrete, irrefutable evidence that nobody could dispute. But to obtain that he needed to get Bernard Grimshaw to share what happened to him. And that was proving to be difficult. He needed a plan.

PC Jones on the other hand did have a plan. Admittedly it was one fraught with problems but that was not of concern to her because the fire of revenge on behalf of her sister burned ever brighter, especially now that a perp was at hand. Any psychiatrist worthy of their profession would diagnose PC Jones as schizophrenic, a condition that had been dormant within her until her late teens (she was now 21). Her friends tried to ignore the combination of hallucinations, delusions, and extremely disordered thinking and behaviour that impaired her daily functioning but were too scared to mention it - at least to her. Added to this toxic mix of abnormality was being gay – not that there is a problem with that – but it tended to exacerbate the symptoms especially when testosterone laden men were on the scene.

She tried it once with a man but found the experience too trying, especially when he was so frightened of her that he called the police to rescue him. (he did recover after intensive counselling) When they arrested her, she found the experience exhilarating and considered further extreme behaviour but decided a better course of action would be to join them, and so she joined the force, discovering that she could mask her symptoms well and so negotiated her way through the psych tests.

Since being suspended - for what she regarded as good policing - she had time on her side to placate the voices in her head that were clamouring for attention. She studied the picture of the escaped sex offender she knew lived locally – a classic example of cognitive dissonance, i.e., when in a reasonably saner place, she would see it couldn't be Bernard Grimshaw, but her psychosis convinced her it was.

She looked closer at the eyes and shuddered. They say (whoever they are) that the eyes are windows to the soul, and in this case to an arshole. Her sister's tears made her eyes sting, and she swiped them away muttering to the photo, 'Your escape is about to end mate.'

Her main hobby was American crime documentaries and as far as she was concerned, he was going down for the max stretch, hopefully to fry in the electric chair. She needed a confession, and the old-fashioned method of policing was a waste of time. It needed her brand of interrogation, fear.

DI Query decided he would do whatever was necessary to convince Bernard to open up. He wandered through to reception where Sergeant Turner was reading the racing times. 'Quiet today Sergeant.'

Sergeant Turner put down his paper. 'Sometimes is at,' he checked his watch, 'sixteen forty.' He yawned, 'Mind you, who knows what schemes are being hatched behind closed doors eh Detective?'

DI Query stretched. 'Two things are infinite: the universe and human stupidity; and I'm not sure about the universe. Albert Einstein was right. I mean we do see some crazy shit here.'

'Can't argue with that.'

PC May entered. 'Two hours to go and I'm off.'

Sergeant Turner asked, 'So I understand your partner is suspended?'

'Yes, despite my best endeavours she refused to calm down.' He leant into them both, 'She was like a bloody rottweiler. No restraint. I think she has a mental illness, certainly not right material for a good copper.'

Di Query patted his shoulder. 'Which you are.' PC May nodded gracefully. DI Query asked, 'So got a new partner?'

'I'm sure you are both aware of the saying "from the frying pan into the fire"?' They both nodded. 'That's all I'll say at the moment.' He left.

PC Jones had formulated her plan, with the assistance of two voices in her head arguing as to the best one. The loudest voice won and she made her preparations.

***

Bernard sat in his lounge staring at the drawn curtains hiding the ever-growing crowd of reporters and weirdos camping on his lawn and adjacent grass area. Ingrid was out doing whatever it was she did - he didn't care anymore and hoped she would get arrested. There was the constant thud of helicopter blades above as the media eagerly awaited the next instalment. Well, they could go to hell. He was already there anyway.

He wandered out to the shed - from habit usually to avoid Margaret – and forgot the monster inside waiting to tear him limb from limb, although it did calm down when he put the lead on last time and accidently dropped it leading to injuries to a reporter. He glanced at the lead and for an instance considered whether Fluffy needed more exercise but decided against it, reminding himself of two impending court appearances for smuggling and assault. Fluffy must have forgotten Bernard's kindness in taking him out because he launched himself against the cage door in what appeared to be the most frenzied attack so far.

Bernard sidled over to the workbench and sat down running a finger along the furrows in the worktop. What had his life come to? Probable divorce and prison. One out of two an improvement he thought sullenly.

The spider did not like being disturbed – doing whatever it was spiders do - and made an exploratory dash for the tin of wood primer. Its decision to move house was made because the toxic atmosphere amongst the tins was intolerable since the last spray attack. Bernard jumped up as the spider briefly appeared before disappearing behind the wood primer. His angst was at maximum and he crashed around looking for the aerosol. The spider knew another dose of *that* would be fatal and made a mad dash for open ground along the shed wall behind Bernard.

PC Jones parked her fiat 500 on a side road and sidled around the enormous crowd. She hesitated for a second as to whether to get a burger from the mobile café now set up and which was making a roaring trade, or the ice cream van. She decided against it because she was in uniform. She was prepared for contact with the enemy and it was only seconds before a reporter stopped her. 'What's he done now?'

She smiled sweetly. 'Just a formality.' She rested her hand on her riot stick. 'Please stand aside.' She entered the side gate and went around to the back of the house. She might be as mad as a box of frogs, but she had checked out the layout of the property and from perusing police documents knew about the shed and the dog. As she approached the shed, she heard Bernard shouting, 'You can't hide you bastard!' There was a crash and silence for a moment before he yelled, 'Now look what you've made me do!' She seized her opportunity of surprise and burst into the shed. Fluffy stepped up a gear and seemed to fling himself in all directions barking and snarling as she stopped mid step. Bernard was on his knees mopping up a spilled tin of paint with one hand and in the other waving an aerosol. He shouted. 'It's curtains for you, you bastard!'

PC Jones assessed imminent risk to herself and decided pepper spray insufficient and went straight to Taser. Bernard went into shock as the voltage froze him, his muscles in spasm. She grabbed his arms and handcuffed him dragging him to his feet. 'Right, you perv. Confession time.' She quickly looked around and seized an old blanket which she threw over him. The effect of the Taser was beginning to wear off and he could walk - albeit stiff legged as if he had had a toilet incident – with her holding an arm. She hurried him out and held up her Taser in her free hand as the press saw her. 'Police business! Stand aside or I will Taser you!' Not surprisingly she had a clear exit and dragged him to her car where she shoved him in the passenger seat.

***

DI Query parked in a nearby street and headed for the Grimshaw house. Not hard to find considering most of the media from the free world was camped outside Bernard's house. As he made his way through the crowd he wondered how they would react if a UAP appeared now. His thoughts were disturbed by a fervent devotee of the "Krishna UFO group" who blocked his way and with darting eyes of desperation asked, 'When are they coming?'

'Don't know mate. Now move aside I'm here on police business.'

A reporter nudged him. 'You're too late. One of your lot has already taken him. Talk about the left hand and right hand...'

DI Query ignored him and knocked on the front door. The letterbox flap opened a tad and a voice from inside announced, 'Dad's not here. Mums gone. Grans out. Go away.'

He stared at it for a few seconds, shrugged and pushed his way back through the crowd. Something was wrong, and he needed to find out what it was.

He entered the reception area and Sergeant Turner was tidying up the desk. 'I've just been to the Grimshaw's house and, it appears, he's been arrested.'

'Arrested by whom? Not much gets past me DI Query.'

'True. But according to a reporter - of which there are many camped outside the house – a female police officer took him away with a blanket over him.'

'Interesting.' He leaned on the counter. 'Far be it for me to make assumptions but PC Jones has been suspended.'

'And for what? As the great man said, "Everything should be made as simple as possible, but not simpler." Perhaps there is connection to Mr Grimshaw's disappearance.'

'If I maybe so bold as to make a suggestion?'

'Please.'

'Talk to PC May again. He is – in my humble opinion - level-headed and a rare commodity in the force i.e. an old-fashioned copper. She was his partner until she was suspended as you know.' He smiled. 'He did his best but she was beyond his control.'

PC May drove steadily, aware of his new partner, PC Damien Green filling the seat beside him. In fact he overflowed onto the handbrake making it difficult for PC May who was trying to make the best of it but was realising that his new partner was just as difficult although in totally different ways to PC Jones. One major difference was that whereas PC Jones was thin and lithe, PC Green was not. In fact the very opposite. PC Green was also very hot on being politically correct and woke. Something PC May found hard to accept or understand. A call had come in relating to an altercation outside a pub and they were on their way.

PC May said, 'Don't know what we'll find so follow my lead.'

He pulled up outside the pub where two youths were brawling in the road. He got out and took out his riot stick as he approached them. PC Green followed, after struggling to get out of the car. The fracas was soon ended and the two youths put against a wall to be searched.

One of them looked PC Green up and down and sneered. 'What you lookin at fatty?'

PC Green looked hurt. 'I would like to voice how incredibly hurt I am by your comments.'

The youth grimaced. 'Do what?'

'I have chronically low self-esteem,' he fought back a tear and said bravely, 'but I love my body.'

The other youth looked to his mate and laughed, 'Don't know why fatty.'

PC May poked the youth and said, 'Ok lads. Enough.' He turned to PC Green. 'Go and wait in the car.' He stood back from the two youths. 'Right. Nobody hurt, too much to drink, I suggest you both go home.'

He got back in the car to find PC Green had turned off the engine, something he never did, not sure why but it was policy, perhaps in case he needed to make a fast pursuit. 'Why did you turn off the engine?'

'We need to be aware of being carbon neutral Sir.'

'I see.' He watched the two youths stagger away. 'You need to toughen up PC Green.'

'Why did you let them go Sir?'

'Because they were two idiots. Nobody was hurt. '

'But surely we should be seeking gacaca?'

'Pardon?'

'Restorative justice Sir. It's another cultures ways of dealing with crime. It comes from Rwanda following the genocide.'

PC May sighed. It was going to be a long night.

***

Margaret parked outside her cousin's house and switched off the engine. Having driven for an hour she had been able to gather her thoughts and come to the conclusion that nothing made any sense. Inside the quiet of Cousin Mable's bungalow she settled down with a cup of tea. 'You know Mable I could never have thought all this up in me wildest dreams.'

Mable busily knitted and talked while she furiously worked the needles. 'I'm sorry to be the one to say it Margaret, but he has been nothing but trouble to you since you got wed. I mean the trouble he caused on't honeymoon. We all thought about you luv.' The needles moved even more furiously. 'How long were you up there?'

Margaret sipped her tea and put her cup down. 'I suppose taking all into account, including fire service, it were about five hours.'

Mable stopped for a moment and looked up. 'Eh, you wouldn't catch me up on one of them contraptions.'

Margaret nodded as she looked out of the window remembering. 'Not been to a fairground again.'

'Why anyone would want to go up on one of them bloody whatever you call them wheels is beyond me.'

Margaret picked up her cup again and paused. 'Ferris. Ferris wheel Mable.' She sipped her tea. 'Like the Everly brothers song.'

Mable paused the whir of the needles and smiled. 'I liked them. My George was mad on em.'

Margaret watched fascinated. 'What are you knitting luv?'

Mable stopped and thought for a moment. 'Fucked if I know Margaret. pardon my French.' She glanced at the ever-growing length of knitting gathering between her pink slippers. 'Started off as a jumper I think, but now I just keep going.'

'Right… Mind if I turn the news on?'

'No go ahead luv.'

Margaret picked up the remote and switched on the tv. A murder documentary commenced. 'You watch FBI files too.'

'I do Margaret. I like to see the bastards get their come-uppance. There was one where this lot of bank robbers were being chased all over bloody place. Ended in a bloodbath and they all got shot. That wer good one.'

'I think I saw that one.' She searched and clicked on the BBC news. 'If he hadn't been such a loud mouth it would never have happened you know.'

'Who, the bank robber?'

'No. Bernard. Telling the man in't car above us to shut his girlfriend up. Mind you was she screaming and crying a lot. Not as much as I was though at end of five hours in pouring rain. Crying that is. I stopped screaming after I went hoarse.' She waved the remote at an unseen memory. 'It started raining after the first hour.'

'What happened luv? You've never talked about it.'

'The man got shirty and of course Mr loudmouth had to wind him up. It got very loud with all the shouting, swearing and his girlfriend sobbing. Then the storm broke and it rained like bloody stair rods, thunder and lightning the whole bloody lot. Then Bernard realised he had gone too far when the man climbed out of their car to get to him. The lightning strike did something to the workings and the wheel stopped. Of course the bloke controlling the wheel called the police and fire services.' She sipped her tea. 'We had to be at the top of course. Bloody high that is Mabel.'

Mable paused her knitting and gave her a supportive smile. 'Did you ever get your wedding dress repaired.'

Margaret sighed. 'Nope. After they pulled it out of the workings, it was a bit shredded and all the grease and shit got ground into it when they dragged me out of the car into the fireman's box thingy. You know, on top of one of them big ladders. I kept it though. Every now and then I get it out and leave it on't bed for him to see what a complete pillock he's been.'

'Don't blame yer luv. I thought George was bad but compared to … 'Anyway, put news on, let's cheer ourselves up.'

'It seems the man from Ramsbottom known as the underpants man, has hit the headlines again. Over to Simon outside the house of Mr Grimshaw.'

An earnest young man addressed the camera in pouring rain. 'Yes Michael. It appears that Mr Grimshaw has gone missing again. He was taken away by police earlier today. Some speculate that it is all just a publicity stunt. However, Mr Grimshaw refuses to talk to us and explain what he is up to.' He gave a wry smile. 'Being abducted by aliens is not very likely.'

Margaret switched off the tv. 'Arrested again? For what?' I've got to go back and find out what the hell is going on.'

***

Margaret carelessly parked in the police station carpark and stomped up the steps. Sergeant Turner picked up his pen in eager expectation, knowing the Grimshaw saga was gathering headway by the second. 'Mrs Grimshaw.'

She gasped, out of breath. 'Why have you arrested him again?'

'I can assure you I haven't arrested anyone for some time now, being stuck behind this counter. My knees you see.'

'Well someone did, it were on bloody news just now.'

'I see. He checked the log. No sign of him here Mrs Grimshaw.'

'Could it be another police station?'

'No. Our jurisdiction you see.'

'Well, according to the BBC he was taken away by a female police officer.'

He smiled ruefully. 'Sadly not an organisation to be trusted. Used to be the epitome of good reporting but not anymore. I believe them to be nothing more than an organ of propaganda for the government.'

'That's as maybe. I want to know where he is.'

'Understandable. Leave it with me.'

'An can't you do something about the mob outside my house?'

'As I told your husband. Too many of them.'

'Right. Then I'll do it meself.'

He shouted as she marched out. 'Don't get arrested.' He thought for a moment and dialled. 'Is PC May down there by any chance?'

Margaret drove onto her drive narrowly knocking over four reporters sitting in deck chairs with umbrellas. She slammed the car door and made it to the front door before being accosted. 'Are you divorcing him Mrs Grimshaw? Do you know the woman he is having the affair with? What do you think about him being abducted by aliens? Have you been taken?'

She put up her arms for silence. A sea of eager faces watched in high expectation. 'I don't know where my husband is, I don't know anything about what has been happening to him, I don't want you here, so go away.' She opened the front door and hurried in as the media crowd went crazy.

Julien appeared. 'When's that lot going?'

'No idea luv. Just ignore them.'

'Hard to do that when I can't get out to go to school.'

'I know, it's hard for us both. Where's your Gran?'

'Out. Don't know where.'

She took off her coat and went into the kitchen. Julien turned on the tv. An earnest concerned looking news anchor on Sky was discussing UAPs with a middle-aged man. 'So in your view Mr Gray they are coming?'

Mr Gray held up a book. 'As I have proved in my book,' he tapped the cover. 'Mr Grimshaw has been selected by an alien race to act as their spokesperson.'

The anchorman nodded gravely. 'But he hasn't made any statement to suggest that is the case so far.'

'Because they are patient. They need to get us frightened; they work on fear. Believe me he will break his silence soon.'

'And what do you think he will say?'

'I believe he will reveal their plans and I don't think we are going to like them.'

'Do you think we are in danger?'

Mr Gray put his book down and looked directly into the cameras. 'I think we are looking at extinction.'

Margaret switched the tv off. Julien asked, 'Is that true?'

'That your father is a spokesman for whoever? No way. Can't even represent wine maker's club wi out upsetting somebody.'

'What do you think is happening Mum?'

'Don't know. But I have my suspicions.'

'Like what?'

'Never you mind. Go and do your homework.'

'I can't. Those weirdo took my laptop remember?'

'Hmm. You can borrow mine.' She rang the police station and asked to be put through to DI Query. She got his answer phone. 'Margaret Grimshaw here. I want to know when my son will get his laptop back.'

***

Sergeant Turner was a man of his word and intended to find out what had happened to Bernard. He was aware that PC Jones had been suspended but not the reason why. He left a message for PC May to contact him. He sat looking out at the autumn weather and sighed. PC May appeared. Sergeant?'

'PC May. A moment of your time if I may concerning Mr Grimshaw?'

'I understand he's missing again?'

'Apparently he was taken from his home by a female policewoman.'

PC May took off his police cap and scratched his head. 'Do you think it was …?'

'I will not jump to any conclusions but you said she was… unstable.'

'That's an understatement Sergeant Turner. She's mad as a box of frogs.' He replaced his cap. 'I'm going to check out her locker. We do have a master key?'

'Of course.'

PC May was joined by his new partner PC Damien Green, eager to start work. 'What are we doing Sir?'

PC May sighed. 'Ok, This is a different sort of police work.'

He made his way down to the lockers, having to hold doors open for PC Green - waddling as fast as he was able - to catch up. He waited at the locker and said as PC Green eventually arrived, 'I would avoid any foot chases if I were you.' He began opening PC Jone's locker.

'Do you have her permission Sir? Otherwise it's a violation of her human rights.'

'So is kidnapping.'

'Kidnapping? Why-'

'It's a long story trust me.' He paused. 'You're straight out of training yes?'

'Yes Sir.'

'Right. Sometimes we need to see the bigger picture.'

PC May opened PC Jone's locker and took out the contents and laid them out on a bench.

He picked up a DIVA magazine which claimed to be "The world's leading magazine for LGBTQIA women and non-binary people." He put it down as if it would burn his fingers.

PC Green picked it up and flicked through the pages. 'Wow. Gender neutral. No body shaming. Amazing.'

PC May continued sifting through the contents but didn't pick up the curled whip, or fluffy pink handcuffs or the nine-inch Auby hunting/outdoor survival knife. But he did pick up the alert circular showing the photograph of the escaped sex offender and was amazed how similar to Mr Grimshaw he was. He turned to PC green. 'Go and make us a cuppa.'

He took the sheet to Sergeant Turner. 'I think we have our answer Sergeant. I think she's kidnapped him.'

From within a car parked in the police station carpark Buzz, a CIA operative, gleefully took off his headphones and exclaimed 'Bingo!' He picked up his mobile. 'Got something. Check out Police constable Mary Jones. I think we've found him.'

BLACK OPERATIONS

Deep within the bowels of the Pentagon a high-level black ops strategy meeting was underway headed up by Dewey Heinzeburgher, a no nonsense General. 'Ok Woody, what ya got?'

Woody Clampitt, selected a Power Point on a screen at the back of the room. 'This guy,' a photograph of Bernard appeared, 'is one clever son of a bitch. We suspect he is setting himself up as the spokesperson for the Perturbians, an alien race that have recently been operating here. We're pulling out all the stops to work them out. He is making out he knows nothing and - and here's the genius – has the world media camped outside his house waiting for a statement.'

Chuck Shellerberger, put up his hands. 'Whoa! Hold up here just a goddam moment. How do we know this. He's probably just a nutter?'

Beau Faartz interjected, 'Agreed.'

Dewey Heinzeburgher slammed his fist down making the glass of water in front of him spill its contents onto the highly polished table and a pile of top-secret documents. He snatched them from the pool of water and snarled, 'Aw fuck it.' He regained control. 'I know this is new to some of you guys, but believe me the CIA have done their research,' he nodded to Chad Biffle, Head of Operations CIA. 'Aint that right Chad?'

Chad Biffle nodded. 'You'd better believe it. My informant, Zac Childersberger has been onto this guy from the get-go.'

Chuck Shellerberger put up his hands again in shock. 'Zac Childersberger? You serious? The guy who failed CIA entrance on the grounds he was unstable?'

Chad smiled. 'In my book that makes him an ideal candidate. Anyway, he is keen to be part of the system and has given us sound info in the past.'

Colt Harkleroad coughed on a mouthful of water. 'Like the last report from him that he was sure the Brits were plotting to take over the USA?'

Chase Gaylord laughed. 'I remember that! You serious about this guy?'

Chad continued, 'Totally, we all make mistakes Chase. This limey guy is an evil son of a bitch. And these guys are serious.'

Chase Gaylord. 'Which guys?'

Dewey Heinzeburgher sighed with exaggerated patience. 'Perturbians?' He nodded to Chad. 'Please continue.'

Chad Biffle looked grim. 'Ok. We know there are a lot of these freaks-'

Dewey Heinzeburgher stopped him with a rueful shake of his head. 'Aliens.'

Chad continued. 'Whatever. These damn aliens have been a pain in our arse since Eisenhour signed the treaty to allow them to take humans for examination in exchange for their tech. That was all fine until these fucking Perturbians arrived.' He snatched a glass of water. 'Now - and you aint gonna want to believe it but it's true - these dickheads only have one agenda.'

Colt Harkleroad, interrupted. 'World domination.'

Chad Biffle smiled grimly. 'Nah. That's the fucking reptiles, they've got that sown up believe me.' He sipped again. 'Check out the Pope, man. See for yourself. Nah. Pleasure. We've got an alien race of hedonists here.'

Dwayne Ridlehoover. 'What have we got they would want?'

Chad Biffle said, 'We thought at first it was drugs. But it's worse. And this is where your guy Grimshaw features. He's been going back and forth seeing these morons and showing em alcohol.'

Colt Harkleroad exclaimed, 'The balls on this guy.'

Dwayne Ridlehoover. 'Damn right. Let's close em down.'

Beau Faartz nodded. 'We need to be satisfied all the criteria are met.' He looked around the table, 'Then we take the son of a bitch out.'

Chad Biffle. 'The other races don't want to be associated with them.'

Dwayne Ridlehoover said, 'Pretty fucked up sit though when we allow these "races" to interfere, experiment on by abducting us and then condemn those out for pleasure.'

Colt Harkleroad nodded sagely. 'Just pleasure huh? remember the Roman Empire?'

Chuck Shellerberger. 'Damn right. That fiddled while Rome burned shit. We don't know what these creeps might do if they got hold of booze. They might take us all out on a high.' He slurped some water. 'Remember the Indians and damn firewater? But my concern is this. How do we know this guy Grimshaw is what you say he is?'

Woody Clampitt turned on him. 'My guy's got it wrong? You sayin the bank of psych tests we've simulated, observations in the field don't amount to diddly shit?'

Chuck Shellerberger smiled. 'All theory Woody. We need the guy strapped to our equipment and get in there and take his brain apart to verify all this. If you're right, ok we fry the motherfucker before he takes us all with him.'

Dewey Heinzeburgher looked around the room. 'Concerns noted. Chad get a team in there and get this guy secured. We've located the site where he is being held?'

Woody Clampitt said, 'Some female nutter has kidnapped him for her on ends. Not a problem.'

***

Four men clad in black armour and armed to the teeth crept silently up to the doors of the garage to number 84, Evergreen Lane. As they reached the garage the leader put up his hand to signal stop. They waited for his signal as he placed a listening device on the garage wall.

Inside, PC Jones was busy trailing two thick leads toward Bernard who was strapped to a chair in the middle of the garage. His eyes stood out like organ stops as he realised the leads were attached to four car batteries. The enormous crocodile clamps made it obvious her intention was not to start a car.

He blustered, 'Look, I don't know anything right? They take me and then bring me back.' Fleeting memories of massively tall figures and drugs passed through his mind lost in the soup of confusion of false memories implanted in him.

PC jones sneered. 'Yeah of course they do. Keep acting innocent. Well I know different. She was thirteen when …that pervert had his way. He was just like you. So now we're going to have a little chat.' She touched the two clamps together making a loud crackling sound and advanced toward him.

The black ops leader was called Clay Thunderhawk, a Cherokee and considered himself a warrior in the style of his ancestors. That was why he was the leader. Nobody could beat him. He was also an enigma or a paradox in that he was extremely violent and willing to kill anything that moved - but also a passionate animal lover, which had caused many arguments when his friends tried to get him on hunting trips. His biggest love was birds.
Now, his focus was totally on the mission and ready to kill without hesitation. He listened intently to his device.

PC Jones thrust the clamps near Bernard's face. 'See these little babies are going to make you sing like a ... whatever.'

Clay mouthed silently, 'A canary.' He smiled. When not blowing up things or people he tended an Aviary in South Carolina.

PC Jones smiled evilly as the voices in her head prompted her. 'Your perversions stop here mate.' She glanced down to his nether regions. 'Once they're fried you won't be a threat to any little girls again.'

Bernard whimpered. 'You've got it all wrong. 'I make wine – bloody good an all even if I say so myself – and I don't even like girls. My wife was one once and look what good it did her.'

PC Jones growled. 'Confession time.'

'Why do you think I've done these awful things anyway?'

She hesitated, dropped the crocodile clamps – a little too close to his feet for his comfort – and grabbed the alert sheet with the photograph of the escaped sex offender. She waved it at him. 'You tellin me this aint you? Looks like you to me and that's good enough.' She bent down to get the clamps.

'But that's not me!'

'Course it's not.' She took out a vicious knife and headed toward his thighs. 'Now then, let's get you out so we can fry you.'

'That's not me I'm telling you!'

The voices in her head knew different and pushed her on. She laughed evilly, 'Frying tonight!'

Clay Thunderhawk put his thumb up to signal action. On his command they crashed open one of the wooden doors and threw in a stun grenade. Bernard thought the end of the world had arrived as the bright flash and bang did what it was intended to do and stunned him rigid. PC Jones was grappled to the floor by three black ops and secured with cable ties.

Bernard gasped as Clay untied him. 'Who the bloody hell are you lot?' He blustered, 'She was going to put-' he nodded at the crocodile clips, 'them on me bits!'

Clay nodded grimly. 'Get that Sir. You're safe now.'

'Who are you lot? How did you know I was here?'

'Need to know basis Sir. Just doin our job.' He stood Bernard up and handcuffed him.

'Eh what you doing?'

'Securing you Sir. Orders.'

'Whose bloody order?'

'Need to know Sir. Come with us.'

'Hold up, where are we going?' he stopped as the thud of helicopter blades became deafening over the house.

Clay roughly manhandled him out to a waiting helicopter. 'Need to know Sir.'

PC Jones sat up on the cold concrete floor shaking her head to clear it. She realised her hands and feet were tied but it was not a problem; she had taken a survival course and knew all the wrinkles.

***

Bernard had never been in a helicopter and decided he would not be doing so again. The black ops team watched him dispassionately as if he was an inanimate object as he wriggled and complained. The transfer to an awaiting aircraft was even worse. After a long and uncomfortable flight The aircraft landed and he was roughly escorted to a hanger, it seemed by the length of the flight somewhere not in the UK. He was taken in a lift to a floor deep below the ground and down a corridor to a room. But this was no ordinary room, it was fully equipped with computers and assorted equipment that looked total beyond him. He was roughly seated onto a chair and secured to it.

An extremely muscled soldier stood behind him. A man entered and sat opposite Bernard. 'Welcome to Hanger 51 Mr Grimshaw. My name is Silas Ramirez. We're hoping you can answer a few questions for us.'

Bernard puffed himself up defiantly. 'Questions? Well, I've got some bloody questions an all. Like who are you bloody lot and why am I here?'

The man smiled as he looked up at the soldier. 'All in good time Mr Grimshaw.'

Bernard began to wriggle, and the soldier pressed heavily on his shoulders. Bernard sat still. Very still.

'That was Kayden introducing himself. He doesn't say much.'

'Let's talk about wine Mr Grimshaw.'

'You could come to bloody wine making club meeting then instead of all this nonsense.'

'Tell me about the deal.'

'Deal, what bloody deal?' He sniffed, 'No good talking in riddles.' He thought for a moment. 'We do have a bring - and - buy evening.'

Two massive hands dug into his shoulders and a deep sonorous voice said, 'You think this is funny Grimshaw?'

Bernard flinched and shook his head.

'Wine Mr Grimshaw.'

Bernard tried to shrug his shoulders, but two massive hands prevented him.

'Let's cut to the chase. We can do this the easy way or the hard way. I think you would prefer the easy way, much less stressful. We know you've been taken a few times. We know you had a bottle of alcohol with you when you were first taken.'

Bernard raised his eyebrows. 'How do you know that?'

Silas smiled. 'We know a lot about you, Bernard. You don't object to me calling you that?'

Bernard tried to shrug. 'Call me Shirley for all I care, just let me go.'

A massive arm put him in a choke hold as Kayden applied pressure.

Bernard waved his arms at Silas to get him released, his eyes bulging and his face becoming a deep purple. He gurgled, 'Ok.'

Silas waved at Kayden and air returned to Bernard's lungs. 'What do you remember of being taken?'

'Nothing.' A memory flashed of massively high figures with four arms threatening him. 'Big tall ones.'

'Very good, go on.'

'That's all.'

Silas smiled. 'False memory implant. We expected that.'

'Can I go now then?'

'Mr Grimshaw, we've only just started. You need to remember, or we will give you something to speed the process up. It's not a pleasant drug - nasty side effects.'

A deep laugh came from Kayden. 'You'd better believe it. You recall, Silas, that little guy you got the dosage wrong? Boy he sure spilled the beans ... before he went batshit crazy?'

Silas smiled. 'Got it right now though. Bernard here will be begging us to stop the drip!'

Bernard yelled, 'Alright. I had a bottle of blackberry and garlic red. Nice little wine. They kept it.'

'And?'

A memory stirred of thoughts in his head that were not his, asking what the object was.

'I said wine.' He looked puzzled. 'They tried it.'

'And?'

'I wer in carpark.'

'What about the second time from the ferry?'

Bernard looked shocked. 'You've been following me.'

Silas shrugged. 'We've been monitoring these guys since they appeared a few months ago because we were told by the Reptilians to watch out for them. They are a race of pleasure seekers, evidently irresponsible and just out for a good time.'

Bernard said. 'What's it got to do wi me then? So they like my wine - not surprising, it's a good drink.'

'You act stupid Bernard.'

'Thank you very much, I don't think.'

'It's a clever act, but we've got you taped, literally.' He switched on an audio player.

Bernard's voice was clear as he said, 'Come an get me. I've got weapons you won't like. I'll be the one to tell the world. Power will all be mine. Wine will rule. I will be your spokesman my friends. The world will hear all about you and bow down to your perfection. You think you can beat me? I'll be the one. The spokesman. they'll have to listen to me. The power is mine. We will work together!'

Bernard's mouth dropped open. 'You bugged my shed?'

Silas laughed. 'Sure we did you are a big blip on our radar.'

'But that was on me own when I got drunk. Not surprising considering pressure I've been under.'

Kayden poked Bernard in the back as he looked at Silas. 'Cleverer than we thought.'

Silas nodded. 'Nice try Bernard. But we've got you on tape. Can't argue with that.'

'I bloody can. I wer talking to dog about me wine. 'He shuddered. 'More like a bloody monster.'

'Ok Mr Grimshaw gloves off. Admit your plans with theses damn aliens and you can go.'

'How can I admit to summat I've not done? I work for building control in local council not bloody MI6.'

Silas looked up at Kayden with a quizzical look. 'MI6? They playin their games again?'

Bernard shrugged. 'One of them spy things anyway.'

'See Bernard, we don't believe you. So, we go to phase two.'

Bernard looked around for a way out. 'Phase two?'

Kayden whispered in his ear. 'You're gonna love this.'

Silas gave Bernard a sympathetic smile. 'We gave you a chance to come clean. Now we'll try the drug way. And you aint gonna like it.' He glanced up at Kayden.

'Aint that the truth.'

***

Dewey Heinzeburgher stared at his phone in disbelief. 'Your tellin me Silas, the damn drug didn't work?'

'Correct. We even increased the dose. Nada. Either the guy is so well trained or he's telling the truth and we've got it wrong.'

'We can't be seen to get it wrong.' He thought for a moment. 'Ok. We know the Perturbians are nut cases out for pleasure, that's been confirmed by the Reptilians. My gut feeling is this guy is nothin but a damn Limey in the wrong place at the wrong time. If I'm wrong we take him out. Nuke the town or whatever, create a cover story like, I dunno, something we can blame on global warming or some shit.'

'What do we do with him?'

'Make it look like he was taken by them. Dump him in a store carpark in his Jockeys. And he was never here.'

***

PC May and his new partner, PC Green were on patrol when a call came in to investigate an incident in Sainsbury's carpark. PC May turned to his partner as he pulled into the carpark. 'Now, don't take everything so personal. We're professionals.'

'PC Green looked anxious. 'I know Sir, but my therapist says I need to own my feelings, to be authentic.'

'All very well PC Green, off duty, but telling a shoplifter you have an urge to steal is not conducive to an arrest.'

'But I must speak my truth. I know I take things personally, but he was horrible to me.'

'Criminals are not renowned for their kindness and social awareness PC Green. I'm sure when he called you-'

PC green burst into tears. 'A fat git was the exact words he used. Sometimes I just want to curl up and die.'

'Have you thought perhaps the police force is not the best career option?'

He pulled up near to the entrance and got out to join a Sainsbury's staff member pointing to a row of trolleys. 'He's behind them.'

PC May had a suspicious feeling he knew what he would find.

PC Green caught up with him puffing after a struggle to exit the car. 'What is it Sir? A drug dealer?'

'No. I think it's probably somebody I know from previous encounters in similar situations.' They walked around the line of trolleys and PC May smiled. 'Thought so. Hello Mr Grimshaw. Becoming a regular occurrence.'

Margaret trotted tiredly up the steps to the police station and sat on the bench waiting for an aggressive youth to make a complaint.

The youth thumped the counter as he yelled, 'Fourth time mate. I'm mindin my fuckin business and you lot stop me on me bike. And what for? Nothing. I know my rights mate.'

Sergeant Turner finished writing and stood straightening his back. 'You have to admit Daryll that being in the middle of an industrial estate at two in the morning with a crowbar and hammer in your rucksack, could be seen as suspicious?'

Daryll picked at a nail. 'Yeah, granted but I wasn't doing nothing.'

Sergeant Turner could not resist it and smiled. 'If you were not doing nothing, you would be doing something. Double negative you see.'

Daryll snorted, 'Whateva. Listen I want compensation mate for wrongful stopping and searching.'

'I see. Whilst we are on the subject of compensation, have you considered giving any to the fifty people you have burgled?'

'Can't mate, on the dole you see.'

'Ah, of course. I will record your complaint Mr Snott. Is that all.'

Daryll huffed, 'Stott.' He stomped out.

Sergeant Turner beckoned Margaret over. 'I assume you are here for your husband,' he smiled kindly, 'again.'

She gave him a look that suggested he should tread carefully. 'In't carpark again I understand.'

'Yes. Sainsbury's this time. He seems to be making the rounds so to speak.' He thought for a moment. 'Or going upmarket.'

'And bloody underpants again.'

'Afraid so. At least they are clean.'

She said through gritted teeth, 'I have my standards, even if he doesn't.'

'Of course.' He stooped to writing and said without looking up, 'He'll be with you shortly. Unfortunately, because he did not return our blanket we have had to improvise.'

Bernard appeared accompanied by a female police officer. Margaret did a double take and exclaimed, 'Is that the best you could do?'

The police officer smiled apologetically. 'Fraid so.' Bernard stood forlornly dressed in a bin bag with holes cut out for his head and arms.

Sergeant Turner said as he bent down to write. 'Sadly, our blanket was not returned hence,' he waved an arm in Bernard's direction.

Margaret grabbed Bernard by the arm and dragged him out onto the steps where a massive group of reporters and general public waited in eager anticipation. A wave of microphones surrounded them with questions coming from all directions.

'Why do they keep taking you Mr Grimshaw? Is this a publicity stunt? Are you covering for your affair? What message do you have for us? Is the world going to end?'

Margaret stood in a daze with Bernard out of it staring at his feet. 'Lot of bloody good you are Bernard. Shaming me again in public like this.'

Sergeant Turner appeared like a knight in shining armour and cleared a path to a waiting police car. 'There you go Mrs Grimshaw.'

Margaret stuttered. 'Thank you Sergeant, I don't know what to say.'

He smiled and opened the door for her. 'My pleasure Mrs Grimshaw, you have enough problems without the media interfering.' He closed the door and waved the police driver to go.

Margaret sighed and relaxed a little in the silence of the car. Bernard sat staring ahead as if in a trance.

The driver said over his shoulder, 'Home, or a planet of your choice?'

Margaret rounded on him. 'Shut it.'

He drove in silence.

Back home she waited as Bernard stood in the middle of the lounge staring ahead, the bin bag stretched tight over his large belly.

Margaret prodded him. 'Oi. Any one in?' He did not respond, so she prodded him harder. 'You can pretend all you like Bernard. I don't believe a word you say about damn flying saucers.' She got in his face. 'If I find out it's that whore, you'll rue the day. Bernard!' He remained still staring ahead.' She decided to call his bluff and rang the doctor's surgery muttering to herself as she dialled, 'We'll see what you're up to you fat git.'

'Hello Swanley surgery.'

'My husband appears to have had a mental breakdown.'

'I'm sorry to hear that. What's his name?'

'Bernard Grimshaw.'

'Ah.'

'Yes that's right, the idiot in't papers and tv. He's standing in my lounge staring at carpet. I need him assessed.'

'The best thing Mrs Grimshaw is to take him to A and E.'

'Really?'

'We have nobody here to make a mental health assessment you see.'

'Right.' She slammed the phone down. 'We're going to hospital and get you assessed. Hopefully they'll agree with me that you're faking it. If not then they can put you away, because Bernard,' she got in his face, 'I've had it up to here with your nonsense. If you want her that bad then be man enough to say so and,' she poked him hard enough tin the belly to make a hole in the bin bag, 'fuck off.'

It was a long wait in the emergency waiting room and Margaret had given up trying to get a response from him. After four hours they were beckoned into a cubicle, and he was helped to sit on the examination bed.

A young doctor appeared obviously at the end of a very long duty. 'Mr Grimshaw?'

Margaret sighed. 'I'm his wife. This is how I collected him from police station after he was found in't underpants in Sainsbury's carpark.' She sneered, 'Behind trolleys.'

'I see. Can I ask why?'

'That's why I've brought him in. I can't get anything out of him.' She considered for a moment. 'Not that he ever makes much sense.'

The doctor looked puzzled. 'Why is he in a bin bag?'

Margaret shrugged. 'Ask him.'

He examined him and declared. 'He's in a catatonic state.'

'What the bloody hell is that? So in other words, he's faking it?'

'Definitely not. It's a state of shock that basically shuts all functions down.'

'So?'

'So, it is just a matter of time Mrs Grimshaw. But I will do bloods on him to be sure.'

Margaret sat in the emergency waiting room. It was 3.00 am and she was fighting to keep awake. Bernard's condition had not changed. The doctor appeared and sat beside her.

'I've got the results of the blood test. It's intriguing.' He yawned, rubbing his eyes to keep awake. 'There was a drug in his system we have not come across before. I've done some checking and-'

'If he's been taking summat I'll kill him.'

'He wouldn't have got hold of this drug Mrs Grimshaw.'

'Why?'

'It's something the military use. It induces a psychotic state.'

'A what?'

'Basically, it made him willing to reveal anything he was keeping secret.'

'Like a truth drug.'

'Exactly. All you can do is let him come out of it slowly.'

CONFUSION

Margaret rang DI Query and explained Bernard had been in a - she couldn't remember the term – dopey state for two days.

DI Query was intrigued. 'How is he now?'

'Still drowsy. I can't make any sense of it. Doc says he's been given some sort of secret drug. Like the military use. And bloody media camped outside house doesn't help.'

DI Query jotted down "Poss truth drug, Military. Black ops?" 'I believe I can help. Can I visit and chat to him?'

'That would be helpful.'

Ingrid arrived home in her wheelchair piled high with shopping. 'I have been busy in shops.'

'I can see that.'

'How is walrus face?'

Margaret sighed. 'No idea. Still drowsy and not making any sense.'

'I do not think he ever does.' She proceeded to her room and shut the door. Margaret suspected she was up to something but didn't have the energy to confront it. She went into the kitchen and put the kettle on. The phone rang. 'Hi Mabel.'

'I saw him on Sky Margaret. Why was he in a bin bag?'

'Long story.'

'Have you got to the bottom of it yet dear?'

'No. But I will. He's got some weird drug in him, made him catlike or some sounding thing, too tired to think Mabel.'

'Is he just sitting there, staring into space?'

'Yes. His eyes did flicker once this morning.'

'It's called a catatonic state.'

'How do you know that Mabel?'

'I watch a lot of police programmes and forensic investigations.'

'I see. I've got a Detective coming here soon to try and talk to him.'

'Worth a try luv. Mind you, he doesn't make sense at the best of times.'

'True.'

'They might have to put those electrodes on his head and shock him out of it. I saw them doing it in a documentary about a lunatic asylum. Mind you I don't think they were much good after it, sort of vegetables and staring-' There was a scuffling noise and Mabel exclaimed, 'Fuck it. Dropped the bastard needles. You know Margaret, I think my eyes need testing.'

The doorbell rang. 'Got to go, the detective is here Mabel.' She let DI Query in and led him into the kitchen. 'I'll get him.'

A few minutes, later Bernard appeared with Margaret leading him by the arm. DI Query stood and offered his hand. Bernard looked at it and sat down at the kitchen table. DI Query sat down and said, 'So Bernard, been taken again.'

Bernard shook his head.

DI Query looked questioningly to Margaret who shrugged. He asked, 'He was found as before but in a different store carpark?'

'Yes.' To Bernard. 'What do you remember Bernard?'

Bernard stirred and tried to focus. 'Drug. Made head fuzzy.'

DI Query nodded. 'I think the military – got to be the Americans – are very interested in you Bernard. I think the two strangers who took the laptop were connected to them, we call them Men In Black, they seem to pop up when an abduction had taken place.

Margaret said. 'Right weirdos an all.'

DI Query sat back and studied Bernard. 'I don't think he will remember much. The best way to access his memory is by hypnosis. There's more going on here than I thought. If the American military are involved, you can bet it is not in our interest. They've been covering up alien visits for years.'

'What on earth do they want,' she nodded at Bernard, 'with im. I mean he's hardly spy material, is he?'

'It's not about spying Margaret; it's about keeping us from knowing what they're up to.'

'Well, whatever it is, I've had enough. What can we do?'

'Hypnosis. I know somebody who is ideal for this.'

***

Bernard sat in the office of Cynthia Warner, hypnotherapist. Margaret was sceptical but willing to explore anything that could explain what was going on. DI Query sat beside her and Bernard sat opposite Cynthia.

Cynthia spoke softly and had a comforting aura about her. This did not have much of an impression on Bernard who sat uncomfortably on the edge of a sofa. She smiled at him. 'Have you been hypnotised before Bernard.'

He bristled. 'I certainly have not. It is in my opinion a load of mumbo jumbo.'

Margaret sighed and said to DI query, 'I told you he was himself again. Better when he was drugged.'

Cynthia was unfazed. 'A lot of people are apprehensive Mr Grimshaw, but soon find the experience very pleasant.'

'That's as maybe. As far I'm concerned, I'm here so I can get back in't me own bed.'

Cynthia glanced at Margaret who smiled tightly, 'The only way to get him here was to tell him he can sleep in't shed until he agrees.'

'I see. Anyway, Mr Grimshaw - can I call you Bernard?'

'Call me what you bloody like, just so I can get out of here.'

Margaret glared at him. 'Take part properly or stay in't bloody shed. Up to you.'

Bernard sighed. 'You can call me Bernard. What do I have to do?'

'That's the beauty of hypnosis Bernard, you don't have to do anything. In fact, if you can switch off your brain all the better. But it doesn't matter because hypnosis bypasses your conscious mind and goes to the subconscious where your memories can be accessed.'

'Right. Let's get it over with then.'

Cynthia said softly, 'Sit back and relax, I'll do all the work.'

After a few minutes of her talking him into hypnosis, his eyes shut and he began to drift under. She soothed, 'You are deeply relaxed, comfortable, without a care in the world. We are going to go back to the last time you were taken.' He shifted a little. 'You are safe here Bernard, just recall what happened.'

He gasped, 'Loud bang, soldiers. Helicopter, airplane don't bloody like it. Bright room lot of questions. Horrible needle and fell asleep.'

'Who took you Bernard?'

'Bloody army types, American.'

Cynthia glanced at DI Query. 'Then what happened?'

'Took me clothes off, put me in't carpark.'

Cynthia said to DI Query, 'Does that make sense?'

'Certainly does.' He turned to Margaret. 'American secret operations. The two men who came to your house are part of it. It's all a big cover up.'

Cynthia said, 'Leave that place now Bernard and go to when you were taken before that. You are safe.'

He didn't respond at first but suddenly became rigid. 'No!'

'It's ok Bernard, you are safe here, Observe from a height and tell me what you see.'

'Big tall monsters.'

'How big?'

'Eighteen feet.'

'And what are they doing?'

'Don't know.'

'Look closer, tell me what you see.'

He tried but shrugged. 'Too misty.'

'Is it daytime or night?'

'Don't know.'

'So now go to the time before that.'

Bernard shuddered. 'Bright light. Flying. Aaargh. Horrible.'

'It's not real Bernard, just a memory. What happens next?'

'Take me clothes off. Lay on cold table.' He began writhing.

'Just a memory, observe from a height.'

'They talk to me but in me head. Wine.'

'Wine?'

'Ask about it. What does it do?'

'Go on.'

'Tell me to get more. Want to experiment. Bright light. In't carpark.'

'Now go to the time before that.'

'Bright light, flying. In bright room on a cold table. They want to know about it. Liked the wine. Voices in my head then bright flash and in't carpark.'

'And before that?'

'Walking to wine club with bottle of finest.' Big smile. 'Bright light above then big white flash and flying up. In big room on cold metal table. Sticking things in me. Carpark.'

He remained still. 'Is there anything else you can see Bernard?' He shakes his head and begins snoring.

'Wake up Bernard.' He stirs and opens his eyes. 'You're back in the room, safe.'

'Bloody hell.'

DI Query asked, 'Can you describe them?'

'Short little bastards, big eyes, no hair, talked with their minds in me head.'

Cynthia asked. 'Do they have a message for us?'

Bernard nodded.

'Is it about bringing peace to the planet. Stopping wars?'

He shook his head.

DI query asked. 'So what do they want?'

'Wine. Blackberry and garlic, my speciality.'

ESCALATION

Bernard was back to normal. Whatever state that would be, and his mouth dropped as Ingrid announced, 'So I have flat.'

'How bloody hell did you manage that?'

She shrugged. 'I know people.'

'Bet you do an all.'

She tried to hide a smile but failed. 'They have rule though.'

'Like what?'

'No dogs. So Fluffy will have to stay here.'

'No way.'

'Yes, I think it is way Bernard. Julien likes him, they are good friends.'

'What about charges for growing bloody drugs?'

'It has gone away. I have friend – he is also good client – in police and prosecution people. So it is all good now.'

'Is it now. How nice for you.'

She smiled sweetly. 'I will get removal people tomorrow. It is nice flat.'

'Plenty of room to grow cannabis I assume?'

She laughed. 'Of course. Perhaps you will miss me?'

'Nope.' Bernard leapt up and strode out to the shed. Fluffy went berserk and crashed against the cage door. Bernard eased past the mobility scooter and glared at the crazed animal from the safety of the workbench. 'If she thinks you're staying here making me life a misery she's bloody mistaken.' Bernard looked around for the spider, 'And you an all.'

The spider peeked out from behind its new home behind the flymo – not ideal as when it became warmer the intruder would disturb its domicile - and sensed tensions in its shed were becoming dangerously high, and that usually meant something nasty and most likely toxic, heading its way. It once again considered moving to the noisy thing the other side of the shed, but that meant a long trek over open areas where it could be hijacked. It decided to stay where it was.

Bernard's eyes swept over the remain s of his haven – now no more than a kennel and mobility scooter storage facility. And of course, home to the spider. But then he noticed two plant pots with tall plants in them. Not having any interest in gardening, he could be on a winner to think it had something to do with his mother. And they had to be cannabis. And if found by the police another reason to appear in court.

Margaret opened the shed door and looked around it with disapproval. 'You could at least keep it tidy Bernard. DI Query will be here soon, and I don't want him seeing it like this.'

Bernard ignored her. 'Did you know the old bat has got a flat? And it won't allow pets.'

'She did mention it earlier.'

'So we have to look after dog, wonderful.'

She poked his belly. 'The exercise will do you good.'

The doorbell rang out. 'He's here.'

Bernard sat in the lounge with Margaret and DI Query who said, 'I think the hypnosis was useful.'

Bernard growled. 'Do you now? And what help has it been?'

'We know they want the wine, crazy as that sounds. And it's likely the Americans and possibly – I suspect – our secret services know too.'

Bernard shrugged. 'So all they want is bloody wine?' He thought for a second. 'Grant you it is one of my best.'

DI Query sighed. 'Not really the point though. We've been visited for hundreds of years by alien races and the first real contact is because they want our wine?'

Bernard tensed. 'My wine.'

Margaret growled. 'We know that, you've made it bloody obvious. So what happens now?'

DI Query shrugged. 'Depends what the Black Ops are planning. If they understand what is going on they might intervene.'

Margaret asked. 'Intervene?'

'If they got the truth out of Bernard who knows what they might do. I don't believe they will allow aliens to continue abducting us if they are drunk.'

Margaret laughed. 'This is not real.'

DI query nodded. 'I agree but it's what is happening, and your husband is at the centre of it.'

Margaret rounded on Bernard. 'Typical. You just have to mess things up Bernard, don't you.'

Bernard bristled. 'Hardly my fault I get snatched by idiots from outer bloody space. Thing is, how do I get away from them?'

'I think you should get on with your life as best you can.'

'Not that easy when bloody media outside front door and I'm suspended from work. Oh and waiting to go to court for smuggling.'

DI Query looked thoughtful. 'I've been watching your house for a while now because I've been tipped off about drugs being sold from here. I'm satisfied you are not involved Bernard. So what about your mother?'

'It's bloody obvious. She's dealing. She was growing cannabis in't flat and I found two plants in me shed.'

'And the pills on the ferry in your caravan?'

'Her, and that bloke she was friendly with, a typical drug dealer if I ever saw one.'

Margaret murmured. 'Not that you have of course.'

DI Query nodded. 'I see your point though. I'll check her out some more. Especially now she has her own flat.'

***

Two weeks went by and the media began to drift away as no further revelations occurred. Bernard was allowed back to work and he hoped life would return to normal. The underpants had been taken down in his office and colleagues tended to go quiet around him, which he was happy with, not being the first to make small talk anyway.

The wine club elections were pending, and he was determined to continue as Chairman, despite Frank's confidence in usurping him. One thing could be said for Bernard - he did bounce back. As part of his plan to win round support he took a box containing six bottles of his blackberry and garlic wine he was confident would impress his club members. It was early evening and dark when he set off in the car, for the first time in a while feeling his old self or as Margaret described – an arrogant git.

Despite Margaret being present when Bernard was hypnotised, she still suspected it was all a cover to see that whore, Penelope Smythe. And so when he left for the wine club she followed him in her car. She kept a good distance and thought about what she would do if her suspicions were right. Instruments of violent torture sprung to mind. As she rounded a bend she saw his car parked ahead. She knew it was nowhere near the wine club, or *her* house. Was he meeting her there to allay suspicion?

She pulled up behind his car and was about to leapt out ready to confront them when a flash of light above his car blinded her for a second. As her vision cleared, she saw him floating up within a beam of light, the box of wine with him. Her mouth dropped open as she saw him enter a massive round craft hovering above. A second later, it simply vanished. She sat in shock for a few minutes before gingerly getting out and looking into his car. The ignition keys were in place, but he definitely was gone - and so was the box of wine, proof she had not been hallucinating.

Zac Childersberger ducked down as Margaret drove past him. He was confident she did not notice him as her expression suggested she was in a state of shock. After what he had witnessed, so was he. That was definitely a box of wine being taken up to the space craft. He dialled his mobile. 'Confirmation Sir. I've just seen him taken and he had a box of wine with him. My theory is right. They are interested in alcohol and he is supplying it.'

Margaret entered the police station hoping Sergeant Turner was there but instead at the desk was a female she had not encountered before.

As Margaret approached the counter, Sergeant Boothe looked up and studied her with a less than friendly face. Stern in fact. Even judgemental. Her tone even more so. 'Can I help you?'

Margaret, for once was unsure how to proceed. 'I er, is Sergeant Turner around?'

'I'm duty sergeant.'

'Yes, only it's about something he understands.'

Sergeant Boothe's face adopted an even less friendly expression. 'I can assure you I am equally,' she sniffed, 'possibly more so than Sergeant Turner, able to assist in your enquiry.'

Margaret went for broke too tired to argue. 'I've just watched my husband go up in a beam of light into a flying saucer with a box containing six bottles of wine.'

Sergeant Boothe considered the late shift too taxing and sighed as she picked up the internal phone. 'Sergeant? I have someone here asking for you.' She looked up to Margaret to ask her name when Margaret could hear Sergeant Turner ask, 'Is it about a missing person by the name of Bernard perhaps?'

Margaret nodded. Sergeant Boothe said, 'Looks like it.' She disconnected and smiled tightly at Margaret. 'Take a seat, he'll be out in a minute.'

Margaret nodded and sat at the bench. A few minutes later, Sergeant Turner appeared dabbing his mouth and holding a Tupperware box. 'Mrs Grimshaw.'

She tried to smile but it came out wrong, distorted no doubt by shock. 'Sergeant.'

He sat beside her and gave her a reassuring smile. 'I assume he is missing?'

A fierce looking elderly man strutted in and confronted Sergeant Boothe. 'I reported my cat missing four hours ago. What are you lot doing about it?'

Sergeant Boothe drew herself up to her full five feet and pointed to a sign on the wall reminding the public that threatening or violent behaviour toward staff would not be tolerated. Margaret was temporarily distracted as Sergeant Boothe said, 'I am sure someone is looking into it Sir. Can I have your name please?'

The man blustered, 'I've given you lot all the information you need. I demand to see someone in authority.' He stiffened and said loudly, 'I have friends in the council.'

Sergeant Turner smiled to Margaret and said, 'Just give me a moment.'

As Margaret watched she couldn't help thinking how much the angry man reminded her of Bernard…

Sergeant Turner went over to the counter and said, 'Good evening Sir. I believe my colleague is doing all she can to assist you but perhaps I can shed some light on your problem. You see I was present when you came in earlier to report said cat was missing. I also recall you threatening me in a similar manner. I know for a fact that my colleague PC May found your cat an hour ago - it was stuck up a tree I believe – and despite his dislike for heights, and cats, rescued it and returned it home. Presumably you have not been home?'

The man's face dropped. 'I've been busy.'

Sergeant Turner, having been around for a long time, sniffed and quickly put two and two together asking politely, 'Busy at the pub I assume.'

The man huffed and marched out. Sergeant Boothe said. 'Thank you, Sergeant. I owe you one.'

Sergeant Turner returned and sat beside Margaret. 'Now where were we?'

Margaret whispered, 'I've just seen him go up in a beam of light into a flying saucer. With a box of wine. Think I'm going crazy as im.'

'You're sure it was not an hallucination or mental aberration brought on from shock?'

'No. I know what I saw.'

'Given he has turned up every time,' he mentally counted, 'five times, I think we can assume he will again and I'm inclined not to write this up.'

She said absently, 'It wouldn't make a lot of sense anyway.'

He smiled kindly. 'No. But what I will do is make sure DI Query is aware because I understand he is taking a special interest in your husband's … difficulties.'

Margaret smiled weakly. 'Thank you, sergeant. You are very understanding.'

He stood. 'I do my best.'

***

PC May sighed as he pulled into Waitrose carpark and without asking staff – because he had a sneaking suspicion – headed straight for the trolleys. PC Green asked,' What is about Sir?'

'I think we will find a gentleman becoming well known to us sitting in a dazed state.'

PC green looked starstruck at PC May. 'How do you know Sir?'

'It's not the first time. PC Green.'

Margaret tiredly mounted the police station steps and approached the desk. Sergeant Turner smiled. 'We have him safe and sound Mrs Grimshaw. Although different apparel for a change.' She gave him a resigned look. He smiled, 'All will become clear.'

A female PC appeared with Bernard who shuffled alongside her. He shuffled because he was wearing pink slippers and wore a pink nightdress. His hairy legs protruded from the bottom and his hairy chest through the top.

Margaret gasped. 'What the – how?'

Sergeant Turner sighed. 'Unfortunately, our responsibility stops at providing cover – usually our blanket but that has not been returned to us - hence he remains in the apparel in which he was found.'

Bernard stood in a trance-like state as Margaret grabbed him by the arm and dragged him out to the car. 'I don't know what's happening Bernard, but one thing I know for sure is for once you're telling the truth.' She sighed as she tightened his seatbelt, 'Thing is what do we do about it?'

Back home Bernard seemed to wake up and looked around in confusion before realising what he was wearing. 'What bloody hell is this?'

'That's what you were wearing when they returned you.'

He spluttered, 'But why?'

She put her hands up. 'No idea, nothing makes any sense. Does this happen to other people?'

He shrugged, 'I don't know, but it's bloody happening to me and I've had enough. Newspapers want to hear about it then I'll bloody tell em – but they will have to pay me for it, and plenty an all after all the stress I've had.'

There was a bang on the door and he strode over snatching it open to find the two men in black. 'Not you lot again. Just p-'

They pushed past him and sat on the sofa side by side. He slammed the door and stood in front of them arms crossed. It hadn't occurred to him that a pink nightdress and pink slippers did not portray a picture of authority as he said, You have no right coming round here asking stupid questions and making threats. Oh, and I want me son's laptop back.'

They looked at each other trying to makes senses of the object standing in front of them, clearly confused. One of them looked Bernard up and down and said, 'We know your plans.'

'Do you now? And what would they be pray tell.' He crossed his arms defiantly and noticed he had pink fluffy arms. He looked to Margaret who hurried upstairs. He puffed himself up. 'I've had enough of you lot. I'm going to the press.'

'You will not.'

'I bloody-' Margaret thrust her green dressing gown at him. He took it. 'Is this all you got?'

'You refuse to wear one remember?'

He pulled it on but it wouldn't make it over his belly. He gave up with it. 'Anyway, I'm going to the press.'

One of the men in black took out a phone and held it up. 'This is you?' He tapped it.

'Come an get me. I've got weapons you won't like. I'll be the one to tell the world. Power will all be mine. Wine will rule. I will be your spokesman my friends. The world will hear all about you and bow down to your perfection. You think you can beat me? I'll be the one. The spokesman. they'll have to listen to me. The power is mine. We will work together!'

He stopped it and stared at Bernard for before putting the phone away. 'We will use this. You will not be going to the press.'

Margaret gasped, 'What in't bloody hell Bernard?'

'I wer in a bad place in't shed. I was a little … the elderberry is a particularly strong wine.'

'So who were you talking to?

He shifted uncomfortably the pink apparel not helping. 'Me bottles of wine Margaret, there, I've said it.' He regained his composure – as much as was possible given the circumstances - I want world to know how good it is.'

The two Men in Black stood at the same time and left without a word. Bernard turned to Margaret. 'Do they look real to you?'

'No Bernard, they don't. I don't think anything is real anymore, I don't know what to believe, especially after seeing that space thing and the light.'

He growled, 'And they've got a box of my wine an all. Bloody good bottles meant for the committee.'

She went into the kitchen and shouted over her shoulder. 'I think that boat has sailed Bernard.'

He absently picked at some of the fluff on the night dress. 'I don't.'

LOSING IT

Bernard awoke to the sound of clanking. Puzzled, he went to the window and pulled back one of the curtains to be confronted by a man at the upstairs bedroom window trying to look in. it took a few seconds for it sink in before he shouted, 'Who the bloody hell are you?' He turned to Margaret who was sitting up at being woken so abruptly. 'You see this! Bloody media.'

'Shut the curtain then you idiot.' She pulled the duvet up to her chin. 'Or push im off.'

Bernard poked at the window. 'Go away. This in invasion of bloody privacy.'

The man eagerly held up a microphone. 'They say you might be the One.'

'What bloody one? Who said? You lot are going to regret this. If you don't get off I'm … how did you get up there?' He looked down to see a scaffolding had been erected which explained the clanking. He looked past the man to see the whole media circus was back complete with burger van, ice cream van and a mass of cameras. He pulled the curtain shut and slumped onto the bed. He groaned realising he slept in the nude.

In the kitchen Margaret was eating some cereal as Bernard hurried toward the backdoor. 'Are you going to get rid of them lot outside Bernard? I feel like I'm living in a goldfish bowl.'

'Me an all. How do you suggest I do that?'

'Well, they're here because of you so figure it out.'

'Helpful as ever.' He went out to the shed to find Julien feeding Fluffy. Bernard climbed over the mobility scooter to the relative safety of the workbench. 'Don't let that bloody thing near me.'

Julien said as he fed Fluffy, 'Gran worked it out. It's because of your moustache.'

Bernard thought. 'Aye, the reporter he went for had one. Well, I'll not be getting rid just because of that.'

Julien led Fluffy out of the shed saying as he went, 'Your funeral.'

Bernard got out a box and loaded six bottles of wine into it. 'We'll see about chairman position.' He peered out of the shed window and was hit by a blinding wall of camera flashes. A man banged on the shed window with a microphone. 'Mr Grimshaw! Are you the One?'

Bernard sighed and strode out to the front of the house where a sea of reporters surrounded him. He looked around in disbelief at the numbers of tv vans, cars all along the road and adjoining gardens. The same reporter thrust a microphone in his face. 'Are you the One Bernard?'

'The one what?'

'It's said you might be the new Messiah.'

'Is it now? And who said that may I ask.'

'The President Bernard. His astrologer told him.'

'Well, he's needs to get a better one then. Now leave me alone.'

'But we've heard the recording.'

Bernard groaned. Obviously it had been leaked. He knew he was wasting his time and pushed passed him to his car. He drove off not caring if knocked one of them over. As he drove up the road through the designated areas cordoned off by plastic barriers he was stopped by Dave Shaw from number 23.

'You've certainly got a following Mr Grimshaw.'

Bernard wound down his window. Do what?'

'I said you've got a following. Fortunately they have been very generous and offered everyone good money to use their gardens.'

'Have they now?'

He leant in closer. 'They're saying your special, going to save the planet. I understand you are to be the mouthpiece for the aliens who are coming.'

'Really?' He shook his head and closed the window.

Dave Shaw banged on the window. Bernard opened it a little. 'Is Ingrid helping you?' He smiled evilly, 'Or is she sending drugs to them?'

Bernard stuck two fingers up at him and wound up the window. He pulled away and past Doris who involuntarily put her hands to her throat in fear giving him a glare. He drove on and parked in Aldi carpark. Seeing the trolleys gave him an involuntary shudder and flashes of memory produced a wave of anxiety. He steeled himself and entered the store, grabbed a basket and headed down the aisle toward the crisps. He was stopped by an earnest young man, 'Are you Him?'

Bernard put his head down and grabbed a family pack of cheese and onion. He moved on and grabbed some other bits and pieces to make up a small feast for the committee members who he knew loved nibbles. He moved on to the cheese aware that he was being watched by everyone in the store. Continuously. A handful of reporters seemed to appear from nowhere and followed close on his heels. 'When will you tell us Mr Grimshaw. Is your silence to build tension? Are we all doomed or can you save us? Is there a heaven?'

He stopped and snapped at them, 'How do I know. I don't know what you're talking about, so leave me alone.'

He hurried to the checkout and groaned to see the aisles full. An announcement blared over the speakers. 'Please open aisle six for Mr Grimshaw.'

He stood not sure what to do when a women in front of him turned to him. 'Go on, it's for you.'

He shook his head. 'This is mad. You're all crazy.' He shrugged. 'But I'll not be looking a gift horse in the mouth.'

Someone whispered to another, 'What did he say?'

'I think he's going to save some horses.'

A voice from behind shouted, 'Don't forget the dogs.'

Another, 'And the whales.'

He got out as fast as he could and ran the gauntlet of other reporters to his car. He got in and slammed the door. They clamoured around the car waving microphones and cameras at him. He sighed and muttered to himself. 'I've had enough of this.' He opened his window and beckoned the nearest reporter to him. 'Best you leave me alone now, I've got a lot of preparation to do.' They hung in silence as he smiled and said, 'I shall be removing global warming tomorrow. On Friday I shall probably nip off to the moon to fill in a few craters. Now if you don't mind…' He wound up his window and roared off.

The journey back to his house was no less stressful and it took a few narrow misses as reports dived for cover as he drove onto his drive. No sooner was he out of the car than they surrounded him. 'When will you give your speech to the world? How will you end global warming?'

He snatched his shopping from the backseat and pushed his way to the front door, turned and put up his hand. 'I have - from deep consideration - come to the conclusion that it matters not a jot what I say, because you lot write what you want anyway. From now on I'm keeping me gob shut so go away.'

'What about your mistress Bernard? Will she speak on your behalf?'

He sighed. 'Which one? I have at least ten. Now, piss off!' He hurried inside and slammed the door.

Margaret came out of the kitchen. 'Just for your information Bernard, all of that was live on sky. That includes the bit in the carpark?'

H emptied his shopping onto the kitchen table. 'I wer just having a bit of fun - for a change – let them get on wi it.'

'Hmm. You really are very naive. What's all this for?'

'Committee meeting tonight. I'm not giving up wi out a fight.'

'So with all this nonsense outside and world attention on your every word, your main worry is staying chairman of a pathetic little wine club.'

'That might be how you see it Margaret and you are of course entitled to your opinion, however, given my life has been hijacked by idiots and things from,' he nodded upwards, 'from wherever, and let me remind you they seem to appreciate my wine, then yes I am.'

'I'm going to stay with Mabel for a few days. I can't get in and out of the house without being questioned.' Her face darkened, 'Especially concerning your mistress Penelope fucking Smythe.'

'I keep telling you-'

'Enough, I'm going.'

***

Bernard was beyond caring about what they wrote as he loaded the box of wine and nibbles into his car.

'Is that for the aliens Bernard? Are they coming today?'

He put up his hand. 'All of the above, now get out bloody way.' He drove off narrowly missing two reporters who dove into the next-door hedge. 'Serve you right an all, blood suckers.'

He parked outside the Goat and Badger and carried his goodies into the pub to be greeted by the landlord who blocked his way. 'I hope you're not here to cause more trouble Mr Grimshaw. I've had the chair repaired and general damage sorted, for which I will be sending you the bill. I am aware you are here for the wine club meeting and will therefore on this occasion allow you onto the premises despite your ban. But I warn you, any more trouble and I'll have you arrested again.'

Bernard nodded and proceeded to the back room where the wine club met. As he entered the room a silence fell over the committee members seated around a rectangular table upon which were various bottles of wine and glasses together with bowls of crisps, nuts and a platter of cheeses. Bernard stood and surveyed the sea of blank faces watching him.

The secretary, Cecil Thornton stood and hurried over to him. 'Bernard, we didn't think, er you know, press and all that, you would-'

'Well I have. Not best idea to listen to what media have to say, bloody liars the lot of em.'

'I'm sure your right... thing is you see,' he glanced back at the other committee members, 'we have the national wine makers association to consider ... membership criteria etc?'

'Right lot of bureaucrats if you ask me.'

Michael French the treasurer came over. 'Thing is Bernard, we don't have any choice.'

Bernard pushed them aside and placed his box on the table. 'I see you've got a few bottles, but here are six of my best, blackberry and garlic.' He leaned on the box and looked around at the various expressions ranging from fear to anger. He avoided Frank sitting smugly at the head of the table. 'We're bigger than them lot out there gentlemen.' He glanced at Mavis Shrew. 'And ladies ... lady. As chairman of this club I can assure you-'

Frank stood and smiled. 'Only you're not as from, 'he checked his watch, 'five minutes ago.'

Bernard checked his watch. 'I'm only seven minutes late and given bloody circus out there making my life a misery, I don't think that's too shoddy.'

Frank smiled and held up his wrist. Rolex, old chum. Synced to GMT on the internet. We kicked off at exactly 7.00 pm.'

Bernard stiffened and looked around. 'Well you've not wasted anytime have yer.'

Frank smiled. 'I did warn you old mate.'

'You are not - and will never be - my mate. This is mutiny. I have always done my best-'

Cecil returned to his seat. 'Sorry Bernard, that's how it is.'

'At least try my wine.'

Frank stood. 'As the new chairman, I must insist that you leave the meeting Mr Grimshaw.'

Bernard grabbed his box and looked around the table. 'Traitors, the lot of yer. Should be ashamed.'

Mavis stood. 'You may say that Mr Grimshaw but we've had nothing but harassment from the national board since your revelations in the newspapers and on television. For goodness sake, they're saying you're the new Messiah.' She stopped puzzled for a second. 'Not that the new Messiah would not be good of course, anyway, the claims you have been making have made our lives very difficult.'

Bernard glared at her. 'Very difficult? I'll tell you what being very difficult feels like. I open bloody curtains to find a bloke trying to look into bedroom.'

Cecil said. 'We know. You were naked on BBC this evening. And evidently, you are going to solve global warming. You can't go around making claims like that Mr Grimshaw.'

'I wer bloody taking piss!'

Graham Smith stood. 'Language please. We have a lady present.'

Bernard was reaching boiling point as he looked around the room. 'Pray tell where.'

Mavis leapt to her feet. 'How dare you.'

Bernard sneered, 'That's not what you said behind bike sheds luv. I seem to remember you let all of us have a feel,' he smiled evilly, 'with knickers round bloody ankles an all.'

Mavis rushed out of the room in tears. The landlord appeared. 'I warned you.'

Bernard turned to him. 'Don't worry I'm going. Rubbish beer anyway.'

Frank came around the table and grabbed Bernard's arm. 'Time you left old mate.'

Bernard dropped his box ignoring the breaking glass as he launched himself at Frank.

ROCK BOTTOM

Margaret sighed and turned to Mable. 'Thanks for understanding Mabel. Just a few days and I will be ok. Just had to get away.'

Mable smiled as she furiously knitted, the needles clacking loudly. 'Don't worry dear, it's nice to have the company. Since George … you know.'

Margaret smiled sympathetically and asked softly, 'How long is it now?'

Mable glanced down between her feet at the steadily growing pile of knitting. 'Don't know luv I just keep going.'

'No I mean since George passed.'

'Oh.' She stopped knitting for a moment and thought, 'Ten years I suppose.'

'It must have been a shock.'

She began knitting again. 'Not really dear.'

Margaret was distracted by the television news on the tv to see a reporter outside the Goat and Badger pub. 'I don't believe it.'

'Nobody did at the time.'

The reporter looked seriously into the camera and said, 'It seems controversary follows Bernard Grimshaw known as the underpants man as yet again he has been arrested, from the pub he was earlier banned from, for causing a violent scene. It seems he has done it again.' He turned to the landlord and asked grimly, 'I understand he had been banned by you.'

'That's right. He turned up here drunk and started attacking my customers.'

'I see. So what happened tonight?'

'He attended a wine makers committee meeting and got into an argument.'

'Do you know what the argument was about?'

'I think he had been told he was no longer their chairman and he lost it.'

'Thank you.' He turned back to the camera. 'I've been told the policeman injured in the fracas is in hospital but making a good recovery.'

Margaret switched off the tv and turned back to Mable. 'Sorry, got distracted, he's been at it again. What did you say Mable?'

Mable smiled as she furiously knitted. 'That's alright dear, I get distracted by it all the time.'

'You were talking about George.'

'Yes. I said nobody did at the time.'

Margaret watched fascinated as the needles clacked and the stitches seemed to multiply at an amazing rate. 'I don't know what's going on Mable, I really don't.'

'I'm sure you don't dear.' She kicked the pile between her feet under the chair. 'I didn't for a long time.'

Margaret was not sure how to respond. 'I don't-'

'Don't worry dear, you weren't to know. You see we don't always know what is going on because we sort of look the other way?'

'I don't know which way to look Mable to be honest.' She sighed. 'If you saw what I saw that night…'

Mable was lost in a memory of her own. 'Of course I did in the end.'

'Right.'

'I found he wasn't going to the fishing club at all.' It didn't seem possible but the needles clacked faster. 'The bastard was going somewhere else.'

'Oh.'

Mable stopped for a second and looked at Margaret. 'Up Angela Dickson to be precise.'

'Oh.'

'Yes, it was a bit of a shock but I knew really, just couldn't accept it.'

'I didn't know.'

'Nobody did.' She looked up and smiled, 'That's how I got away with it.'

Margaret struggled to understand. 'Got away with it? Sorry luv I don't understand.'

Mable stopped and connected another ball of wool. 'Killed the fucker.'

'You-'

'I did.'

'But...'

'You mean how?' Margaret nodded. Mable started knitting again. 'I poisoned the fucker. Did it slow like. Used rat poison.' She smiled to herself. 'He suffered for days. Served him right.'

Margaret glanced anxiously at her cup of tea as she asked softly, 'Did nobody suspect anything?'

'Well I suppose if they had done one of them auto things-'

'Autopsy.'

'That's it one of them. Then I suppose they would have. I mean over a few weeks I must have given him enough to take out most of Bolton.'

'So...'

'I put him in his beloved shed and set fire to the fucker. No evidence you see. Just an accident.'

As much as Bernard drove Margaret to the edge of her sanity, she could not envisage poisoning him. Strangling maybe... 'It's all getting too much for me Mable, but I can't stay here forever.'

'You're fine dear.'

Margaret asked, 'Upstairs?'

'Yes dear, the downstairs blocked.'

Margaret hurried up the stairs still shocked by Mable's confession, if that is what it was - it seemed more a matter-of-fact discussion of an event. She opened what she thought was the bathroom but it was a bedroom – full of piles of knitting, like square pillars. She quietly shut the door wondering if she should go home sooner than planned.

Mable looked up as Margaret returned and sat down. 'All good?'

'Yes, fine. Are you getting a plumber in to fix the loo?'

Mable shook her head as the needles clacked away. 'Don't want the hassle.'

'I think they're quick if you find a good one.'

She stopped for a moment and said, 'I used to have a cat.'

'Did you?'

'Hmm. Horrible little bastard, kept bringing in dead birds and seeing as I belonged to the RSPCA it didn't feel right.'

'I see.'

'So,' she nodded toward the downstairs loo. Margaret followed her eyes. 'That's why it's blocked.'

'Umm not sure–'

Mable laughed. 'I stuffed the little fucker down it. I thought he would flush away but he hasn't. I suppose eventually he will fall to bits and slip down.'

Margaret shifted uncomfortably. 'Mable …'

'Don't worry dear, you're quite safe,' she smiled again, 'just don't upset me.'

Margaret laughed nervously. 'Do you want a brew? I'll make it.'

***

PC May leant against the reception counter as Sergeant Turner completed an entry. 'So then we got the call.'

'To the Goat and Badger. Who thinks up these names?'

'I told PC Green that he needed to toughen up, but he couldn't hear past his pc correctness and wokeness or whatever they call it.'

Sergeant Turner sighed. 'It's a strange world we live in PC May. I shall be glad to retire.'

'Me too. Anyway, I responded to the call and was surprised to find Mr Grimshaw on a table throwing cheese and onion crisps bags at a woman cowering in the corner. It's odd isn't it, how quickly we make assumptions of our,' he smiled, 'customers. I mean on the two occasions I have met Mr Grimshaw he has been in underpants, oh and the most recent of course in a night dress. So to find him the centre of a punch up was odd.'

Sergeant Turner nodded sagely. 'The vagaries of our job eh PC May?'

'The very thing I've been trying to get over to PC Green. But it was to no avail. He got in there before I could and attempted to talk Mr Grimshaw down, of course with little effect as said perp was in full rant on the table, swigging from a bottle and throwing cheese at a group of men – presumably the committee members – shouting that he was the real chairman. When I entered the room the pub had been cleared by the Landlord who was heading toward the room with a baseball bat.'

'One can do considerable damage with one of those. Wish I had one behind here sometimes.'

'I had to restrain him with cuffs so that I could rescue PC Green who was hiding under the table, the woman by now was hysterical, as was PC Green come to think of it.'

'I don't think he is the right material for our line of work.'

PC May sighed. 'I don't seem to have much luck with partners recently.'

'No. But you have done your best. By the way, what has happened with PC Jones?'

'Gone to ground. Now I know I can speak candidly to you Sergeant,' he leaned in and said quietly, 'she was fucking crazy.'

'Hmm. Another example of where it has gone wrong.' He thought for a moment. 'Was Mr Grimshaw released?'

'Yes, on bail to next week.'

'Perhaps I'd better ring his wife.'

Margaret had insisted on cooking their meals; something for which Mable was very grateful. She was tidying up the kitchen when her mobile rang. 'Sergeant Turner?'

'I thought I would see that you are alright since your husband was arrested again for a violent affray.'

'That's very kind of you. As much as he is a bully, he has never threatened me with violence.' She felt a wave of guilt considering the acts of violence to which she had subjected him. 'I'm not at home for a few days, I'm staying with my cousin in Bolton.'

'I understand. Just wanted to be sure.'

'Thank you Sergeant. I do appreciate your concern, and how you do your job.'

'It's my pleasure Mrs Grimshaw.'

Margaret carried two teas into the lounge and sat beside Mable who was furiously knitting. 'Doesn't that make your fingers ache?'

Mable nodded. 'They go numb after a few hours.'

'Do you ever stop?'

'No.'

'Right. Here's your tea. Fancy a takeaway?'

***

Bernard arrived home from the police station and narrowly avoided killing three reporters as he carelessly parked his car. He shoved them aside and crashed into the house. Ingrid looked up as he stormed through into the kitchen. She wheeled herself after him. 'I see you on news again. You are becoming popular person I think.'

'Think what you bloody like. I'm going to bed and not getting up again.' He trudged up the stairs throwing his clothes on the floor and getting into bed. So this is what his life was going to be from now on. He laid in the comforting silence for a while then noticed movement at the window. 'Not bloody again!' He leapt out and snatched open the curtains to see the same face at the window again. 'Right!' He threw open the outward opening window and shouted at the figure descending fast toward the ground, 'Serves you bloody right!' He got back into bed and groaned as he laid there. Suspended from work, laughing stock of the town, hounded by the media, lost the wine making club, facing court for smuggling and assault, haunted by his evil mother and nagged by Margaret. He sighed, 'What else good go bloody wrong?' He turned over to sleep when the doorbell chimed. He ignored it. It kept chiming. His patience running on vapour, he leapt out of bed and snatched on Margaret's dressing gown past caring what he looked like - and let's face it he had been naked on the media around the world. He opened the door ready to blast an inevitable reporter. He was taken by surprise as Daphne Pearce from the golf club smiled at him. A very young and attractive Daphne Peace. A Daphne Pearce who had occasionally featured in his fantasies.

'Hello Mr Grimshaw. Can I come in?'

He squinted suspiciously at the reporters gathering like vultures to see what the next instalment of his misery would be as he hurriedly ushered her inside and slammed the door, his belly on auto as it drew in. 'Aye come in. Them lot out there are right pain.' He couldn't ignore her doing her best to not notice the green dressing gown. 'Ha! Grabbed it by mistake like, brew?'

'That's very kind of you Mr Grimshaw.'

His belly couldn't keep up the pretence and relaxed to its full extent forcing the dressing gown open. She quickly averted her eyes and scurried through into the kitchen. She asked anxiously, 'Mrs Grimshaw not around?'

He returned from the hall wearing his overcoat. 'At a friends for a few days.' He nodded at the front door. 'Them lot.'

'Yes it is a very large gathering.' She sat at the kitchen table and crossed her legs. 'I've seen the news; you appear to be flavour of the month.' She attempted a smile but was too tense. 'That's why I'm here Mr Grimshaw.'

He switched on the kettle and took down two mugs from a cupboard. 'Uhuh.'

'Thing is -'

'Sugar?'

'Erm, no thanks. You see Mr Grimshaw -'

'Milk?'

'Yes just a drop. So -'

He asked softly, 'And how is David?'

'Oh. David. Yes, he's fine. Just got a promotion actually.'

He checked the kettle with one hand, 'Promotion you say? Very good.'

'Yes, yes it is. Thing is Mr Grimshaw-'

The kettle began to boil. He switched it off and said, 'You should never let it boil for making tea. Did you know that Daphne?'

'I, err no I -'

'And for the perfect cup of tea, always put the milk in first.' He did so. 'See? Perfect cuppa.'

'I didn't know that.'

'No, why should you. You come from the South, not been here long enough to pick up the old ways.' He stirred his mug. 'How long have you been up here Daphne? Two years? No three is it?'

She shifted uncomfortably sensing all was not well on the Mr Grimshaw front and beginning to regret visiting. 'Two.'

He smiled sweetly as he sipped his tea. 'Two years and already Vice President of the golf club. Impressive.'

'Yes, thank you. Which is why I am -'

He put up a hand to silence her, 'To inform me that I am suspended?'

She glanced at her tea still on the worktop as he took another large sip of his. He nodded at it. 'You're wondering why I haven't passed you your tea?' She nodded imperceptibly. He picked up her mug. 'So I assume then that your visit today is not to check on my wellbeing?'

She blushed. 'I am of course concerned for your -'

He tipped the tea down the sink. 'Bollocks. Let me save you the trouble of pretending and say it for you. I'm suspended.'

'Your membership has been withdrawn Mr Grimshaw.'

'Ah, straight to jail like.'

She was perplexed. 'Sorry?'

'Monopoly, look it up. Anyway, much as I would like to stand here and pass the time of day with you, I would prefer it if you left.'

'We will of course refund any outstanding fees.'

'How fucking generous of you.'

She stood and shifted uneasily toward the lounge as he finished his tea. She was deeply regretting volunteering to undertake - what was becoming - an extremely uncomfortable experience. 'Please, Mr Grimshaw there's no need for such language. I am only -'

He placed his mug down heavily. 'Only?'

She backed toward the front door. 'I'm leaving now. You will receive a formal letter in the next few days.'

He noticed the handle of the mug was no longer attached to it as he waved it at her. 'I can hardly wait. Pray tell, Daphne, which prat on the committee suggested I be expelled?'

She reached the door and felt behind her for the handle. 'It was unanimous.'

He moved toward her waving the handle at her, 'And based on the lies those morons outside have put out.'

She tried to smile but it gave up and came out as a grimace. 'That and the statements you have been making. The committee felt your actions were not in keeping with the ethos of the club.'

'Ethos of the club. I see. So a committee of stuck up, pompous twats, got together in a little huddle and chucked me out.' He began to pace. 'You come round here with your airs and bloody graces, you know what? Stuff yer bloody golf club. I've two minds to get a JCB and dig bloody lot up.' He sneered, 'Seeing as you've never done proper days' work in yer bloody life and certainly not a building site I am sure - with yer high heels and tight skirts. So a JCB is a bloody big digger.'

She managed to open the door and frantically slipped out slamming it behind her. She turned to be faced with a sea of microphones. 'Did he give you a message?'

She pulled her coat tight around her and pushed through them to her car. 'He certainly did.'

'What was it?'

'He told me to piss off.'

Bernard staggered back up to his bedroom throwing his overcoat down the stairs, followed by Margaret's dressing gown. He muttered to himself as he got back into bed, 'Come round here like that, and to think I used to fancy her.'

***

Bernard stirred and realised it was dark. He got out of bed and pulled the duvet around him. He muttered to himself, 'Mouth like bottom of bloody parrot cage.' He stumbled to the stairs and saw the lounge light was on. He checked his watch to see it was 7.30 pm. He made his way down the stairs almost tripping over the duvet when he looked up to see the lounge now resembled a communications command centre. Ingrid appeared to be the Commander surveying a row of mobile phones.

'What the bloody hell is all this?'

'Hello Bernard. It is nothing important.'

'Nothing important? ... what are all these phones ... I don't it. This is for dealing bloody drugs.'

'Is just business.'

'Illegal business, in't my house. I'll not be condoning it.'

She chuckled. 'I understand, after all you must go to court for smuggling.'

'Aye, because you and that git on the boat, set me up.'

She smiled. 'I know nothing about it Bernard.'

'Of course you don't. Get this lot out by morning or I call police.' He smirked. 'You didn't think I know but I do. You see, I've been a tad busy what with – according to media - saving bloody world, but I've had time to reflect, *mother*.'

'What is this reflect on Bernard?'

'Don't play dumb Russian with me. See, I know you have a house near winery. So that means you have been lying. And that means you've got a problem.'

'Problem?'

'Yes mother, a big problem, unless,' he got down to her level, 'you get your arse out of here tomorrow.'

She smiled. 'Is not a problem. I have new flat I can go to.'

'Good and take your phones with yer.'

They both looked round as a key turned in the front door and Margaret entered, surrounded by a sort of halo forming around her from behind making her saint like from the arc lights of the media. She slammed the door, 'What are you two doing? What are all those phones for?'

Bernard nodded to Ingrid. 'Ask her. I've had it. I'm having a brew and going back to me pit.'

'Charming.' She focused on Ingrid as he shuffled into the kitchen. 'Well?'

'Is nothing, little experiment.'

Bernard shouted from the kitchen, 'She thought she could run a drugs business from here but I've just put her straight. See Margaret, we forgot she has a house near the winery. She also has a flat so she can piss off there tomorrow and take this lot with her.'

Margaret shrugged. 'I'm past caring. I've got used to arriving at the house like it was red carpet at the Oscars ... minus the star status of course.'

Bernard slurped his tea and shuffled past her upstairs. 'I've had it an all. I'm going to bed and staying there until further notice.'

Margaret shouted to him as he disappeared up the stairs. 'I've made up a bed in the spare room, so you can have our bed to yourself.' She leaned over to shout at his receding backside. 'And you can have the media all to yourself an all.'

He mumbled as he slammed the bedroom door, 'Whatever.'

She went into the kitchen and made herself a cup of tea as Ingrid wheeled herself into her temporary bedroom and shut the door. She picked up her mobile and thought for a few seconds then put it down again. She sighed. She had been married long enough to know that Bernard was not right. Accepting he had never actually been "alright" he was now definitely even more not alright, to the degree she was actually worried about him. She became aware of feeling a little out of control – as if she was being pushed toward something she was not actually aware of - and yet needed to explore it, whatever "it" was. She picked up her mobile and hesitated for a few seconds then dialled. 'Is Sergeant Turner on duty tonight?'

Bernard lay in the dark - as much as the arc lights outside would allow despite the blackout curtains Margaret had hung in a fit of frustration. His mind was flitting from crisis to crisis the least being that of the impending court appearances. And his suspension from work. And his mother. And the media. He groaned and turned over half aware the front door had opened and shut. He vaguely heard the reporters but drifted off.

IT'S COMPLICATED

As if not really in control she walked quickly up the steps into the foyer of the police station. Sergeant Turner looked up as she approached. He smiled enquiringly. 'Don't tell me…'

'No, he's taken to his bed. I've not seen him depressed like this since the fiasco at the wine tasting.'

'Yes, I understand from my colleagues that was quite the event.'

'I'm going in the spare room for a while, the media outside are awful, and so is his snoring.'

'Something I shall be doing myself,' he checked his watch, 'in about two hours.' He smiled, 'Don 't know if I snore though, nobody to tell me you see.'

'You live on your own then?'

'Yes I do. I have chosen it as being the lesser of two evils; on the one hand I do get lonely, but on the other no hassle.'

'I can understand that. My life is nothing but hassle at the moment.'

'You have certainly had your share it's true.' He thought. 'Do you have someone you can confide in Mrs Grimshaw?'

'Thought I had but Doris is a gossip, don't trust her anymore.'

'I see.' He looked thoughtful. 'Trust. Not something I've been too good at if I'm honest.'

'Has there ever been, you know …'

'A lady friend?'

'Hmm.'

'There was once,' he looked sad for a second before the concrete defences reappeared, 'but it was not to be.'

'I'm sorry to hear that Sergeant.'

'Thank you Mrs Grimshaw,' He took a deep sigh, 'But all in the past. Water under the bridge etc.'

She smiled feeling more relaxed than she had for a long time. 'Call me Margaret, after all we have been through a few odd experiences together.'

'We have …Margaret.' He leaned over to her and said quietly, 'And you can call me …Sergeant!'

She wasn't sure how to react for a second but then he laughed. 'Alternatively, you can call me Bob. Robert is too formal.' He smiled. 'My mother used to call me that when I had misbehaved,' he looked thoughtful, 'probably all that mischief led me to be a copper.'

'And I think a very good one …Bob.'

'That's very kind of you …Margaret.' He straightened his back. 'Was there something you wanted?'

She smiled. 'I don't know what I want Sergeant.'

'Do any of us when we stop to think about it.'

'We just go on every day I suppose,' she sighed, 'until it's too late.'

'Perhaps your tired, that makes our thinking go off track, and you have had a lot of stress.'

'You're right there. I'm right knackered.'

'Then best you try and get a good night's sleep.'

'Yes, I will.'

'I am always willing to listen.'

'Thank you.'

He smiled as he picked up his pen. 'Are you still confused?'

'Not anymore.'

He watched her as she left and went back to his writing. DI Query appeared. 'Was that Mr's Grimshaw?'

Sergeant Turner was busy writing. 'It was.'

'He hasn't gone missing again.These guys are really after him.'

'No. She wanted to talk, that's all.' He straightened his back. 'I think Mr Grimshaw is in a bad way mentally.'

'Not surprising.'

'Perhaps your expertise in the … alien department might be helpful to him?'

'Maybe. Depressed do you think?'

'Very likely. He strikes me as pessimistic.'

'I'd rather be an optimist and a fool than a pessimist and right.'

'That would be a quote from our friend I assume.'

'Certainly is.'

'Very apt I'm sure.'

DI Query looked thoughtful. 'I'll go and see him.'

Sergeant Turner was feeling mischievous. 'Albert?'

DI Query had to think for a moment. 'Ah, a joke Sergeant, very good. I mean Grimshaw and at the same time I will see what transpires with his mother.'

'Dark horse, me thinks.'

'Absolutely. Thing is Sergeant we old school, don't give up easily do we.'

'No, we don't.' He went back to his writing, Never know what to expect.'

***

PC Jones rubbed her sore wrists as she stared at herself in the broken piece of mirror. She hadn't expected half of the American SWAT team to get in the way. Giving up was not in her nature and her experiences on the survival course for preppers was paying dividends. The wind was picking up making the sides of her one-person (not a one man in her world) tent flap furiously. Being in the wild – if the wood near to Ramsbottom park could be described as thus – enabled her to think out her strategy without interference from the outside world, namely fellow police sisters – fellows was not in her vocabulary either. Her plan was simple if not fraught with problems; something she thrived upon and provided the energy required to reach her goal, which was to secure the perv once and for all. Her police uniform lay crumpled beside her – there wasn't much point in keeping it pristine given her time in the police force had come to an abrupt end. Now it was civvies, which were better suited to her plan.

She was disturbed by a torch beam cutting through the tree trunks before stopping on her tent. She leapt up ready for action as she heard feet rustling through the wet leaves approaching her. She rushed out to see the perv furtively exploring the outside of her tent. She grappled him to the ground and applied a choke hold satisfied his weakening response indicative of surrender. He groaned and went floppy. She quickly secured him with cable ties – a little too tightly remembering her recent experience – and sat him up shining her twenty thousand lumens tactical flashlight in his face. The light bore through his eyelids and he was instantly awake – perhaps not present but certainly awake – and shook his head to get the blood flowing again. She grabbed his coat collar and got in close, the light inches from his face. A realisation struck her and she growled, 'Stay there or I'll gut you.' She launched herself into the tent and reappeared grasping the police alert picture of the escaped sex offender which she held close to his face. She looked from one to the other and exclaimed, 'It's you! There's me planning to get you and here you are.' She studied him for a few seconds, playing the piercing light over his face, 'But why? Why would you give yourself up, and how did you know I was here?' She placed the torch on the ground shining in his face, stood and began pacing back and forth. 'Think Jones.' Her need to apprehend the perv who represented all pervs – especially the one who violated her sister was a driving force that tended to make clear thinking an impossible task, clouding any rational thought. She stopped and looked at him. 'Right,' she held up the picture, 'this is you right?'

He squinted and muttered in a Sottish accent, 'Canna see from here, the lights in my face.'

She grabbed the torch which was now encompassed in a mist as it heated up the wet leaves and shone it on the picture. 'This is you, right?'

He knew his run was over and nodded. 'Aye that's me lassie. I'm tired of running anyway.'

Referring her to a dog did not do him any favours and she got close to him with the torch. 'Hated that programme.' A fleeting memory of her sister crying hit her. She bashed him over the head with the torch. 'You're right there, mate, you're going down.' She secured him with more cable ties and began pacing again. Something was not right; at some level of her tired mind a thought was fighting to surface. She stopped and pointed a finger at him, 'You're Scottish right?' He nodded. She paced again. The thought was beginning to surface through the murk of her anger – almost but not quite obscured by her sister crying and the need for revenge expressing itself as the need to rip his head off. She stopped and studied him again. 'Sure you're Scottish?' He nodded. She paced again and suddenly the thought crashed through the murk to be examined. 'When I was interrogating you, I'm certain you weren't Scottish then.' She stopped. 'But you are now.' She knelt down and grabbed his collar. 'What game are you playing?' She pointed the torch close to his face making his moustache sizzle.

He whimpered, 'No game. Just tired of running, I was looking for somewhere to hide.'

She stood and paced again. 'If you're Scottish and you weren't when I was interrogating you, that means …' she frowned fighting to make sense of the thoughts fighting for attention, 'You're somebody else. But that doesn't make any sense. Who are you?'

He began sobbing, 'I confess, it was me. I want to change, please help me.'

The thoughts struggled as her psychosis took hold, and one in particular made itself heard. 'You're his twin. You're covering for him. He operates from that house because that's where I took him. Sooo, you must be his … his twin! Clever. But it won't work. You're staying here and I'm going to go and get the real perv.'

He cowered. 'I'm not his twin…'

'Course you're not. I did my psychology training mate, and I know all about blood's thicker than water shit. He's your pervy brother and you have to protect him. Well good try, but no go. I know your brother is the real perv cos he's not Scottish.'

The realisation that he was in the company of a nutcase softened his reply. 'Ok.'

***

Chip Haslow pulled the collar of his coat up tight as he locked his car and headed toward Earl Street, what he considered downtown Ramsbottom. Hell, he considered everything to do with the North of England downtown. He pressed the bell and looked around with distaste at the old buildings and tiny cars parked in rows along the street. A middle-aged woman opened the door and smiled, 'Hello.'

He attempted a smile, but it didn't work. 'I'm visiting Zac Childersberger.'

'Please come in and I'll let him know you're here.' She showed him through into a room obviously used for meals and currently with breakfast bowls set out. 'Won't be a moment.'

He nodded and checked out the photos on the walls of rock climbers ascending what he considered to be an impossible vertical rock face. He muttered to himself, 'Goddam crackbrained donuts.'

The woman appeared, 'Room five on the first floor.'

He grunted thanks and made his way up the stairs noting more pictures of nutcases climbing stupid rocks. He was not in a good mood as he knocked on the door of number 5. He was aware of the woman peeking up the stairs as Zac opened the door.

'Chip?'

Chip pushed past him and took off his coat. 'This the best you could do?' He looked around the tiny room with distaste.

Don't want to draw attention Chip. Protocol.'

'Yeah I know. So this limey guy Bernard Grimshank.'

'Grimshaw.'

'Whatever. You've caused one hell of a shitstorm son.'

'Just reporting what I've observed.'

'Ok.' He sat on the bed. 'You sleep on this?'

Zac shrugged. 'Not too bad once you get used to it.'

Chip got out his phone and scrolled. 'Ok.' He thought for a moment. 'You live over here, like permanently?'

Zac nodded. 'In Bolton, renting this to be close.'

'Why would you choose to live in this godforsaken country anyway. And Bolton? Never heard of it.'

Zac smiled. 'Not so bad once you get used to the weather.'

Chip shook his head. 'If we're going to reduce this place to ground zero, I want to know it's based on sound intel. So, let's focus here, get the landscape on the table. You first spotted this guy when he was found in a carpark in his jockies. What made you suspect he was the real deal?'

'I've been following UFO abduction cases for years. This one felt different.'

'How so?'

'A gut feeling I guess. Then I saw with my own eyes that box go up with him. From the phone tap I knew it was wine. And then the statement leaked to the press.'

'World domination shit. Yeah, that was chilling alright.'

'The media are not giving up Chip. This guy is the real deal.'

'Ok. I'll file my report. I suggest you keep away from Grimshaw's house, its gonna burn like a motherfucker.'

Zac sighed. 'Sounds pretty extreme Chip. Why not just take him out?'

'We don't know the extent to which this nutter will go. He might be in with the Chinese, making a bomb, who the fuck knows. 'Too much media presence. We can't be seen going in there, so … boom.'

***

Deep within the bowels of the Pentagon a high-level black ops strategy meeting was again underway headed up by Dewey Heinzeburgher. 'An update gentlemen.'

Serious faces nodded around the table. Chuck Shellerberger said, 'So intel was right. Goddam.'

Dewey Heinzeburgher nodded. 'Chip has spoken to Zac who filed the initial report. He's since seen clear evidence of a box of wine being taken up into the craft with Grimshaw.'

Chad Biffle said grimly, 'My guy is sound. The best in his field.'

Beau Faartz. Leapt to his feet. 'Then we act.'

Woody Clampitt nodded. 'Everything points to this nutter setting himself up to be one powerful dude. With the backing of the aliens he could do whatever he wanted.' He sighed. 'These damn aliens are losing the plot and it's got to be because,' he stood and banged his fist on the table, 'they're fucking drunk! You know he was found in a woman's dressing gown?'

Colt Harkleroad stood. 'Like I said. World domination. And now while being damn alcoholics.'

Dewey Heinzeburgher put up his hands. 'Ok guys, let's cool it.' They both sat down. He continued, 'We can't let him make any more announcements. I recommend we send in SWAT and remove him.'

Chad Biffle looked worried. 'What about the media presence? We can't be seen going in.'

Colt Harkleroad nodded. 'Correct. There is an alternative.'

Dewey Heinzeburgher sat forward. 'Go on.'

'Do as we originally considered.'

A deathly silence descended over the room. Chad Biffle sighed as he rubbed his eyes, 'You serious?'

Colt Harkleroad put his hands on the table. 'Nuke the whole dam area.'

Chad Biffle gasped. 'The fall out would be massive.'

Beau Faartz nodded. He's right. Massive.' He smiled, 'But we can control the media.'

Chad Biffle sighed. 'I was referring to the radioactive fallout. It will contaminate the whole of the country.'

Dewey Heinzeburgher smiled grimly. 'Sure, but it's not like one of our states, right?'

Woody Clampitt nodded. 'We've always considered it as like an aircraft carrier for our planes anyway. But I suggest instead of a nuke - which will be difficult to explain away - we send in a couple of missiles.'

Chad Biffle nodded. 'High collateral damage but we can handle that. Might have to take out a few other local facilities to make it deniable.'

Dewey Heinzeburgher. 'Then it's agreed. I'll set it up with General Mervin Zuckerhieser.'

A collective gasp went around the table. 'No!'

Dewey Heinzeburgher put up is hands and sighed. 'Above my pay grade guys. No choice.'

Woody Clampitt said softly, 'We've made the right decision, but to implement it with General Mervin Zuckerhieser?' Chad Biffle said angrily, 'I want it recorded that I strongly disagree with the choice of General Mervin Zuckerhieser.'

Dewey Heinzeburgher. 'I know your concerns, but I've conversated with him and he has assured me he is now recovered.' Chad Biffle sighed, 'Does anyone come back from that sort of breakdown?' He looked anxiously around the room. 'Talking him down from the roof? Jeez.'

***

PC Jones parked away from the media crowd and made her way past the various food stalls along the estate road. She was tempted by an ice cream, but the queue was too long and she had business to take care of. So were queues at the burger stall, specialist coffee marquee (which was full to the brim) and a Jehovah's Witness stand beside which was a table with UFO paraphernalia. Her rucksack was cutting into her shoulders, but it was not a problem to her because she was on a mission. It had taken some effort to obtain the equipment she required but the application of her femininity proved effective – if not distasteful. She rounded the corner to see Bernard's house in the distance, not hard to miss as it appeared every news outlet in the world was there, along with members of the public. She made her way around the tents and deckchairs so that she had a clear view of the front door.

She decided she needed to establish some intel and stood beside a young man sitting on a camping chair.

He looked up as she unslung her rucksack and rubbed her shoulders. 'Looks heavy.'

She turned and smiled down to him. 'Yes. Are you a reporter?'

He stood. 'I am. Can't afford to miss anything.'

'No. What is actually going on?'

He gave her a look which suggested she was from a different planet. 'Really? How could you not know?'

'I've been busy.'

He shrugged. 'Too busy for the biggest news story this century?'

She smiled shyly. 'Sounds lame doesn't it? My name is Mary. What's yours?'

He offered his hand, 'Tim.'

'So…?'

He studied her. 'You really don't know?'

'Nope. I was passing and saw the crowd. Believe me or not but it's true. To be honest I've been off grid. Roughing it so no internet or phone.'

'Get you. Well, in a nutshell, the guy who lives in this house is called Bernard Grimshaw…'

She was finding concentration difficult and the voices in her head kept grabbing her attention.

She zoned out not interested because she knew the man in that house was a perv and she had his twin brother - who had tried to divert her from her mission – secured. She gave him the occasional nod as she watched the front door. It was going to be tricky and she would have to follow him until he was away from the crowd, then she could apprehend him and continue her interrogation.

RECOVERY

It was becoming difficult to access the house without causing a media frenzy and with the agreement of the neighbouring house a temporary access was made to the back garden. It was not ideal as it required ducking under the low branch of an oak tree and avoiding a very angry hawthorn hedge that wanted to snag everybody who had the audacity to pass it.

Di Query took on the challenge and managed to get to the back door with only a few scratches.

Margaret opened the back door to him. 'Thanks for coming. I can't get him out of bed.'

DI Query smiled. 'Not a problem. There's certainly a crowd out there.'

She ushered him in. 'Seems to get bigger every day.' Tiger slinked in and gave DI Query a haughty look before rubbing itself against Margaret's legs. 'Brew?' The cat was too tired to cause a fuss and lazily jumped onto the sideboard and settled down on the router.

DI Query sat at the kitchen table. 'Please, two sugars, little milk. Is he prone to depression?'

She switched on the kettle and took down two mugs – distracted that a mug was missing from the shelf- and thought for a second. 'He's never been what you would call happy - too busy moaning – and I suppose his belief that he is a gift to the world has prevented him from needing to be depressed.' She dropped two teabags in the mugs, 'This is a first, but then,' she nodded in the direction of the media, 'them lot haven't helped.'

'I'm sure, but first we need to get him out of bed and thinking straight.'

She poured the teas. 'So you're interested in all this UFO stuff?'

'I am Mrs Grimshaw. Been an interest since I was a teenager.' He picked up his mug. 'I had an experience when I was eighteen.'

'Oh. A bad one?'

'Depends how you view it I suppose. I don't talk about it to many people because they are brainwashed into considering it stupid.'

Margaret sipped her tea. 'What do you mean?'

'The American government have been in contact with aliens since the fifties. They made an agreement that they could abduct us for experiments in return for their technology.' He sipped his tea, put down his mug and looked at her. 'I was taken. I had missing time, confused, disoriented. Luckily, I had a friend who understood and persuaded me to be hypnotised.'

'So that's why you suggested it.'

He nodded. 'Hoped it would work, like it did for me.'

'I suppose it did,' she studied her tea, 'I'm not used to all this stuff. Knit and natter is about the sum of my education since leaving school.'

'And now?'

'I'm confused.' She thought of Sergeant Turner. 'In lots of ways.'

'Let's see if we can get your husband to get up.'

She studied him. 'You lot have restored my faith in the police.'

'Glad to hear it.'

Margaret opened the bedroom door and nodded at the arc lights outside. 'Hope that's not coming off my bloody elec bill. Bernard?' She shook him. He grunted. She shook him again. 'Bernard, DI Query is here to see you.'

'Come back and arrest me tomorrow, too tired.'

'He's not here to arrest you, he's here to help, isn't that right DI Query?'

DI Query leaned over the bed covers to the mound of depression beneath. 'Just want to help.'

'Don't see how, best leave me alone.'

DI Query sat on the edge of the bed, 'Let's see. Get up and we'll talk about it.'

'Too tired, can't be bothered.'

There was a tapping on the window followed by a man's voice. 'Hello. Mr Grimshaw. Can you give us an update?'

This served to provide what DI Query was unable to as Bernard snarled and sat up. 'I've had it up to here with bloody press. He struggled out of bed making DI Query look away as of course, Bernard slept in the nude. He strutted over to the window and snatched open the curtains.

A man was on a ladder with one arm in a sling. 'Please don't open the window again Mr Grimshaw.'

Bernard's hand was on the window clasp as he growled, 'You've got a bloody cheek. See if you bounce shall we?'

'No, please, we just want to know if you're alright, seeing as we haven't heard for a while.'

'Get stuffed.'

'Can I quote you on that?'

'Do what you bloody like.' He drew the curtains and headed back to the bed.

DI Query averted his eyes and said, 'Now you're up come downstairs and have let's have a brew. Perhaps with some clothes on …'

Bernard realised he was naked and dragged the duvet around him. 'Go down and I'll join yer in a mo.'

Margaret muttered. 'For everyone's sake.'

In the kitchen Margaret boiled the kettle again. 'At least he's up.'

DI Query sat down. 'I can understand his frustration.'

Bernard appeared and sat at the table. 'Has she gone?'

Margaret sorted the mugs. 'If you mean your mother, yes she has.'

'And taken that bloody great scooter out of my shed?'

'Yes. But not the dog.'

Bernard sighed as he rubbed his eyes. 'I used to love that shed – until she came here and ruined it all.'

Margaret made the teas. 'Well she's gone now.'

'Except bloody wild animal in't cage.'

DI Query said, 'I could help with that.'

Bernard perked up. 'Pray tell.'

'I've got a mate in the canine division. He could get me something you could give it to calm it down.'

Margaret exclaimed, 'Drug it? Poor little thing. Talk about cruel.'

Bernard snarled, 'You don't have to sit in there while it watches yer, its eyes just follow every movement, waiting, plotting-'

DI Query put up his hand, 'No nothing bad, just a mild tranquiliser, he uses them on fireworks night sometimes.'

Margaret asked, 'So how come Julien can walk him ok then?'

DI Query smiled. 'It's a rescue dog, I think it has been traumatised, probably by a moustache.'

Margaret frowned. 'By a moustache?'

'By a man with one. The same as Bernard's.'

Margaret passed them their teas. 'Better shave it off then Bernard.'

'I will certainly not. Aye get the stuff, let's try it.'

Margaret couldn't resist a dig. 'That just leaves the other monster then.'

Bernard bristled. 'You can mock.' He looked to DI Query. 'Bloody spider in't shed been the bane of my life. Eyes like bloody saucers, and it watches me, waits, and then runs about.'

Margaret sipped her tea. 'We have half the world's media outside damn house, and here you are whittering on about a tiny spider in't shed.'

Bernard muttered, 'Certainly not tiny.'

DI Query interjected. 'It doesn't appear that these aliens are going to leave you alone Bernard.'

'They want the wine. Took whole box of me blackberry and garlic.'

'And that lot out there believe you have a message for them.'

'Not helped by something I said in't shed being leaked and totally misinterpreted.'

'Yes. I must say it puzzles me why an advanced race should be so obsessed with alcohol?'

Bernard straightened and sipped his tea, 'It is my finest.'

'I don't question your prowess at wine making, it just doesn't make sense.'

'So what do you suggest?'

'Standing up to them, defying them.'

Bernard eyed him suspiciously, 'And what if they don't like that and zap me with some bloody ray gun thing?'

'I was thinking more along the lines of trying to reason with them.'

Margaret asked, 'And what about them lot out there?'

DI Query sighed. 'I've got an idea about that. Leave it with me.'

Tiger slinked into the kitchen from where it had been watching proceedings whilst sitting on the Wi-Fi router.'

Bernard pointed as it jumped down and crouched down in hunting mode. 'And that's why tele signal is bad, cos router's full of bloody cat hair.'

Margaret said defensively, 'He likes it on there, it keeps him warm.'

'Then tell it to sit on radiator then, and perhaps we could watch tele in peace without buffering all the bloody time.'

As if in reply, Tiger ran across the lounge and pounced on Bernard's leg embedding its claws through his joggers.'

'Aaargh! Thought you said you'd cut its claws?' He fought to get it off as it buried its teeth in his leg.'

'I was but your dramas got in the way.'

***

Bernard sat in the shed glaring at Fluffy as the dog impassively watched him seeming - to Bernard - as though he was to be its next meal. The difference being that since administering the tranquiliser Fluffy had ceased to launch himself at the cage door and was now more contemplative – perhaps imaging more than acting out his need to rip Bernard apart.

Bernard felt caged in the shed by the mob outside and had given up leaving via the front door and instead used the temporary exit through next door's garden as if escaping from a prison camp. There was not much reason to leave the shed he thought glumly, given that he was suspended from work, expelled from the golf club and ostracised by his fellow wine makers. Life was not good and he was considering returning to his bed.

The spider also wished he would leave it alone as it eyed the partially completed web it was in the process of spinning when the interloper appeared. Life was supposed to be the simple search for food and the production of a good web to obtain such, not having to constantly be on guard against being zapped by a fly swat or gassed. Since the other unwanted guest appeared to have calmed down, it was considering whether the move to that side of the shed might be a possibility once again.

Bernard was aware it had crept out from behind the white emulsion and glanced at the aerosol spray but didn't have the energy to reach for it. Thus, the spider felt emboldened to explore a possible route to the other side of the shed and made a dash for the tin of creosote at the end of the shelf.

The sudden movement made Bernard jump which was sufficient to stir Fluffy from her dazed state and start barking.

Margaret looked over the various combinations of clothes on the bed and chose the first one she had tried an our ago. It still fitted – just about – and then it was which shoes. There were eight pairs of high heels on the floor and after consideration chose the first pair she had tried.

She slipped them on and immediately wondered why she didn't wear them more often. Not having being encouraged to show them off was the main reason, given they never went out anywhere. She checked herself out in the mirror and was satisfied with the result. Sue had done a great job on her hair – not that anyone had noticed - as had Greta with her nails - now a deep shade of red, and why not?

She was trying hard not to think about why she had made all the effort, to many conflicting thoughts and emotions crowding her mind, but she had to acknowledge the predominant one was that of excitement. Something she had not felt for a long time. A very long time. She was spraying some Jean Paul Gaultier Classique Eau De Toilette when she heard Fluffy barking. She sighed and pulled on her coat.

Margaret snatched open the door to the shed. 'What's the noise about? I thought you had doped it or whatever?'

Bernard hovered with the aerosol in the direction of the tin of creosote. He did a double take when he turned to her. 'Going out?'

She shrugged, 'Meeting Doris, I've got to get out.'

He nodded vaguely as he poked around amongst the tins.

She said, 'So, I'm going now.'

He shifted the creosote tin, 'Right.'

Margaret sighed and escaped via the back garden to the adjoining street where she had parked her car, having given up on their drive. She sat and pulled down the vanity mirror, took out her lippy and applied it. She gave a little rub to her eye shadow and said to herself as she flipped up the mirror. 'You've still got it.' She flipped the mirror down again and looked at herself. 'It's just a drink.'

She drove to the dog and whistle, a pub sufficiently far away that she was confident she would not be known.

Her stomach was in knots – more bats than butterflies – and she noticed her hands were shaking. This was mad. It was wrong. It was deceitful. But it was exciting. She pulled into the carpark and for a moment considered driving out again but parked and got out. She locked the car and headed toward the entrance.

Sergeant Turner was waiting at the entrance and waved to her. She waved back and again felt the urge to turn and run away, instead she quickened her step and joined him. 'Hello Bob.'

'Hello Margaret.'

He was lost for words so she nodded at the doors and said, 'Shall we, bit bloody cold out here.'

'Yes, time of the year. After you.'

They got drinks and found a table in the corner which provided some privacy. Bob sipped his beer. 'Well, here we are. I was pleasantly surprised when I received your message.'

Margaret picked up her rum and coke. 'I can't believe I left it.'

'But you did. And here we are.'

'Yes.' The bats had now become - whatever birds were bigger than bats, her mind was spinning – stirring her stomach to the extent that she was developing wind. Not conducive to whatever she had in mind although what that was still eluded her. 'I really appreciated your attention when we chatted the other evening in the police station. I was not in a good place. Still not to be honest.' She picked up her drink noticing her hand was shaking. Not good. But exciting. 'I'm not sure why I'm here.'

He smiled. 'That's ok.'

'Is it?' She sipped her drink feeling the rum behind the coke relax her a trifle. 'I'm married.'

He smiled again. 'Yes, it had come to my attention. I think it was the Mrs that gave it away.'

She laughed. Something she had not done for a long time. 'You are funny.' She studied him. 'It's nice.' She took another drink. 'Who would have thought we would be sitting here.'

'Indeed. I certainly never entertained the thought. Not that I wouldn't … erm-'

She laughed again. 'You're sweet. It's a change to meet a man who isn't full of himself.'

He tipped his head in acknowledgement. 'That's very kind.'

'I think you are very kind. It must be hard doing your job not to become hardened.'

'It is, and some of my colleagues have. I try to see the bigger picture you see. Having been brought up with four sisters and five brothers I've learnt to be tolerant.'

'Blooming heck. I thought one sister was enough.'

'Yes, It was a good grounding for life in some respects but not in everything. It is why I have chosen to be on my own.' He laughed. 'To have some peace and quiet.'

'You said the other evening that you feel lonely at times.'

'I do, but I have interests that occupy my mind.'

'Like?'

'DIY around the house. I've lost two of my brothers and one of my sisters and the remaining don't all have handy partners so I help them out with odd jobs, shopping etc.' He took a mouthful of his beer. 'You on the other hand? Married early?'

'Too young. But it was what you did then.'

'Regrets?'

She picked up her drink. 'Yes. Should have played the field.' She took a large sip. 'Bernard was my first you see.'

'Ah, hence your apprehension tonight.'

'Your very perceptive.'

'Comes with the job.'

'I don't want much. Just to be appreciated. Noticed now and then.'

'And you are not?'

'It was bad enough before all this nonsense started. Bernard is not a bad person, he's just …. self-absorbed. I think it stemmed from being abandoned by his mother. The first few years were ok but I suppose we grew apart. Children were not something either of us wanted and Julien was a surprise. I was in my early forties and that has its risks, but he's fine. Well I say that but he is struggling coming to terms with being gay; something Bernard has an issue with.'

'I understand.'

'Yes, you do which is why I'm here I think. I wanted to be noticed.'

'Then you have succeeded. I think you are a very attractive woman.' He looked into his beer. 'And I came tonight because I was intrigued. Not many woman notice me you see. Also I do not have a wide social profile as it were, choosing privacy over socialising.'

'But we're here.'

'We are. Has it helped you?'

She smiled, 'I think it has.'

He smiled kindly. 'We won't be meeting again though I suspect.'

'Why do you think that?'

He smiled shyly. 'Oh, years of doing my job, reading people.'

'You're probably right, but not for any reason other than I'm married and - although he drives me mad – Bernard is a good man and deserves another chance.'

'Then it has not been a waste of time Margaret.'

'Very definitely not.'

REVEALED

Bernard had entered a staring game with the dog but had to accept it was winning - judging by it not blinking once – and him a few times. He realised that Margaret was wearing her special perfume, something she had not done for a long time. Odd. But then who could understand the vagaries of a woman's mind? For instance, if he wanted a pair of shoes he would go to a shoe shop try a couple on and buy them. Whereas Margaret would visit every shoe shop in the town and then buy the first ones she saw. Same with shopping. He would – like a guided missile - head straight for the things he wanted and that would be that. Margaret on the other hand would graze up and down every aisle. He would never try to understand what went on in her mind.

He was about to enter into another staring competition with the dog when a shimmering form appeared in the corner of the shed. For a second he thought he was hallucinating but it continued until it took the form of a small being. Not human or monstrous; just odd. It had a large head and big black eyes, the same that had haunted him for the past few days. It wore a tight fitting, almost like a skin covering of some sort and it appeared to be struggling to maintain its shape; becoming transparent and then an arm would vanish and reappear.

Bernard reached for a chisel to defend himself but stopped as a voice in his head said, 'Don't be frightened Bernard. I'm not here to harm you, on the contrary I want to help.'

'Do you now? So taking me up to your thing and doing, 'he shuddered. 'whatever it was you did, oh and taking my bloody wine.'

'We apologise for that. There is a small faction within our community who have become interested in alcohol, something we discourage. Unfortunately, the Reptilians have used it to draw attention away from them. Nothing could be further from the truth, but we have not tried to dissuade them because it suits our purpose.'

Bernard was angry which made him bold enough to argue. 'And what might that be?'

'We are here under cover you might say. The Reptilians that are destroying your planet by manipulating your leaders and those in authority. We want to expose them. The media outside are at last all together and we can now show ourselves. What we need is for you to get our message to them.'

'Why me?'

'Pure chance. But we think you have the potential to do something worthwhile.'

'Like what?'

'Save your planet.'

'Bloody hell.'

The apparition vanished leaving Bernard wondering if he had been dreaming. Judging by the dog fast asleep he decided he had not. Although he did not know what was going to happen it felt as though he sort of knew it would and that he would know what to do. This was certainly something he could not have imagined and suddenly he felt a pressure had lifted. In fact he felt a new man. He would have a shower and shave and a good trim.

Margaret drove home glad the butterflies or whatever flying things in her stomach had gone. Sergeant Turner had proved to be the perfect gentleman and good company. But she knew that was all it had been. She was relieved. Bernard of course remained a challenge.

She opened the front door to find music playing, her sort of music, Motown, not something she thought he liked. She went upstairs to find him in joggers and a T shirt trimming his moustache. Are those my kitchen scissors-'

'No Margaret, they are the bathroom ones.' He held them up, 'See?'

'Right.' She checked him out. 'You seem in a better mood.'

'I am. I've had a visitor.'

'Who?'

'This you will find hard to believe.'

***

General Mervin Zuckerheiner surveyed the aerial photos and bit on his cigar. 'This is one clusterfuck boys. We're gonna need to get in there and quick. I want infantry, tanks, ground support-'

Tank Schmunk interrupted. 'Ground support Sir? Aint that for-'

'Don't interrupt me boy, I was pickin shit like you outta my teeth afore you were born! Argue with me Goddamn it. We've got a situation her of clusterfuck proportions, and it's up to me to deliver a final solution. Now, get me those tanks. And a coffee!' He studied a map of the area. 'Shit, these Limeys sure live close to each other. Might need a little repair once we're done… But hell that's not my problem, leave that to the government boys.'

'What about the media Sir?'

'Not worth the spit on my shoe.'

Tank looked concerned. 'They're pretty powerful Sir.'

'Not compared to the US of A goddam military son.' He examined the chewed remains of his cigar. 'Get me those tanks boy. And while you're at it, an air strike. My Daddy always told me "Strike hard, strike first".' He paused deep in thought and muttered. 'There's only one damn right solution, and just cos it's hard don't mean we can't make it.' He glared at Tank. 'Order a tactical nuke strike.' He drew on his cigar. 'You still standin there boy?'

***

Despite Margaret having made the decision to try again with Bernard, she still felt confused. The circus outside did not help. Or those alien things. She rang Mabel. 'Can I visit for a bit?'

'Of course dear.' She had a little chuckle to her voice. 'You can stay over if you want. You don't have to worry you know.'

'I know.'

It was an uneventful drive and Margaret had used the time to think about her life. It didn't resolve anything other than to remind her that she was confused.

Mabel poured the tea. 'One sugar right?'

Margaret nodded. 'Thanks.'

Mabel laughed as she handed the cup over her. 'Put the shits up you luv? Last time you were here?'

Margaret smiled awkwardly. 'Suppose so. Didn't know what to think Mabel.'

'Not surprised. It's not every day you find your cousin is a murderer.'

Margaret picked up her cup. 'It was a shock.'

'But you're here again dear.' She sipped her tea. 'So, what's up?'

'I've met someone I found ... interesting.'

'A man.'

'Yes.'

'Who is he?'

'He's a policeman.'

'Fuck me Margaret.'

'I would never, you know, say anything.'

'I would hope not. It wer told to you in confidence like.'

'I know.'

'So, this man. How many times have you seen him?'

'Other than over the police station reception desk, once. We met for a drink.'

'I never trusted them. Mind you they didn't cause any problems over George,' she looked thoughtful, 'but then there wasn't much left of him.' She sipped her tea. 'That was an odd time in me life Margaret, what with George and then Nevil.'

Margaret clasped her cup with both hands. 'Nevil? Don't remember-'

'You wouldn't dear, he was my neighbour.' She picked up her cup, 'Nasty little shit he was an all.'

Margaret was beginning to discover she did not know her cousin at all. She was intrigued. 'Why?'

'You see, the final dose that saw George off left him on the kitchen floor. So I had to get him in't shed.' She sipped her tea.

Margaret was deep in thought. 'I remember George was a big bloke?'

Mabel put down her cup and picked up her knitting. 'He was. Nineteen stone. And there's me, eight stone.'

'So how did you get him into the shed?'

The needles clacked furiously. 'Well, George was a builder as you know, and he had this big wheelbarrow with them pump up tyres. So I used that.'

Margaret felt she was in an alternative reality and would wake up any minute. 'But how did you get him into the wheelbarrow?'

'I knew he was going to croak some time, just couldn't say where, so I had a good look in the garage and found a hoist, you know, one of them things for lifting up heavy weights. Well George was heavy alright, but it did the job.' The needles ceased for a moment. 'Mind you, it put me back out something awful, still get a twinge now and then.' She looked toward the kitchen, 'You can see where I screwed the thing to the door frame. He didn't know it, but over the years I learnt a few things from him so I knew how to do it.'

Margaret looked toward the door. 'Oh, I think I can see them.'

'They're filled well enough.'

'You mentioned your neighbour.'

'Oh yes, Nevil, little shit.' The needles picked up speed. 'I had nearly got George to the shed,' she stopped to think for a moment, 'That was my mistake see, I thought 11.00 at night, nobody would see. But he did. I found out he had that – what do you call it? When you can't sleep?'

'Insomnia.'

'Aye that's it. So nosey little shit was looking out window and saw me. He said he could see me struggling, well I was, look at size of me, so he came round wi bloody big torch.'

Margaret gasped. 'What did you do?'

'What could I do? I'm not a dope Margaret, but could you think of a reasonable explanation?'

Margaret watched the needles almost whir as they clacked. 'No Mabel, you've got me there.'

'I had to think quick like cos he was suspicious.'

'Not surprising I suppose.'

'Suppose not Margaret.' The needles stopped and she looked up. 'So I grabbed his torch and bashed him over t'head wi it.' Margaret gasped. The needles started up again. Mabel said, 'It stunned him like, and he went down on his knees which gave me enough time to grab a shovel from the shed.'

Margaret whispered, 'What happened then?'

'I finished im off. That didn't do my back any good either. Dragged im into shed and set light to bugger.'

'But how did you explain two bodies in the shed?'

'Luckily, they did sometimes sit out there with a beer. So I said they must have been a bit drunk and fallen asleep.'

'So the police believed you.'

Mabel smiled, 'Of course.'

'Did it not bother you?'

That's what I'm getting to Margaret. George was a cheat and a liar. I thought hard before I did it and decided he deserved what he got.'

'What about Nevil?'

'He was a nosey little shit.'

'Right. I suppose when you put it like that.'

'What I'm getting at Margaret, is I've learnt to live with what I've done and understand I'm a tough old bitch.'

'I see.'

'Hope so dear. You can't afford to feel guilty. You've not done any harm, just thoughts in't head.'

'Thanks Mabel.'

'Put tele on dear let's see news for a laugh.'

Margaret switched it on and gasped. 'Bloody hell Mabel!'

A sky reporter was talking into the camera whilst on a helicopter circling her house. 'It appears that a major development has occurred at the Grimshaw's house. I can see tanks lining up along Birchwood street, and behind them infantry. I'm sure they are American, certainly the tanks are.' He looked closer as the helicopter circled. 'There is a SWAT team assisting the police to - I think the term is Kettle - the reporters into a small, grassed area. Mr Grimshaw has not appeared yet but I understand he is due to make an announcement on behalf of the aliens.'

Margaret pointed at the screen. 'That's my bloody house!' She leapt up. 'I'm not sitting ere watching that! I've got to go.'

Mabel stopped knitting. 'Don't forget what I told you dear.'

Margaret kissed her cheek. 'No, I won't. Thanks.'

***

Deep within the bowels of the Pentagon a high-level black ops strategy meeting was again underway headed up by Dewey Heinzeburgher. 'We have a situation, gentlemen.'

Verry serious faces nodded around the table.

Chad Biffle looked serious under that façade but in reality, felt a little smug. 'General Mervin Zuckerheiner. Told you guys he was a bad choice. Hell, a monkey would be more responsible.'

Chuck Shellerberger said, 'We're into damage control now.'

Dewey Heinzeburgher looked around the room. 'Ideas Gentlemen?'

Woody Clampitt said quietly, 'Remove the son of a bitch before he nukes the whole damn country. Much as I hate the damn Brits we would have difficulty denying that.'

Colt Harkleroad nodded. 'You're right there Woody.' He pinched his eyes, 'I suggest we send in a hit team and take him out.'

Dewey Heinzeburgher nodded. 'Radical, but I think it's the only way.'

ARMAGEDDON

PC May put on the blues and twos and accelerated. PC Green was anxious but also a little excited. 'Got to be the escaped sex offender Sir?'

'We can't make assumptions PC Green, but it certainly looks that way.' He drove as fast as was safe given it was dark and soon reached a layby with a footpath into a wood on the outskirts of Ramsbottom. 'This looks right according to the call.'

He got out and shone his torch down the path. It didn't take long to find the caller with a dog standing beside a man tied to a tree. PC May instructed PC Green to return to the car and call it in.

The man was visibly relieved and was grateful to be untied. As PC May led him handcuffed to the car the man gabbled. 'I was attacked by this mad woman who was convinced I am somebody's twin. She wouldn't listen to me.'

Back up arrived and took the man into custody. PC May looked to PC Green. 'Let's see if I'm right.'

'Sir?'

'Given he is the spitting image of Mr Grimshaw, it is my guess that PC Jones has gone to his house.'

'But it's crazy with press Sir.'

'I know, but I suspect Jones is past caring.'

'Why's that Sir?'

'Because she's psychotic.'

They parked as near as possible to Bernard's house and made their way around the crowd of kettled reporters held in by police, some of whom PC May recognised. Bernard snatched the door open eyeing the reporters. 'What yer arresting me for now? Stepping off bloody pavement or summat?'

PC May smiled. 'We're here because we have arrested a man who claims he was held captive by a ... woman who has a grudge against you Sir.'

'Tell her to get in line then.'

'Can we come in Sir?'

'Help yer bloody self.' He stood aside.

PC May said, 'Can we look around, make sure she's not here in hiding.'

'Is she dangerous?'

PC May nodded. 'Yes.'

Margaret came in. 'What's he done now?'

Bernard said, 'They said some mad woman is coming after me.'

Margaret huffed, 'Better not be that-'

'Will you give it rest?'

She shook off her coat and looked around. 'Where's Julian?'

Bernard shrugged.

PC May turned to her. 'Is he usually home at this time?'

'Yes. Usually takes the dog out.'

PC May turned to Bernard. 'Can you see if the dog is there please Sir?'

Bernard reluctantly went out to the shed and returned. 'Dog is not there. He must have taken him.'

Margaret checked her watch. 'He should be back by now; he hates that lot out there so he wouldn't hang about.'

PC May turned to PC Green. 'We'll go and see if we can find him. Just in case he's run across this woman. Where does he take the dog?'

Margaret said, 'Out back through neighbour's garden and left along main road.'

They made their way carefully past the hawthorn hedge - which was very fed up with constantly being disturbed and did its best to cause some damage - exiting onto the road. In the distance the grinding roar of tanks drew their attention. They rounded a corner and stood in awe.

A row of tanks unable to drive down the street to Bernard's house because of parked cars, were taking an alternative route through front gardens, mowing down fences as if they were matchsticks. Hedges were uprooted and dragged into the caterpillar tracks as the tanks trundled relentlessly toward the house. Dave Shaw at number 23 watched in horror as they passed his front window. His mouth dropped open as an American trooper nodded to him, cigarette hanging from his lips. He called his wife over to look. 'I don't believe this Dot. My lawn, shrubs, not to mention the fountain, all gone.'

She peered out and sighed, 'Fuck me.' She shuffled back into the kitchen.

***

Within the hastily erected control centre at Burtonwood airbase, General Mervin Zuckerheiner barked orders at his subordinates as he studied aerial surveillance on a screen. He tried to ignore the extreme twitch his left eye lid had developed blurring his vision of the tanks moving steadily toward the Grimshaw's house. 'Corporal!'

An exhausted young man rushed in and saluted. Sir!'

'I'm takin some shut eye boy. Alert me with sit rep when house is secure.'

'Sir, yes Sir!'

General Mervin Zuckerheiner saluted and marched to his private quarters. He entered and slipped off his jacket. He muttered, 'Too Goddamn old for this shit Merv.' He took out a bottle of bourbon and had a large swig. He considered his options - concerned that a level of confusion not experienced before had settled on his fast-becoming bewildered mind – and decided he could not make sense of them. He had ordered the tanks and infantry to descend on the house but was not sure why. He had a vague recollection of being ordered to order a missile strike but not sure by whom. The bottom line was he had total autonomy and that was messing with his head. But worse still, the nuke strike was set for two hours. He bit a nail wondering what idiot had ordered that. His hot line rang, and he snatched up the earpiece. 'Speak.'

'The President has confirmed the strike is to go ahead Sir.'

A wave of confusion and anxiety flooded him, 'Missile?'

'Nuke Sir.'

'Right. Just confirm time of impact.'

'Two hours Sir.'

Get right back to you son.' He gently put the phone down and muttered, 'Shit.' An emotion unknown to him appeared and smashed him in the head - fear. It was accompanied by another unknown - panic. He picked up the phone. 'I need an airlift asap.'

'Destination Sir?'

He bit through a well-manicured nail. 'Bermuda.'

PANIC

Bernard paced the lounge. 'The whole bloody world has gone mad.'

Margaret was making a cup of tea. 'If anything has happened to Julien…'

'Nobody's going to threaten him wi that bloody monster wi im. Get torn limb from limb.'

'Might be so Bernard if they had a moustache like yours, but bearing in mind it is a woman, not very likely.'

'Good point.' He stopped as the general noise outside changed. He peered out of the front window, 'Something going on out there.' He pulled on his coat and went outside. He noticed the reporters were all gathered in a small area looking very unhappy. He approached them drawing immediate attention, expecting microphones pointing at him but they seemed more concerned with escaping the police cordon.

Bernard put up his hands. 'Wait up. What's going on?'

'The nearest gasped, 'Got to get away! They're going to nuke the place!'

'Do what?'

'Leaked info one of us picked up on a waveband. Two hours. I'm off.' He shoved hard and managed to slip away. He shouted over his shoulder, 'Run if I were you mate!' Another reported leant over to him. 'It's true. A tactical nuclear device.' He shoved against a policeman near to him, 'And they won't listen.'

Bernard took in the tanks lined up outside the house and infantry behind them. 'I've had enough of this! Bloody nuke? We'll see about that.' He stomped back into the house and searched for his car keys.

'What's happening?'

'You don't want to know.'

'I think I do Bernard.'

He stopped at the backdoor. 'Let's just say a factor 50 in't going to help.'

'Do what?'

He opened the door and turned to her. 'They're going to drop a nuclear device on't bloody house, and I'm going to stop it.' He growled, 'I've just got me shed back and I'm not losing it again.' He hurried out to the shed and opened and shut drawers taking out items and laying them out on the furrowed workbench. The spider peeked out from behind the creosote tin and assumed the interloper had moved its attack to Def Com three. There was no choice but to make a dash for the other side of the shed in the hope it would provide more protection. Bernard stopped for a second as he spotted movement near the creosote tin out of the corner of his eye. His instinct was to panic but there were greater stakes at hand and he stoically began to assemble an old alarm clock (the sort with two bells on the top) two candles and an old mobile phone strapping them together with black insulating tape. He sat back and studied it. 'Looks like bloody bomb to me so it should fool em.'

With his device he hurried out of the front door to his car. The kettled reporters erupted with questions, 'Have you got an announcement? Are they coming?' A louder voice filled with fear shouted, 'Is it true they're going to nuke us?'

'Not if I have my way.' He thought it best to conceal the fake bomb considering there was no time to explain it to the police, or – it appeared – most of the American army. He jumped into his car and manoeuvred around tanks and armoured vehicles. He thought for a moment about the assorted American presence and decided there was only one place they could have come from. Burtonwood airbase. He knew where it was and set off as fast as the old focus would allow.

***

Julien was patiently waiting while Fluffy sniffed yet another lamp post. He was deep in thought about a flat he had seen and wanted to show Sebastian. Granny Ingrid had convinced him that anything was possible so why not. She had also introduced him to weed but since being arrested he was more cautious using it in public. He tugged on the lead to drag Fluffy away from the sniffing and thought he saw a figure moving in the bushes. He shrugged thinking all the recent happenings had made him paranoid. 'Come on Fluff.' He pulled impatiently at the lead and stopped as something cold poked into the back of his neck.

'Move and I'll blow your head off.'

Julien struggled against the rope tying him to a tree in a wood off the main road. PC Jones was pacing muttering to herself occasionally looking at Julien. 'Think he can fool me with his twin brother.' Julien kicked Fluffy trying to get him angry but he was content licking his private parts.

***

Bernard had had enough. His patience was at an all-time low – something not to be ignored as it was always virtually at zero anyway. He pulled up outside the gates of the airbase and with his device hidden behind him approached the two guards.

He puffed himself up and announced, 'I have important business inside with your – he wasn't sure what the man in charge would be called – manager.'

One of the guards said off handedly, 'Go away, nobody allowed in.'

Bernard moved a little closer. 'Is that so?' He revealed the pretend bomb. 'I've had enough so if you don't let me in I will explode this right now, cos I've got nothing to lose see?

So tell your manager or whoever that I need to speak to him.'

The two guards exchanged glances and decided they had better things to do and let someone on a higher pay grade deal with it. 'One of them got on the phone. 'Tell the General we have a situation at the gate, there's a guy says he will blow us up if we don't let him in.'

Tank said, 'The General can't be disturbed.'

He looked out of the window to see the General carrying a suit case heading quickly toward a waiting helicopter. 'Erm,' He looked around the makeshift HQ and realised he would have to make the decision. 'Ok, let him through.'

Bernard screeched to a halt outside the command centre and hurried inside with his bomb held up in front of him. 'I'll set bloody thing off if you don't let me in.'

Tank opened the flaps of the marquee and gulped as he saw the bomb. 'No need to be hasty Sir, we can talk this through.'

'No time for talk. I'll not be letting a bloody nuclear device go off near my house, I've spent too much time on lawn. Now connect me up to TV I need to make an announcement.'

Tank hesitated, given his commander was currently getting into a helicopter and therefore not available to make decisions he was next in command. 'I don't-'

Bernard moved closer. 'Do you know who I am?'

Tank shook his head. One of the operators in the HQ shouted. 'That's Mr Grimshaw, the guy on the tv?'

Tank looked blank. 'I don't-'

The operator shouted. 'Let him in!' Tank stood aside in shock unable to think clearly. Bernard marched in and said, 'You lot are about to drop bloody nuclear device on't my house and I need to stop it. Put me on't tele, 'he thought for a moment, 'Sky, they'll do. And tell whoever makes decision to stop bloody bomb. Tell them to watch tv.'

'I can't just-'

'Well I've had it up to here and if you don't I'll blow us all up.'

Panic ensued as urgent phone calls were made.

Deep in the bowels of the Pentagon the Black Ops meeting was once again in progress.

Dewey Heinzeburgher looked around the table with a grim stare. 'We have a clusterfuck of major proportions.'

Chuck Shellerberger nodded. 'And let it be noted I said he would be a disaster.'

Chad Biffle smiled. 'Aint the time to gloat Chuck.'

Dewey Heinzeburgher nodded. 'Weve got a situation we need to contain.' He looked around at the gloomy faces, 'So what are we gonna do, cos the President is up my arse. He's authorised a tactical nuclear device to be dropped in under two hours.' He sighed. 'And we have this nutter form the UK saying he will blow up our command centre.'

Colt Harkleroad snarled, 'What is General Mervin fucking Zuckerheiner doing?'

Dewey Heinzeburgher rubbed his eyes with exhaustion, 'On his way to Bermuda.'

Dwayne Ridlehoover leapt to his feet. 'Bermuda? Are you kidding me?'

Dewey Heinzeburgher nodded. 'I know. We'll deal with him later. We are now into a damage limitation situation.' He looked up as a television screen lit up to show Bernard in the command centre holding a microphone.

Bernard drew in a deep breath and checked the microphone was on. 'I am Bernard Grimshaw. I don't think I need an introduction as - without my permission – I have been all over tele recently. So here is the announcement you have been waiting for.' He looked around. 'I'm in't an American army command centre and they are about to drop bloody nuclear bomb on my house. Of course, that will do a lot of damage to a lot of people but they don't care. All his started because some alien race abducted me when I was carrying a bottle of me finest – blackberry and garlic wine. Now it seemed the military thought it wer for my wine - which is of outstanding quality – and they would get out of control.

But it turns out they are really here to show up what these so-called politicians are really up to. Now I don't know for sure, but I've been told by these aliens that there are some nasty ones here and controlling so called world leaders for their own ends. I for one don't approve and it has to stop. The bloody newspapers and tele have only been interested in't making news for money, they don't care if what they say is true or not as long as they profit. Time to wake up, there are aliens here and we have to talk to them. Our governments are corrupt and we must change em. Now, I don't want nowt from all this other than to make me wine and the occasional round of golf. The media have set me up, now they need to do the right thing and show up these politicians.' He sighed in frustration. 'Why can't we all just get on wi living without all this fighting.'

Dewey Heinzeburgher stared at the screen and uttered, 'Gentlemen we are, as the great man once said, fucked.'

Bernard put down the microphone as Tank said, 'The strike has been called off. I think the President is pretty mad.'

'Good. So get all them bloody tanks and whatnot off me lawn.'

Margaret watched open mouthed as Bernard spoke to the world. 'Bloody hell.' She sipped her tea as a tv presenter came on earnestly addressing the cameras.

'It seems from the dramatic revelations form Mr Grimshaw that we have all been fooled by the world leaders and politicians. Unbelievable but it seems there are aliens here,' he was interrupted and looked even more shocked. 'We have to go to live cameras at the Grimshaw's house where world shattering events are taking place.'

The camera shifted to a reported in a helicopter circling the house, 'Yes Todd, beneath me I can see the tanks and army withdrawing but – oh there is something happening to our left. We're going to move away to get a better view.' The helicopter swooped down and away to the right to reveal chaos below. 'It's a giant spacecraft descending over the house, people are running in all directions, the army are firing at it but to no effect but wait, it has a brilliant light piercing the darkness below and – I don't believe it, there seems to be a fire fight, a battle, no it's just one individual with it appears a machine gun firing at the soldiers who are returning fire. The craft is hovering over the scene, its light on the battle below. I don't know what is going on but it is dramatic.'

Bernard's voice boomed out of the craft, "Why can't we all just get on wi living without all this fighting.' It repeated it a number of times. The reporter gasped, 'It seems thy are playing part of Mr Grimshaw's speech. This proves they are here to help us and what he said was right.'

As Bernard's voice boomed out the soldier stopped and looked at each other. PC Jones stopped firing as his voice distracted her.

PC May stopped PC Green and whispered, 'Over there in the wood. Someone is firing at the soldiers. It's my guess its PC Jones - and she has Julien as hostage.'

PC Green nodded and said, 'I'm going to rescue him Sir.' He started to move toward the wood. PC May tried to stop him but he was too quick. He crashed through the bushes and landed on PC Jones who was trying to reload her machine gun. PC Green struggled with her and eventually secured her with handcuffs. 'I've got her Sir.'

PC May arrived as PC Green was untying Julien. 'Well done. You might just make a good copper yet.'

RESOLUTION

Bernard sat in his shed still in shock not believing what had happened. The pretend bomb was proudly displayed between the creosote and white emulsion, and he kept looking at it and smiling. The spider had no idea what it was but decided it was too much to risk and once again made its way to the other side of the shed. Bernard noticed and smiled. 'I would prefer it if you were on't other side of shed so off yer go. Better put words into practice eh?'

Margaret poked her head around the door. 'Just made a brew.'

'I'll be right in.' He looked at Fluffy who was following his every move from within its cage. 'Not sure bout you though.' He went into the kitchen where Margaret was watching a small tv. 'They still going on about it?'

Margaret pushed a mug of tea over the table to him. 'They are. Evidently, the media have swapped sides and are exposing all the dodgy goings on with these world leaders and politicians.'

'About time an all.' He sipped his tea. 'I've been invited to wine club meeting tonight.' He put down his mug. 'But I'll not be going if Frank remains chairman.'

'So you can change the world but not swallow your bloody pride.'

He nodded. 'I'll let him make a balls up of it and be re-elected next year no doubt.'

'Still a stubborn old git, but you've changed - for the better I must admit - at last.'

He smiled, 'There were nothing wrong wi me from start.'

She laughed. 'Oh I think there was.'

'With the money I've got from these tv appearances, we could go on't little holiday Margaret.'

'And you haven't changed?' She reached over and touched his arm. 'Biscuit?'

'Aye, why not.' He stood and stretched. 'New beginning.' He went over to the lounge window and surveyed the carnage outside. 'Aye, there's some cleaning up to be done. Council, going to be busy.' He gasped, 'I don't believe it.' Margaret joined him. His mouth dropped as he pointed at a motorcycle and sidecar weaving around the detritus left by the reporters.

She laughed. 'That's-'

'It is. Silly old bat.'

Margaret squeezed his arm, 'Let her be Bernard.'

***

Bernard stood outside the backdoor and sipped his wine. He held up the glass and smiled, 'Competition for you next year lad, we'll show em, eh, blackberry and garlic, who would have thought.' He glanced up at the evening sky and saw three lights moving in unison. He raised his glass and smiled.

Tiger had been eying him from the sideboard and dropped to the floor, keeping low as he stealthily crept up on his prey. Bernard shrieked in pain as it leapt and embedded itself on his leg, claws fully extended. Wine slopped from his glass onto his coat as he fought off the cat. 'Margaret!'

THE END

Printed in Dunstable, United Kingdom